SWIMMING WITH

SWIMMING
WITH GHOSTS

Laurence E Fisher

KITE PUBLICATIONS

SWIMMING WITH GHOSTS
ISBN 978-0-9547585-2-3

First published in 2007 by
Kite Publications
42 Village Court
Whitley Bay
Tyne and Wear
NE26 3QA

Cover illustration by Mick Oxley
www.mickoxley.com

Produced by John Saunders Design & Production, Abingdon OX13 5HU
Printed in Great Britain by Biddles Ltd., King's Lynn

For Alison

"True love is always quiet."
Elizabeth Jennings.

SWIMMING WITH GHOSTS

Part One

ABSENCE

I was angry, then numb, in shock. My body was going through the motions, no more, simply following orders. It's the only explanation. The woman I loved was dead. The one I had been waiting for. The one I was meant to be with. My life as I knew it was over. I hope this is of use to you.

Some people are dead while alive – they have no heart, no soul, no real passion. This was true of me, my only thoughts consumed with hatred and regret. They ate away at me like poison, gnawing one part at a time, destroying all goodness. I was being sent from Malta back to England. Ordered! To marry and start a family with someone I did not know anymore, someone I barely even liked. Gwen. The name alone sent shivers through me.

I remember little of leaving the island, my home of four years, recalling bare fragments of the voyage home. The boat was already full of returning men. They were excited and jubilant, so unlike me, and I took refuge in the crowded dining room, any thin scraps of sleep snatched while collapsed on top of a fixed table, rolling in time with the vessel. Nan, my love, was gone forever. Taken away from me, leaving the future a dead land where I had no desire to tread. I lay still, avoiding all conversation, a mask-like expression fixed rigid on my face. I was determined not to cry in front of the men – I had never succumbed to this on nursing duties, not once, despite the twin hardships

11

of siege and illness. I was not going to start now, but it was so hard. I felt polluted with bitterness, wishing for a second chance, that I might have fought harder for Nan to stay and then she would still be alive. I might have saved her life. Even the blood that flowed in my veins was contaminated. I remained a broken man.

The sea ran mountain high, many men were sick, and I did not care. I suppose I must have breathed the rank air in and out. My heart must have continued to pump, despite this weary indifference. I don't remember. I still could not wholly believe it, the brown stain of memory repeatedly collapsing my world. It was Matron who had broken the news, in the hospital gardens outside F Block. No survivors. Nan's boat had sunk. Mere fragments of the conversation remained.

Matron's concern had been genuine, of that I felt sure, when she had sometimes appeared so hard and distant. For once, all her barriers had come down. Major Merryweather had described her as great, and he was not far wrong. What was her name again? Perry, that was it. She was kind and wise; I had come to realise this over time. Somebody had once told me that she used to keep goldfish and I couldn't associate this with such a pragmatic individual, although nothing would really surprise me about her. She seemed a lady capable of anything. Now, onboard, I tried to use her as an example, clutching for inspiration. For strength. How would she have acted, if she trod in my shoes? It was impossible. I was lost. All help was beyond me now.

We sailed without interruption and did not moor again. If we had, I wouldn't have noticed as I rarely ventured up onto the deck – someone would always attempt to strike up a conversation, and I had no desire for this. It was preferable to spend the time alone with my anger, to wallow in the trench of memory and painful regret. The black horizon of the sea was of scant interest to a broken man such as myself. The company of men could bring me no comfort.

Four years had been spent on Malta, long months of this endured under constant attack and siege. It was a lifetime. We were the most bombed place on the planet, a living hell, but I had Nan and she could make everything bearable. I was happy in love, fulfilled, and would not have swapped places for anything. War was far preferable than peacetime, or the peacetime to which I now returned. When the summons had arrived and the Colonel ordered my departure from the island, it made no sense. Gwen had never expressed a desire for my return, and definitely no wish to start a family. The Colonel had actually told me she was a suicide risk.

I continued to question her motives. We had not been a proper item for a long time and Gwen was a fake; there had to be more to it than met the eye. My anger was paired with suspicion. What did she hope to gain from all this? I still could not bring myself to believe that we might be married, our relationship long since finished. Surely she realised that? Of all things, Gwen had never been one for self-deception.

The boat docked at Greenock on the Clyde. A labourer on the quay told us that it was the first week of December, and that much I do recall. His accent was horrendous. It was 1944. Freezing cold, after the heat of the Mediterranean. We were separated into regiments then loaded onto buses, before travelling in slow convoy to Glasgow Central. The sky was porcelain white, the river a murky brown. Everyone was smoking. We were not allowed to leave the platform, fed greasy egg sandwiches where we sat, and then a night train eventually showed up to transport us south. I would be returned to Boyce Barracks where we had been prepared for war so long ago. Everything was different. Nothing remained the same. I did not know what I would do – I was living someone else's life now.

Bright stars punctured the night sky on this, the longest journey. The constellations appeared strange and unfamiliar after my time on Malta. I remained silent, squashed in the corner of a shabby compartment while clutching my meagre belongings. Shadows of the country floated before my eyes, fleeting, leaving no trace, while all thoughts refused to leave Nan. I remained numb with the shock of it all. It seemed that my life had been blown terribly off course just when it all appeared settled. What if we had fought to stay together? Nan and me. What then? Surely we would have stood a chance? I could have remained on the island and continued to work as a nurse. If I had converted to Catholicism, then her family would have accepted me. It all would have worked out in the end. It had to. We loved each other. What was more important than that? The red thread connecting us had been allowed to snap, and for this I blamed only myself.

The train arrived early, allowing time for a simple breakfast. I was not hungry and chose to wash and shave instead, then collect my pay and leave pass. I was delaying the inevitable for as long as possible, the final leg of the journey to Rayleigh, Essex. It was all I could do to put one foot in front of the other – Gwen waited there with friends. A message had been left for me at the Barracks. Our wedding had been arranged for noon.

I was not properly alive. I had no soul, no passion. I remained in shock, paralysed to act. It's the only explanation – how else could I have gone through with things? Still, it made no sense. The train ride passed with cruel speed, and on some level I started to panic. It remained an effort to keep back the tears. How I missed the silk blue Mediterranean, the pure unsullied sky, the soft buzz of the hurricane lamps. Hell, I even missed the carbolic acid smell of the hospital. I wanted to be with Nan again, my lost love, reliving the velvet tenderness of our shared nights. I loved her so completely, in a way I had never believed possible. Nothing of our time together was forgotten. Nothing would ever be forgotten.

The train pulled into the station. The end of the line. I spotted Gwen immediately from a winter of faces, standing alone at the edge of the crowd in front of what appeared to be the waiting room. She had not seen me yet, and I watched her wrestle her features into some semblance of happiness. It did not come easy. She took out a mirror, studied her mouth, then applied a little more red. She tugged at the hem of her skirt, a drab brown affair, and straightened her jacket. She appeared colourless, and I wondered could she not have made more of an effort? We had not seen each other for four years, and she had always been so vain in her Garbo imitation. One hand reached up to tidy her

14

hair, nervously stroking it into place. The corners of her mouth, those thin lips, twitched downwards. For some reason, the voice of Joyce Grenfell began to sing in my head. *London Pride*, a verse of *All My Tomorrows*; a bitter sound to a man who considered he had no future. I grabbed for my bag and jumped reluctantly onto the platform.

Gwen's features sharpened in recognition. She hurried forward to greet me, one hand gripping tight on my forearm when she kissed me.

"Welcome home, Harold. How are you? Have you missed me?" Her eyes were cold, so empty of love, unable to conceal the truth. It was all I could do to remain upright, and I buried my face into the barbs of her lacquered hair. The smell was chemical, overpowering. Suddenly, I was all too aware of the reality of my return.

"So how are you then? You look well – lucky you to have a sun tan!" She continued to speak, while I withdrew once more into silence. I did not know what I could do. Gwen released her grip and stepped backwards to look at me directly. Bright gaudy lipstick stuck to her upper teeth, making her appear cheap, no better than a Sherry Bandit on Malta.

"Harold, aren't you going to say something? Have you lost your tongue?" She ruffled my hair. " I haven't heard your voice in years, you know."

I knew this only too well. I would have been happy never to see Gwen again, if Nan had lived. She had never used lipstick, no need of such fake decoration. Gwen's mood appeared anything but suicidal, which only added to the bad feeling and bitterness I now experienced.

"I'm dog tired, that's all. I haven't slept in days. It was a tough journey." The words were dragged out of me.

"But you're home now." She smiled. Home. Gwen could not have picked a more unfortunate word.

"Am I?" I snapped. "Really?"

"Yes, darling," she ignored the tone of my voice. "We'll get you back for a change of clothes, and then it's straight to the wedding. It's what you always wanted isn't it, to make an honest woman of me? Come on, we mustn't be late."

She grabbed my hand and started walking briskly towards the exit. There was an edge to her voice, a sharp reminder of the old days, and meekly I allowed myself to follow. I had no stomach for an argument, not yet.

The crowd had quickly dispersed. We made our way uninterrupted, too fast, way too fast for my liking. Life was spiralling out of control. It was as if someone else now walked in my shoes, a stranger. Detached, I noticed the sky was grey; funeral grey, my father would have said. A fine mist swirled in the air, soaking us through. The light was poor, appearing muddy after the clarity of Malta. If my hair was long enough, it would start to go curly. Nan had always liked it when it did that.

Grace and Lionel waited in the car, both erupting into wide smiles when they noticed our approach. A skinny Lionel jumped from his seat and out of the vehicle, clapping one arm about my shoulders.

"Welcome home, old chap. Good to see you safe and sound. Journey all right?"

They were originally friends of Gwen, but decent people and I was happy to see them. Lionel appeared to be genuinely delighted, and I was glad not to have to deal with Gwen on my own. In front of company, she put on a suitable show of joy at this heroic return, while I felt nothing but shame. I should never have come back like this – it was all wrong. My work and my love had been taken away, the two reasons I had to keep breathing, and now it seemed there was nothing left to live for.

We drove to their house on the outskirts of town. I said as little as possible, feigning exhaustion, and seemed to get away with it. Gwen did most of the talking, the centre of attention as usual. She ushered me out of the car and up the stairs to get changed – time was running out, the ceremony would soon be upon us. I discovered she had collected an ancient grey suit and white shirt that I had owned for years, dating back from my time spent working in *Rutherfords*, a gentleman's clothing shop in Folkestone, before my time at the National in London. Before I had even begun nurse training. Putting them on was a strange, disconcerting experience, like climbing into the skin of someone who no longer existed, someone who was long since dead.

We drove to the Registry Office in Southend, where Grace and Lionel acted as our witnesses. The words, the vows, were so difficult to say – still, it was as if an intruder stood in my place, wearing my body, my clothes. I could not look Gwen in the eye, staring determined at my shoes, willing it all to be over. The service was short and this was the only good thing about it. Truly, I could not have coped with anything more. It was one month before my thirty-fourth birthday and I felt completely empty inside. I could not imagine how things might ever improve.

The reception took place in an old hotel overlooking the sea, the four of us enjoying an expensive cheerless meal in one of the supposed finer establishments in town. Grace and Lionel had soon realised that something was seriously wrong, probably attributing this to the shock of my war service and abrupt return. I had no words for any of them and remained largely silent, picking distracted at my food. They were obviously embarrassed, but I did not care about this. There were far more important things of concern – how had I got myself into this mess? How would I get out of it? Gwen, my wife, hustled and bustled about the conversation, ostentatiously grabbing my hand and arm, but I could not bring myself to respond. I was still in some form of shock. I remained a shell of a man.

Our hosts tactfully withdrew to the bar, and the real Gwen was quick to come out of hiding.

"So what's going on?" she hissed, immediately. "What's got into you? They're putting us up. They've looked after me while you've been away. Have you any idea how rude you're being?"

"I'm sorry," I lied, while studying my plate and scraping a fork through the congealing fat from my steak.

"Well stop it! Aren't you pleased to see me at all? Harold?" She carried her own suspicions. We had been apart for a long time and nobody emerged from war unchanged.

"I'm tired out, that's all."

"There's more to it than that. I'm not daft, remember. We'll talk later, but buck up. They're coming back now. The least you can do is be sociable." She leaned forwards to kiss my cheek, one hand pinching hard on the back of my neck. "Harold's just apologising," she beamed. "He'll be missing all those Maltese beauties."

☾

We embarked on a two-day honeymoon in Essex. I put off going to bed for as long as possible, making excuses in the hope that I might finally collapse from exhaustion. It did not happen. It never happened. Eventually, I had to lie there next to Gwen, lost and anxious, tossing and turning through long endless nights. I tried to edge as far away from her as possible, avoiding unnecessary contact, as if the touch of her skin might somehow pollute me further.

I thought about Nan. Always Nan. Where was she? How could she die? I'd come to believe in her God, how we were meant to be together, that nothing could tear us apart. But now she was dead. I was deprived of her forever. It had all been a lie. I had put my faith and trust in her God and he had turned me away. If he even existed in the first place. If I had lost her forever, then I had lost him as well. I was prepared for, and welcomed, a life without God.

Again, I remembered Matron Perry. During the war, she and Nan had provided me with continued inspiration, and now only Matron remained. Miss Perry was slim, apparently tireless, and always focussed on her work at the hospital. Her sense of duty was impeccable. She must have been in her forties, but it was hard to guess with any degree of accuracy. She was one of those women who will look the same over a great number of years, neither pretty nor unattractive. Matron had such beautiful manners; she possessed true courage and determination. Again, I wondered how she would react in my shoes. She possessed such grace, a calm demeanour so important in nursing, and a selfless devotion to work. Nothing was more important than duty, certainly not any personal problems. These would never be allowed to intrude on the sanctity of nursing. I tried to borrow some of her determination, this strength and self-respect. I needed to regain some sense of control over my life, but it was no good. I was wasting my time and energy. Matron Perry was a long way away and she could not help me now.

I remembered our patients on F Block, the familiar radiance that followed acceptance of illness or injury. I tried to equate this with my own life and loss, but this also proved impossible. I was not even close. When I looked up from the hotel pillow into the night sky, the stars shone smaller and darker than they had ever appeared on Malta. I fell back into blackness and depression.

I had been ordered to England to marry and start a family. It was awful. My impotence turned to anger. If that was Gwen's game, then I would play my own hand and call her bluff. I would set out to do exactly that, knowing full well that she did not want this any more than I did. It was her rules and I was going to punish her with them. I was a broken man and would pull her down with me – it was largely her fault, anyway. I had her, and it was brutal. I stared at the wall, eyes fixed open, rueing that I had not listened to the warnings of my parents. They had never liked Gwen and tried to warn me away. It had only strengthened my resolve to stay with her. I was always a stubborn fool.

The honeymoon was a disaster. We did not communicate and by the end of it could hardly bear to be in the same room, let alone talk to each other. And on top of everything else, I quickly discovered that my suspicions were indeed correct – Gwen did not want children at all. I caught her using pessaries in an attempt to prevent any pregnancy. It was another in a long chain of lies. Still, I wondered as to the real reasons why she had brought about my sudden return.

Often, I dreamed of Nan, our nights together on the island. How precious these now seemed. I took comfort in their memory, recalling the moan of the rushes in the valley floor when we walked back from swimming at Xlendi, the tiny bats swooping and darting in the warm air about our heads. Nan wore her floppy straw hat and we smelled the orange blossom in the fields; we snacked on fresh cheese pastizzi bought from a stall in the old market square. If I was lucky, I could just about imagine the taste of a *Blue Label* beer.

Nan had always enjoyed the *Café de la Raine,* where the owner was a real character, all smiles and leathery handshake. His eyebrows were joined in the middle and he possessed the most impressive of beer guts. This little fellow invariably spilled her lemonade, never my *Blue Label*, following this with a small bow and the exclamation *So sorry, my friends. So sorry. I'll give you a discount. Tomorrow.* Of course, tomorrow was always the same.

In another bar, we had once been hassled by an ex-service man, an old player by the name of Charlie. He had stumbled in, all trussed up in a shiny suit that might have been the right size ten years earlier. His hair was oiled flat, his complexion a florid spider web of broken capillaries.

"So are you married? Or enjoying life?" He had rested himself on my shoulder, his sour breath rank from alcohol and rotting teeth.

I tried to ignore him, hoping he might move on and bother someone else, but Charlie had other ideas. He nudged my elbow, intrusive, spitting on my face as he asked another question. "So do you love her?"

"That's a bit personal." I spoke quietly, wiping my cheek with a serviette, wishing him far away.

"So do you love him?" he persisted, now directing his attention at Nan.

"I'd rather talk to him about that," she squeezed my leg beneath the table.

We stood and left while he swayed, perplexed, lighting up a horrible Victory V cigarette. Now, on bitter honeymoon, how I wished I'd answered differently. Yes. I wanted to shout it from the rooftops for the whole world to act as my witness. Yes, I love her. I have always loved her, from the very first moment I saw her in the Services Club, and I would always love Nan. Nothing could ever change that.

I dreamt of the church, still at Xlendi. I was alone. I walked slowly along the curve of the bay, the blue-white flickering sea, and then climbed uneven stone steps leading up to the chapel. In my vision, this was no longer the basic building I fondly remembered, but a palace with the grandest of squares, resembling pictures of the Alhambra that I had first seen as a boy. It was decorated with bright painted frescoes, gold leaf, and elaborate mosaics. The sky was a pure unbroken blue. Silence fell over me like rain.

And then Nan appeared. She floated towards me, clad in her lily-white dress, her wonderful eyes shining with purpose, with happiness and love. Her arms were held out in welcome, and she was smiling. She was unbearably beautiful. I stood still and she came near. Everything would now be all right. Her dress shimmered to a celestial wind and I found myself laughing with joy; I was saved. At last, I was saved. Her hand reached out and just as our fingers touched I woke with a start. It was not her who lay beside me but Gwen. I sobbed between the sheets, crushed all over again, prepared for a life long loneliness. The sea remained in my blood, always, and Nan was now in my blood. Death had found home in my blood, but not Gwen. I thought it could never harbour Gwen.

☾

The honeymoon was a sham. Still, we had nothing to say to each other and Gwen must have wondered exactly what she had done; she must have regretted engineering my return from active service. It was a great relief to everyone when it was all over, and I would be able to return to work. Now, I needed some of Churchill's legendary blood, sweat and tears to achieve victory over these personal ghosts and demons. I needed time to heal and braced myself for a swift return to duty, craving any distraction that work might offer. I vowed, again, to copy Matron Perry and ignore as much personal baggage as possible. Nothing would get in the way of nursing.

Gwen and Diana, her daughter from a previous relationship, returned to live with my family in Folkestone. I helped transport their luggage, journeying with them, and it was a relief to find myself back in Kent. It was certainly wonderful to be reunited with Mother, and she fell crying into my arms. Her youngest son was back from the war, apparently unharmed and without injury. Dad had been unwell and was currently hospitalised with a chest infection, a weakness picked up from his own time spent in the services, and she struggled to cope in his absence.

The house was unusually dusty, the toilet dirty and sink grimy. The flowers in the vase in the kitchen had been dead for a long time, but it was still my old home and I felt glad to be there. Happy times had been enjoyed within these four walls and we were able to reminisce over a fresh pot of tea. Mother was obviously delighted to have her Harry back safe, and I promised to return to Folkestone as soon as duties allowed. No vacancies were currently available, to my secret relief. It was Government policy to post men as near to their homes as possible after completion of overseas service, but I remained glad of the chance to escape. This way, I would also be away from Gwen.

The repatriation agreement that had dragged me from Malta left a bad taste in the mouth. I felt tricked – Gwen did not want children as I had been informed, and I still puzzled as to her motives. There was always the nagging concern that it had something to do with Len, who we had boarded with in Harrow. They had always been disappearing together and I'd suspected something was going on. I knew his wife felt the same way, but we had no definite proof.

I think that Gwen must have detected my own love, Nan, maybe through one of her frequent premonitions. She was rarely proven wrong. Perhaps she simply feared the loss of financial support, because I had sent her most of the wages earned during the time abroad. This seemed the most likely explanation, in keeping with her character and selfish nature. I could not stop myself from being argumentative, disagreeing with much of what she said on principle. Madly, I still insisted that we attempt to start a family if this was the reason to drag me back to England. I was in shock, foolish, not aware of the repercussions. Our unhappiness quickly became malignant.

I was in no way sorry to leave Gwen and Diana in Folkestone, preferring to return to the solidarity of male company in Boyce Barracks. There, someone might understand what I went through. I could not be the only one in such a predicament, and still could not grasp that Nan was gone forever, taken away from me. My love had not died – what was I supposed to do with that? Where could I place or direct it? If anything, it became stronger, recalling the perfection of her beauty and personality, comparing her against Gwen. I missed her friendship and touch as much as ever, the kiss from her lips. As she had said to me on our last meeting, love does not have to stop. Not ever. I remained unmoored, cast adrift, the future of no interest whatsoever. As my father had done before me, I chose to take refuge in alcohol.

☾

That winter was extremely cold. The barracks were crowded, unheated, and I volunteered myself for the straw pallet in front of a draft-ridden door. Nobody else wanted to stay there but I did not care. The greater the hardship the better, as far as I was concerned. I wanted to suffer, and chattered to fitful sleep, numb both inside and out, with drink helping increase this unhappiness. I knew it was the coward's way out, even then, and it made no difference.

I developed a new recurring dream to accompany the old ones, and imagined myself climbing the tower of Canterbury Cathedral. With each step I moved faster, in a hurry to meet destiny at the summit. I looked over the edge for a long time, greedy, already savouring the fall. My aim, when I jumped, was where the roof below peaked sharply, in an attempt to chop my body in two. This way, it would mirror what had happened internally, when I lost Nan. Slowly, I raised myself onto the cold stone of the balcony, before leaping out and falling faster and quicker, preparing myself for impact, for welcome oblivion. Always, I woke up disappointed.

It was fortunate that I was transferred quickly, before anything serious happened. This new posting took me to the Cambridge Hospital in Aldershot, where I was allocated a position in stores. It kept me busy for much of the time, free of such terrible thoughts, although I still sometimes dreamed of Matron Perry breaking the news of Nan's death. The sun still shone in the hospital gardens, the lizards sunbathed, and wild butterflies sloped through the warm air. Each time, she was lost to me all over again. It did not get any easier. The pain did not reduce or disappear.

My miserable aloof demeanour did not stop the warrant officer, Iain Sutcliffe, from befriending me. He had actually married, before the war, a young woman who also came from Folkestone. She was called Eileen. Eileen Ward. We had never met, but it was this connection that brought us together. Iain took it upon himself to single-handedly cheer me up, accompanying me through a fine selection of local bars and clubs. He put a stop to my excessive drinking, suggesting it was never a good idea, and regularly bought me a ticket if he was taking his wife to a show at the Hippodrome Theatre. He could have become another Eric Reynolds, my best friend, if I had not been transferred suddenly once again.

This time, I was stationed with the RAMC in Maidstone, assigned to the general surgical wards. The work was satisfying, the duties familiar, but the posting did not last for long. Finally the notice arrived. A vacancy had become available and I was returned to Folkestone. It was the town where I had grown up a lifetime ago. Life was simpler back then, free of such complication and difficulties, but somehow the town was able to provide both security and comfort, acting as a safety net to break this prolonged fall. The Warren was nearby, my boyhood escape. The sea was returned to me. I was home, whatever that meant. Family was restored to me, and I would have to make the best of things. The only alternative was death and, thanks to Iain, this had now lost its recent appeal.

☽

A number of hotels in town had been grouped together and constituted a transit camp for soldiers travelling to and from the Rhine and central Mediterranean forces. I was assigned to the Hotel Wampach inspection room, my role to determine whether those men reporting sick were genuine cases or simply attempting to avoid a return to active duty, having lost the stomach to fight.

The entire staff comprised of four RAMC orderlies, an ambulance driver, and myself. The main surgery had only four beds, where we were authorised to detain the men for a period of up to twenty-four hours. An adjoining sick bay could be utilised for more urgent cases. It was tiny, compared with the one hundred beds that I had looked after on Malta.

I reported to the Officer in Command stationed at headquarters in the Leas Cliff Hall. The last time I had been there was for a dance held long before the war, when the seafront promenade had always been the place to be seen. War had changed everything. Now, he informed me curtly that hours would be nine to five each day, with weekends free, and this struck me as remarkably undemanding after the interminable shifts spent on F Block. I was both keen and ready to throw myself into work, fuelled with the passion of anger and loss. They had picked the right man for the job.

I had absolutely no sympathy for the shirkers. They were getting sent back into action, escaping abroad, and I envied them this future. They would not fool me so easily. It was true that there were a number of genuine psychiatric cases suffering from anxiety neurosis as there had been on Malta, but it was amazing how many soon recovered when detained and restricted to a regime of two-hourly fluids and an absence of food. After I had finished with them, they were soon complaining of headaches and pains in the stomach, declaring themselves fit and ready for immediate active service. We also stitched up cuts, referred hernia cases to the local hospital, and treated a variety of common ailments ranging from toothache to in-growing toenails.

This work was non-urgent, frustrating and sometimes petty. I did not care to deal with men who would lower themselves to feigning illness, and continued to miss the responsibility of F Block. There, my presence had felt important and I was of real use, my skills contributing to the greater war effort. Here, I felt ashamed to be reduced to such a position. My mood deteriorated. I acquired a reputation for being a difficult bastard, and this is how I came home to Gwen in the evenings. The situation between us grew worse.

I had rejoined Gwen and Diana in my mother's house. It did not seem right to parade our problems and fighting in front of her – she had enough to contend with my father's poor health, and I had no wish to continue with this imposition. She had never liked Gwen, and with me back in Folkestone it seemed unfair, an embarrassment to everyone concerned. I hated for

Mother to observe my unhappiness and did not wish to add to her troubles – I knew she would only worry more. Diana ran riot, having grown wild through the war years, and I determined that we should move out as soon as possible. We should be sorting our problems in private, not under somebody else's roof, and when an aunt discovered a home for us to rent as a family it seemed to provide the ideal solution. It was only then that I discovered another unpleasant surprise.

For four years, I had been sending wages home to Gwen. It had struck me as the right thing to do, and there was only so much I could spend under siege on Malta. During this time, she had been in full employment as a ward sister. I thought that we would have saved a considerable amount of money, that renting should be comfortable enough. I was wrong. Less than twenty pounds remained in our joint account. Initial disbelief soon transformed into fresh anger – when questioned, Gwen could provide no reasonable explanation. She insisted that it had all been spent on Diana's private tuition and clothing, when there was no evidence to back this up. Her daughter's clothes were old, her behaviour anything but cultured or intelligent.

At last, I began to study Gwen closely. This had been too hard at the beginning, too painful, compared with the memory of Nan, but now I could recognise how easily she dismissed me, like a cat toying with injured prey. I noticed all of the haughty glances, the criticism, and the constant frown grazing her pale complexion. Her thin lips pursed tight in persistent complaint; the frequent little shakes of the head. It was with some pleasure that I realised how much I annoyed her, and yet it was Gwen who had engineered my return. I could not work it out, still, and the sense of despair deepened. War nestled tight in my chest; bitterness breathed in and out of my lungs.

Work provided the sole escape. It was not enough. On F Block, we had nursed bed after bed of infection and contagious disease. We had kept people alive manually for days on end, and through use of the iron lung. It was difficult and exhausting. It was demanding both physically and emotionally, but I had Nan and love to keep me going, to keep me strong. Now, this had all been taken away.

A bad atmosphere followed me around everywhere. In the inspection room, I barked orders and snapped at my colleagues. I shouted insults at some of the patients. If I suspected someone of shirking, *Ipecac* was prescribed to make them throw up, to make them want to get out of the Wampach as quickly as possible. I acquired a fearsome reputation, but this was just cover for my desperate unhappiness. I had lost all direction in a major way.

It would have helped if I could have spoken to Eric Reynolds, Matron Perry or even Iain Sutcliffe at Aldershot, but everyone had been taken away. The only person who remained was my mother, and I had no wish to trouble her further. These were desolate, hopeless times, with Nan never far from my thoughts. Her absence continued to eat away at me, leaving me empty and hollow inside.

☽

In direct contrast to my own fortunes, news from the war had improved – Jerry appeared to be in fast retreat, pursued by the all-conquering Allies. I imagined the ward of F Block, the smiles of optimism and relief while all patients listened to the words of Winston Churchill, the songs of Vera Lynn. I wondered who looked after them now, and hoped that the gentle Sister Olivia Mercieca still played a prominent role. Over there, I could have shared in this excitement. It was what we had all been hoping and praying for, yet now I felt excluded, a stranger suddenly unwelcome at the party. I became paranoid that people might wonder what I was doing at home, questioning my courage and commitment. I felt a constant need to explain how I had not chosen to come back, that I did not want a life lived safely under the covers of England. I craved the intensity of day-to-day bombing, the trauma of nursing under extreme conditions. Now, as much as ever, I wanted Nan.

Depression cloaked me in poisonous darkness. I struggled to find enjoyment in anything, but it was impossible not to experience a lightening of spirit when hearing reports of Hitler's death, with news swiftly following that Berlin had fallen. On May 8th, 1945, victory in Europe was announced. At last, I did not have to feel so ashamed at being separated from the action. We had won: I had played a part and carried a British Empire Medal as proof of this contribution. In spite of that, I still felt hollow inside. The nagging sensation remained that I was living someone else's life.

The entire army salary was spent on decorating and furnishing our new home. It would have made things easier to borrow money, to save us from scrimping and saving, but I refused to entertain such an idea. It was Gwen's suggestion, reason enough to refuse, and I continued to view our problems as entirely her fault. It seemed only right that she should be made to suffer, to give her a little taste of the reality in which I now lived. We could barely manage to be civil with each other, avoiding contact as much as possible while Diana continued to reap havoc unchecked. She was Gwen's responsibility, certainly no daughter of mine.

I painted the walls like a man possessed, everything a uniform cream – we could not afford the fancy colours or wallpaper. The furniture was selected from markets and second-hand shops, an ugly mix of spartan uncomfortable style. It did not look good. There would be no luxury here. I felt determined to punish Gwen for everything.

☾

Great celebrations were planned in the town to celebrate victory in Europe. Victory flags had sprung up everywhere, stretched along telephone lines and hung up on poles in gardens and out of windows. Folkestone had suffered more than its fair share of bombing and shelling, and was ready to enjoy itself. The locals needed to blow off some steam. From a quiet morning, excitement grew palpable on the streets, leading up to Churchill's three pm broadcast. As far as most people were concerned the war was finally over, forgetting the distant battle in Japan. Such crowds had begun to gather in the streets that I actually struggled to walk home after finishing work.

It was a real surprise to discover Gwen apparently restored to her former self, all Garbo make-up, hair and mannerisms. Slight colour bruised her cheeks. She had dressed smartly in a slim fitting brown suit, and actually smiled at my prompt return.

"Well done, Harold. We did it, we've won," she pecked at my cheek with the briefest of kisses. I knew that she boasted to friends of my BEM, although nothing was ever said directly to me. "Shall we go out? Will you be ready in time?"

"Yes, of course."

I hurried to change. After everything that had happened, this was one celebration that I did not want to miss. I had earned my place in it, and together we stepped out from the house. Quickly, we made our way back into the centre of town. Gwen reached for and took hold of my hand, surprising me further, when we pushed through the masses gathering in Tontine Street. We were aiming for the far end, beyond the damaged buildings and near to the fish market, where we had chosen to listen to the broadcast. There was something different about her, less hostile, and I wondered what was going on.

We stood close, Gwen's breath prickling the side of my face. Wind gusted in from the sea, ruffling my hair and blowing it flat across my forehead. Gwen laughed, her own hair unmoved from its lacquered constraint. No clouds were seen in the sky, as if they had all departed for fear of dampening the mood in any way.

There was silence when Churchill spoke of our victory and freedom, then cheering when he spoke of great days. *God bless you all* he said, and I thought about Nan. Her God had not blessed me, and I wanted nothing further to do with him. People started to sing and to cry and to dance, their bodies propped close and swaying together. The noise grew to rival the Gut in Valletta, although thankfully without the accompanying stink of Victory V cigarettes, and there were definitely no Sherry Bandits here.

People were kissing everywhere, climbing lampposts and knocking off hats. They were laughing. At last it seemed that peace was upon us, with victory snatched and achieved against all odds. I allowed myself a smile of satisfaction; the time on Malta had not all been spent in vain. Something positive had risen from the embers of heartache and loss. I wondered what had happened to Dicky Fuller after his own return from the island, my old mate from the town, thinking it would be good to see Dicky again.

The lights could finally stay on, releasing everyone from a six-year prison of shadows and darkness. Finally, my claustrophobia when outside would be reduced, the night no longer blind. We remained in the crowd for hours, and all of the best buildings were illuminated with spotlights heralding the arrival of dusk. It was glorious. Victory V signs were projected up into the sky, spilling hot light into the previous darkness, and it was with some reluctance that we eventually set about the journey home. Gwen had to collect Diana from my mother.

"Harold," she tugged on my hand. I turned to look at her and she forced out a smile. "Harold, I'm pregnant. Are you happy now?"

We embraced with no further words. I was stunned – we were going to start that family, as ordered by the repatriation agreement. I was going to be a father with Gwen, who I did not love. I felt her tears soaking into my shirt, warm, like blood. What had happened to my life? This was not supposed to be taking place. I looked about me, helpless in the gathering dark: judging from the faces nearby, I was not the only one experiencing such mixed emotions. I recognised all too well the glare of loneliness and loss, a feeling that life during war was somehow preferable to the uncertain, unknowable peace we now approached. I could not help myself, and felt the black hole of depression reclaim me once again, sucking, gripping tight while I slipped further and deeper out of Gwen's reach.

I continued to sleepwalk through life. Work at the transit camp continued with business as usual, our admissions a familiar mix of minor ailments, nothing exciting. The shirkers all but disappeared – there was little incentive to feign illness now that the war was nearly over. Gwen and I chose to avoid discussion of our shared future. Living from day to day proved the easier option for both of us. She did not want the baby any more than I did, and yet we continued to go through some pretence of normality. Hesitant, joyless, we discussed a few tentative names, the prospect of having a boy or a girl.

It came as a great relief to be notified of a further posting in June. This time, I had been selected to work on a new exhibition in London, although I have absolutely no idea how this came about. I would have thought that my reputation would have deterred any such opportunity, but read how all personnel chosen had received a decoration in recognition of services and bravery while serving abroad. *Out From The Battle* was scheduled to run for two weeks, based in the gardens of the Royal residence Clarence House. I had to be ready to leave the following week, and there is no doubt that Gwen was glad to see the back of me. I could not blame her for this. I was glad to be getting away.

In 1945 I returned to London a broken man, much changed from the excited youth who had arrived ten years earlier to commence nurse training at the National Hospital in Guilford Square. So much had happened. Then, I was fresh from tending the reverend and author Joseph Hocking, my last private patient as a trainee. I was happy, enthusiastic, and suitably inspired by this quiet strong man. He had broken his neck in a car accident, surviving against all odds and allowing me to benefit from his calm, considered teaching.

It was the reverend who taught that if others could like me, then I should like myself; to be confident and self-assured, so helping lift me from the depths of recent unemployment. I read his books voraciously during my time at Charnwood in Tunbridge Wells, when I had lodged with his family. *The Purple Robe* and *The Scarlet Woman* were good reads, and I knew that Gwen would approve of his title *All Men Are Liars*.

Now, I recalled the romantic storylines and comfortable solutions, how everything worked out neatly in the end. All lives were tidied up. *Heartsease* was my favourite, a more recent novel, the wholesome plucky heroine reminding me of Nan and her nobility of spirit. I hoped and prayed that something similar might be able to unravel from the wreckage of my own life.

It was the perfect time to be getting away from Folkestone and Gwen, to take stock and attempt to regain some balance and sanity. Finding myself away from home and restored to London, the place that I had dreamt about during the worst of Malta's siege, was exactly what I needed. This city had always been good to me, and it was a real joy to meet up with old colleagues at the RAMC hospital in Milbank, where all army personnel involved with the exhibition were quartered.

The exhibition was certainly impressive, much bigger than I had anticipated. Military marches were broadcast over a tannoy system installed in the grounds, and this acted to attract visitors from the nearby Mall and St James Park. We had all sorts of people turn up, from the wealthy to down and outs, from old dames to young children. Everyone was welcome, and the goodwill directed our way was a true surprise. They treated us like heroes.

Out From The Battle conveyed a picture of the transit of patients from the initial field dressing station, through camp reception, and eventually to the base hospital. I was instructed to relate our specific experiences from F Block, including the polio epidemic, and how we had managed to salvage and construct artificial iron lungs. It was tough at the beginning, some memories too raw to relive and discuss, but over time a sense of closure came my way. This was then replaced with pride to have taken part. I continued to miss Nan as much as ever, her absence felt keenly, but inside a tentative healing had at last begun.

Visitors to the exhibition would often invite us to parties. Rationing was all but finished and it was a superb way to be reacquainted with this great city. I had missed it more than I realised, from the intoxicating mixture of smells to the vast range of cinemas, theatres and clubs. There was something here for everyone; Eric had primed me well, before the war. I had missed the paperboys sprinting through the streets delivering the latest edition, the pretty match sellers, particularly the old ladies selling lavender for luck. There was one old girl who I remembered from my time at St Peters, and to my delight she remained stationed on her usual corner. I bought the sweetest smelling sprig to attach to my lapel and wished her a hearty good day. She had been there when Reg Marriott was hit with shrapnel, near to the Grave Maurice pub. It was all coming back to me now.

It was good to see the smiling policemen sweating under their big hats; the cheeky market traders of Soho, selling anything and everything from singing canaries to copper toothpaste to fight decay; the lumbering fleet of bright red double-decker buses. The buildings appeared so grand, despite the obvious war damage. I loved to hear the chimes of Big Ben from nearby St James Park and outside the exhibition. I loved my local café for scrambled eggs on thick cut toast for breakfast. The city remained alive and glorious, unbowed and swiftly recovering from the recent destruction. It carried an infectious restless energy and, best of all, was the absence of broken glass underfoot. That most dreadful sound from the Blitz was heard no more. It was with a sense of wonder that I began to enjoy myself again. What's more, I began to experience a softening in my antagonism towards Gwen. I was going to be a father. We were going to have a baby. A new life would be created to replace the old one.

London brought with it a return of friends, none more welcome than the sight of Eric Reynolds. I had not heard from him for years, fearing we might have lost contact forever. I did not even know if he was alive, yet Eric somehow managed to track me down. I was busy at work on the exhibition, but noticed his lazy swagger from across the room. This was a man at peace with the world, a man to be taken seriously as the glances he accrued confirmed. Eric had always been a big hit with the ladies and now looked better than ever – he had grown his hair, appeared to have bulked out with muscle, and possessed the most golden of sun tans. He looked indestructible.

"Harry Fisher, eh? Thought they wouldn't be able to finish off an ugly mug like you!" He took me unawares, clapping one hand upon my back and making me jump while I addressed a collection of schoolboys. The lads giggled and moved away.

"Eric! How did you find me?" I was delighted.

"Friends in high places," he smiled, "you know me. So what are you doing tonight then? Been starring in any more films?"

It was thanks to Eric that I had been paid as an extra in a movie starring John Loder and Sylvia Sidney. The director had become considerably more famous, an Englishman by the name of Hitchcock. Eric was responsible for some of my finest memories, including nights out late exploring the city, and attending the Chelsea Arts Ball in the Royal Albert Hall.

"Not really," I grinned. "It's great to see you, mate. So what did you have in mind?"

There was so much catching up to be done. Eric had recently returned victorious from the Allied advance through France, and we arranged to meet at the end of my shift when he took me on a drinking tour around Soho, reliving past glories. He was suitably sympathetic to hear of my relationship with Nan, and how it had ended. He rested one arm upon my shoulders, gesturing to the barman for another round of gibsons.

"That's war, old boy. These things happen. But your lady was right, be grateful that it did happen. Remember, you're a long time dead!"

He appeared genuinely sorry to hear of the problems I currently experienced with Gwen. It was Eric who had introduced us, so many years before. His own charms had not diminished at all, and Eric told me that he had even managed to work his way back into the affections of Margaret McGrath, the stunner from my time at nurse training. He had already broken her heart the once. Eric grinned when he mentioned her name, how her parents had always disapproved of him, and I noticed that he now missed one of his teeth. There was something imperfect about him, after all.

"My war wound," he explained. "The only one, from a stone in the Bully Beef! But what was it your old man used to say, how ladies love scars? Well this will have to do!"

It was wonderful to see Eric again, but his return proved very short-lived. A restless man such as himself could never settle into comfortable peace. He applied to the Colonial Office and was swiftly selected for the police force in Benghazi, leaving the country in a couple of days. I was sorry to watch him disappear so soon, but the important thing was that Eric remained alive. I had no doubt that I would be meeting him again. I have no idea how Margaret took the news of his sudden departure.

Out From The Battle went on to become such a success that

we were granted a longer run. It would have been foolish to close us down all the time we were pulling in the crowds, and people were not ready to stop celebrating just yet. The victory had been hard fought over a number of years. They deserved a chance to make the best of things. It also provided me with more time to enjoy this stay in the city, a real chance for some time on my own, and I explored old haunts and previous lodgings at every possible opportunity.

I discovered a broken St Peters, no longer operative as a hospital, where I had worked after gaining my qualification. Just one part of the building remained, and this was now deserted, awaiting reconstruction. A trip to Elsham Road, and the lovely four-storey building I first shared with Gwen, revealed old Porter had sadly died. He had been such a kind old soul, the best landlord, regaling tenants with constant gifts of tea, wine, and even a turkey at Christmas. His errant wife had since returned to look after their quiet son in the basement rooms. The flat at Marchmont Street, our next place, had been totally destroyed.

With great reluctance, I forced myself to visit Len and Marjory in Harrow. Gwen had been insistent we should keep in touch, but there was nothing about the man that I liked. He was a fake in every respect, and had managed to avoid active service although he spoke as if he had won the war single-handed. I did not trust him, and recalled all too well the way in which he had used to disappear without explanation with Gwen. There was something suspicious about it, leaving Marjory and me to wallow in uncomfortable silence. I remained convinced that there was more to their relationship than met the eye, and kept any visits to see them as brief as possible.

It was on a hunch that I visited Gwen's father, Harry Fletcher, who also lived in Harrow. He remained married to Ruby Lloyd, the singer and supposed bane of Gwen's childhood. On the first night we spent together, Gwen had been quick to detail the alleged cruelty of this woman who had stolen her father away. Back then, it had sounded so terribly plausible, but I now understood how Gwen could twist most things to suit her own argument. I was not so sure of the truth of anything she had said.

Harry and Ruby welcomed me with open arms, although we had never met. He was a big man, with slick back hair and slightly overweight through years of good living. He possessed Gwen's piercing eyes. Ruby retained a girlish figure and outlook, endlessly optimistic and cheerful, her features elfin. They could raise the spirits of anyone, a charming couple, and I doubted further Gwen's stories of alleged hardship. Harry and Ruby were good people, sincere and open, and I knew there would be more to it than I had been told. He said that he felt glad and relieved to know that Gwen had ended up with an honest man such as myself. She had always been one for bad choices. I wanted him to like me and I hoped that, somehow, I might be able to bring about reconciliation between father and daughter. It might help to make amends for some of my recent poor behaviour. Gwen was pregnant with my child, after all, and this had to count for something. I recalled a saying of my father – you play the cards you are dealt with, and my mother's frequent incantation – you make the bed, you lie in it. It was up to me, no one else, to make something good from my life.

Out From The Battle continued to prove a considerable success, although we received noticeably fewer visitors after the tannoy broadcasts were silenced. A complaint had been received from Clarence House; apparently, a Royal nap was being disturbed. The reduction in numbers allowed us to spend a longer time with each interested punter, and I enjoyed this period of the exhibition the most. I understood that it was healthy for me to speak about the war, rather than bottling it all up inside. People wanted to hear about the hardships, the heartache, and it allowed them an opportunity to share their own recollections. Everybody had a story to tell.

I was actually explaining details of the camp reception area and our front-line duties on F Block to a pretty brunette when she took me quite by surprise. The hall was empty; she tilted her head in apparent concentration, smiled, then reached for my hand. I could feel her warm fingers stroking gently between my own, exploring the centre of my palm.

"Would you like to come for dinner tonight? I live alone, and you are a darling. My name is Carol."

She spoke softly, quickly, insistent in a way that I could not refuse. Carol was small, maybe five feet tall, with doe-like brown eyes, her straight hair cut into a bob. Two strands escaped over her forehead, brushing the side of her mouth, her lips.

"Yes, thanks." I did not think about it. The answer was automatic and I dared not consider the consequence. It was Eric's words that roared in my head – *you're a long time dead.*

She provided me with directions and then walked rapidly from the hall, turning once to shoot me a dazzling smile. I watched the seductive swing of her hips, the smooth outline of stocking on flesh. I could not help it. I was a man, weak and out of control. It was not every day that you received such generous offers.

I was the first to leave work from the exhibition, and raced home in time for a wash. Clean clothes were selected, and I even polished my shoes. I shaved, again, and my hair was greased into place. Eric and Dad had always stressed to me the importance of good grooming. I should have remained in the lodgings, I knew this, but left Milbank filled with both excitement and trepidation. I felt alive, the blood pumping hard through my body, cool air rushing in and out of my lungs.

Carol's flat was found near to the muddy river, a fourth floor apartment in one of the oldest tenements. The sky remained blue, yet a pale moon hung low over the water. Carved cherubs hovered lazily above the grand entrance, and she buzzed me inside as soon as I pressed on the doorbell. "Come in darling, it's all ready," she said, hurrying me away from prying eyes.

Conversation came more easily than I had expected, and I found myself quickly relax. Carol did most of the talking, telling me how she had helped out with the women's patrol through the war. She had even met the famous photographer Lee Miller, who had taken her picture wearing a facemask and eye shield as protection from incendiary bombs. I listened enthralled, always keen to hear stories of London during the siege. She had actually been one of the sleeping bodies I had stepped over during the Blitz, choosing to take refuge in the Underground.

Carol prepared the best meal I had enjoyed for years: French onion soup with cheesy croutons, followed with a prime cut of steak and all the trimmings. We drank French wine, then fine cognac. I found myself getting tight while she appeared fully at ease, gliding about the apartment in a flattering black dress that clung to all of her curves. The stockings had been removed, her bare legs shapely and tanned. I knew that Eric would have been impressed. He would have known what to do next, how to act, but I became frozen with nerves and some other indefinable emotion.

"Have you ever slept on a water bed, Harry?" She sat next to me, our legs touching, carrying with her a cafetiere of freshly made coffee and two mugs. She leaned over to pour and I tried not to look down her top, catching the briefest glimpse of black underwear.

"I'm sorry?" I said.

"You heard me. Don't be shy." She sat upright, resting one hand on my forearm. Another smile was shot my way, revealing a perfect set of teeth. Her lipstick remained immaculate and she smelled fabulous. "Wait here for a couple of minutes darling, then come through to the bedroom."

I watched her leave, stunned at this directness; even Gwen had never been so obvious. The coffee would have to go cold. The pendulum of the grandfather clock swung slowly in front of me while I sat anxious, tugging at my hair, unsure if I would be able to see things through to their natural conclusion. Only now, I began to take in the surroundings: Carol's furniture appeared expensive, the apartment kitted out in all the latest fashions. Somebody was paying for all this – a husband? A picture of the sea, white lighthouse in the distance, looked like an original work of art. It was beautiful, much nicer than the printed reproductions I had to make do with.

"Harry, I'm ready."

I rose meekly, following the sound of her voice. The door was left open, the light extinguished and curtains drawn inside the bedroom. I stood still, allowing my eyes time to adjust. A huge bed took up much of the space, a real four-poster. Carol lay sprawled on her stomach on top of the covers, one leg raised up from the knee, her foot twisting slowly from side to side.

"Sit down," she commanded. "Relax, I won't bite you." She was a lady used to giving instruction. The soft voice was hard to refuse and I lowered myself onto the floor, one arm leaning onto the bed for support. She rolled towards me, propping herself up on both elbows. Her perfume was amazing, clouding over me, surrounding me, intoxicating. I had never smelt anything like it. I tried to keep my eyes from her breasts, which nearly spilled out from their flimsy covering. She wore a scarlet negligee, I could now determine.

Carol moved forward slowly, so slowly, before kissing me on the mouth. She smiled, deep sighing, then kissed me again. I felt her tongue graze the edge of my teeth, one hand brush onto my neck. She rested her cheek against my own.

A strange thing was happening. Carol was undeniably beautiful and her actions had a profound effect upon me, but not one that either of us expected – I could not do it. I could not respond, even though some part of me definitely wanted to. I still missed Nan, yes, but it was more than that, much more complicated. I suddenly recognised the emotion that flooded my body and it was guilt. I could not do this to Gwen, my wife. She was pregnant and carried our child.

"I'm sorry Carol, but I've got to get back." It was all I could manage to say, the words thickening in my throat, while forcing a distance between us.

"Why? Don't be silly. Harry, come here and get into bed."

"I'm sorry, I can't."

"Why not?" She was beginning to sense I wasn't joking, that something was definitely wrong.

"I'm with someone else. I'm married."

"Is that all?" She laughed, relieved. "Everyone is with someone else. Where do you think my husband is? You didn't think I was single, did you? Now come on, she'll never find out. Promise I won't tell a soul."

"I can't, I'm really sorry." And I could not, it was true. I stumbled to my feet. "Thanks for the meal – it was lovely."

"Harry, I can't believe you're doing this. What sort of a man are you, not one of those fruits? A nancy boy? Can't keep it up, is that it?"

I hurried from the room pursued by a stream of furious insults. Carol's voice had changed beyond recognition, all trace of seduction removed. My jacket was grabbed and I raced from the apartment, closing the door with an almighty bang as I jogged back towards the river. It was not until reaching the relative safety of the embankment that I allowed myself a pause for breath.

The majestic river flowed sluggish in front of me, as old as time, as young as the sea. Above me, a black sky dripped heavy with stars. It was cold. Windy. The evening had turned into a real embarrassment, but it had washed up one priceless fact. I had not cheated on Gwen. I could not do it. She was my wife, after all. Maybe there was some hope for us, for our future and that of our child. I was finally sorting myself out, in London, getting ready to take on the responsibilities that were undoubtedly mine.

☪

Out From The Battle ran until Victory in Japan day on September 2nd, a two-week exhibition that continued for months. By the end of this time, I was ready to return to Folkestone. I had seen all of the city that I wanted, and all of the people. I remained in touch with Gwen's father, Harry Fletcher. Eric was away in Benghazi and, thank goodness, I never saw Carol again. It was time to pick up the pieces of my life.

VJ celebrations were immense, not least because I remained in London. The war was finally, unequivocally over. All staff were invited to a victory dinner in Milbank, and this marked the official close of the exhibition. I had been away for three months and Gwen was pressing for my return. The baby was expected soon.

I fought my way through huge crowds that had gathered to fill the Mall, in front of Buckingham Palace. We would join this later, after our private gathering. There was so much going on in my head – it was still hard to believe that it could all be over, that we could go home and live in peace. Home – I hoped that I would still have one. It was difficult to gauge Gwen's mood, her letters were always so brief. My colleagues were all getting plastered in spectacular fashion, but I stuck largely to water, fearing the effect of alcohol upon me. I had hoped to finish with self-pity and depression after my time at Aldershot, after the help of Iain Sutcliffe. Drinking had never made me a better man. It had never made me feel good.

It seemed that everyone in the unit remained drunk the following morning, except me. There were some shabby faces, bloodshot eyes and terrible headaches. Responsibility inevitably fell upon my shoulders, and I had to muster the entire company before checking that everything was packed safely onto the designated lorry. It felt like losing the toss and organising the baggage party after arrival on Malta, only this time there was more cursing.

We left the city via Kensington and Hammersmith, the streets still busy with ongoing celebrations. I sat in the front with the driver, silent, while the remainder of our company chose to doze in the back. For a bunch of men who had been awarded commendations for bravery, we did not appear so valiant now. Vicious farts stunk out the cabin, loud groans sounded periodically, together with coughing, an occasional snore.

It took hours to pass Virginia Water and then, finally, we were able to speed through the green Surrey countryside and into Hampshire, eventually arriving at Boyce Barracks late afternoon. The men were tired and grumpy, hungry and thirsty. I could think of nothing but the life awaiting me in Folkestone. Now, it was close enough to touch. Nan was gone and I had to get over it. There was a baby on the horizon. I did not know if I was ready for this, how I would cope living with Gwen again, but then remembered another saying of my mother. *One gift is lost, another comes along, and that's life Harry.* Our baby was a gift. We had another chance. I felt renewed determination to make the best of it.

☾

The company was disbanded in the morning. That last night in Barracks was a particularly muted affair, with little of the joking seen from previous days and weeks. None of us could be sure what would come next; we had become used to living with war. Pay and leave passes were collected, before bidding the usual farewells. We all promised that we should meet up again, knowing this probably would never happen. I climbed onto the train, alone, and made my way back to the south coast.

Gwen looked pleased to see me. She even met me at the station, a practice she had not bothered with for some time, and appeared in reasonable health. Her cheeks were touched with colour, her make-up intact, and she had grown considerably in size. I rested my hand upon her stomach and we kissed briefly, like strangers.

"Welcome back, Harold. Did the change do you some good?"

"It did, thanks," I smiled. "I feel much better. And you look well – blooming. I've never seen you with so much colour."

"It's called foundation, Harold." She placed one cold palm on my face, before taking hold of my hand. "Come on, let's get you home. I know that Diana is keen to see you."

Many old friends had now returned to the town, and we were able to enjoy several reunions and parties. Gwen and I both did our best to appear the happy couple, excited by the prospect of impending parenthood, and she seemed genuinely impressed by the attention that my British Empire Medal inevitably garnered. It was the highest decoration that a man of my rank might receive. Relations between us had definitely improved, and life was becoming easier than I had dared imagine. Everything was on the up, I remained on the straight and narrow, and then I bumped into Dicky Fuller.

"All right Harry! Blimey, can't escape you anywhere, eh? So what are you doing back 'ere then?"

He caught up with me at a party. I had often wondered if and when we should meet, and had always enjoyed his good humour. It was Dicky who had introduced me to Nan on Malta, where he had seemed to grow larger than life. Dicky had always been the life and soul of the party, the centre of attention and any scam that might be happening, but now he appeared diminished. He had lost his suntan and much of his hair. Previous muscle was turning into fat and, when he grinned, his eyes had lost their characteristic sparkle.

"Dicky, how are you? I was sent back not long after you went. I didn't expect it either, but us nurses have to do as we're told. So how's life? Still dancing?"

"Not now. Not now." He shook his head. "The wife's gone right off it – corns on her feet! How the mighty have fallen, Harry. Sorry I disappeared at your party, mate."

The last time I had seen Dicky was at the Sergeants' Mess on Malta, just after I had heard about the commendation. The night had been arranged in my honour, but I had ruined it by drinking too much and making a show of myself. I had even thrown up into my shoe, much to the delight of some colleagues.

"No problem, I understood." Dicky had not wanted to leave the island. He had not felt in any mood for company.

"Still, we should have had one last *Blue Label*, eh Harry?"

It was good to hear his familiar trademark cackle. "So how are things?" I asked.

"So so, mate. So, so. And what happened to Nan? I didn't think you'd be in any hurry to leave her. A right couple of love-birds you were."

With those words, all of the previous depression came crashing and clattering back. I had been deliberately burying these memories, trying to forget how happy I'd been. Seeing Dicky shattered all my defences. I knew that Gwen could never compare with Nan. We had shared something very special and rare; nothing would ever match the purity of our love. We had so much in common – I would never be so compatible with anyone else. My eyes filled with sudden tears, I made my apologies and pushed a way outside to be alone.

It all came back to me then. I remembered her touch, her smile, those dark eyes. I remembered her smell, the curve of her lips, our long afternoons spent hidden in Buskett Gardens. Loving. She had been everything to me and now she was gone. She was never coming back. I sobbed and sobbed, noisy, uncontrollable, out of reach from all present company. I knew that life could never be so good again. My recovery was over. I slipped

43

backwards into memory and terrible grief.

Again, I withdrew into myself, and just when things had started to improve. I could not help it. I felt shattered and torn inside, so alone, still rueing the one chance of happiness that had been brutally snatched away. I railed against God, Nan's God – he had not played fair with us. I railed against the world and against my wife, Gwen. And this time, it was not her fault. Our relationship deteriorated further.

I knew that I'd lost something special – it was so hard to settle for anything less. I kept away from friends and family. Work at the Wampach inspection room remained the sole thing to command my attention, and my reputation as a bastard was confirmed beyond doubt. Some men, on hearing who would be carrying out their medical examination, recovered instantly and dismissed themselves on the spot.

☙

It was during the night of September 18th that Gwen shook me awake from a light sleep. We still shared a bed, a house, but nothing more. I had been back in Folkestone for fifteen days when her contractions began, and Gwen wanted me to summon the midwife immediately. She knew from her own nursing experience that the baby would not be long to arrive.

I threw on some clothes and left the house as quickly as possible. The midwife lived just under one mile away and I attempted a jog. No moon was visible in the black sky and I was surrounded by silence, struggling to collect my thoughts. So this was it then, the decisive moment – it was finally happening, the reason for my return from Malta. We were starting a family. Everything would change once again, the future different and up for grabs. My feet pounded on the cold stone of the pavement and I understood that I had to try and make things better between us. We could not carry on as before.

My breathing was laboured yet I quickened in stride. I heard the bark of a dog, a distant flutter of wings in a tree, the calm hoot of an owl. I ran faster and faster, before breaking into a sprint. It felt good. My whole body jolted alert and awake, and it did not take long to reach her house. The midwife soon appeared at an upstairs window in response to my knocking; she recognised well the frantic hammering of a first time expectant dad. Before I knew it, she was out of the house fully clothed and jumping onto her bicycle. I was instructed to follow her home but keep well out of the way. She would call me when I was required.

And then the waiting began. I tried to sit still in the kitchen, but this wasn't possible. I paced the floor of the living room, making circles and loops, listening to Gwen's screams above the patient urging of the midwife.

"Push. Push. Bear down now, push harder dear."

"I can't. I'm trying."

My own stomach knotted in sympathy. I pressed both hands firmly upon it, willing Gwen my strength, hoping it would all be over soon. She sounded in real pain, making an animal noise that I recognised from F Block. It would have been good to leave the house, to escape this harsh sound that brought with it such painful memories, but what if she asked for me? If the midwife needed assistance? I sat heavily, collapsed on the sofa. It was awful to feel so useless and ineffective; I considered going upstairs and offering to help, but the midwife had instructed me to remain where I was in no uncertain terms. I picked up the newspaper and attempted to read, however the words danced teasing over the page, refusing to be understood.

Instead, I made cups of tea for the women that were left at the foot of the stairs. The midwife called down that everything was going all right, it was just taking longer than expected. I tried, again, to consider the future. There would be a new life, a new gift, to consider. My mother would be a grandparent and I was going to be a father. Despite the persistent screams sounding from above my head, it all seemed so unreal. I experienced a strange dissociation from proceedings.

Dawn broke, the living room slowly clouding with light. Birdsong whispered through the windows and, at last, I heard the sound of a child. Our baby. Everything was going to be fine. The worst time was now over and maybe Gwen had been correct all along, that it was right for me to return to England. The midwife called down that all was well for mother and child, appearing soon after dishevelled and red of face. She shook my hand then marched from the room, to catch up on her own sleep she said. She told me to go and have a look at the baby.

At last, I was able to climb the staircase. Each creak, each step, seemed so important, a lifetime dependent upon these actions. I moved slowly, cautiously, forward, determined to be a good father and husband, determined to make good on the past.

Nobody had told me, but I knew our baby was a girl. I had never once doubted this. Reaching the top of the stairs I paused briefly, before pushing open the door and discovering Gwen helpless with exhaustion. She looked so weak and pale, her hair all over the place, and it appeared she had been crying. Her bloodshot eyes were nearly closed and she struggled to glance my way, nodding once. The room smelled of blood, sweat and something else, something unpleasant. A stale aroma caught in the back of my throat.

The baby lay in her arms, our baby. She looked so small and vulnerable, all twitching little arms and feet as she squirmed defenceless in her new world. She was perfect, a real beauty. I found myself brimming full with love and joy, suddenly understanding that this was the true meaning of life. There was no doubting my intent and emotions now, and I edged closer towards the bed.

"Thank you Gwen. Thank you." I stroked her cheek before reaching, tentative, for one of those tiny hands. My eyes were spilling over with tears. "She's lovely. I'm so sorry for all the pain and suffering I've caused."

I hoped and believed that this could be our new beginning, that we might finally be able to put the past behind us and move on to better days.

"That's the one and only time I'm going through that for you. Never again." Gwen did not feel the same way.

We did not embrace or kiss. We did not talk. I recoiled from the room, stunned, distraught, and this is how Jacqueline came into the world. It was not her fault that Gwen and I were to remain so unhappy with each other.

☾

I left them to sleep and rest, taking refuge first in the kitchen before moving through and into the living room. Once more, I collapsed on the sofa, this time closing my eyes. The decisive moment had arrived and things were no better. I did not know what to do next.

Later, I snatched some sleep of my own, leaving mother and daughter upstairs, already apart and distanced from me. Eyes closed, I dreamed of Nan, her abrupt departure from Malta. The drowning. I had thought about it so much, but this time I imagined myself taking her place.

It was a beautiful clear day. The sailing was smooth, some of the girls sunbathing on deck, and then we hit the mine. Before I knew what was happening, the boat went under with an unexpected rush. Screams sounded loud in my head, resembling Gwen in childbirth. There was panic. It was cold, pitch black, the air escaping so fast. A deafening noise filled both ears, horrible, interminable. The boat was breaking up.

There were emotions. Grief first – I would never be able to see Nan again. Anxiety followed – who would be there to comfort her now? And then there was total despair. I sobbed great racking tears, my chest heaving uncomfortably under the relentless pressure of water. I was suffocating.

And then my body became warm, suffused with a serene sense of calm. I experienced visions: my childhood, baptised with the love of a mother, and then Nan, dancing at the hospital in Malta. Those wonderful eyes shone so brightly. She was on the beach at Dingli, smiling, then outside Xlendi church. She was waving me goodbye, wearing her lily-white dress, as immaculate as an angel. Her dark hair blew loose and free.

I felt at peace. Absolute peace. Unable to distinguish whether my eyes were open or closed, I recognised nothing but total blackness and drifted away to the void, a welcome loss of consciousness.

Later, I woke to a choking silence, disorientated and confused. It took a moment to register the reality of where I lay, in my own living room, the house in Folkestone. I was alone. Terribly alone. Nan was gone, out of my life, and my wife did not love me. Emptiness, an absence, now flowed in my veins.

Part Two

FORGETTING

PAM had never felt so alone in life. She had escaped from Poland, at last, but at the expense of her husband. Her marriage. Paul had not been allowed to leave with her and it was awful. She remembered all too clearly the way the soldiers had dropped to their knees, grabbing at his arm, preventing any chance of departure from his frozen homeland.

The boat journey to England had seemed endless. She lay in her cabin and cried tears of ice, her chest thumping in rhythm to the jagged swell of the waves. The moon shone so cold in the sky above, hidden behind a veil of rain. The stars already looked different when she crept about the deck, attempting to avoid unwanted company. Pam tried to prepare herself for an uncertain future but it was all so difficult. How could she live without Paul?

It was undeniably good to be reunited with family. Her mother and sister, Peg, were obviously delighted to see Pam again, but they could not act as a substitute for her husband, her love. Paul. She felt his absence like an amputation, a part of herself that had been crudely, savagely removed. They were meant to be together, of this she remained convinced. It was obvious, after seven years of marriage. He was her best friend and she would wait for him as long as it took.

Time slipped and fell through her fingers. He did not come. She found a flat in Brockman Road, near to the train station in

Folkestone. It was small but contained everything that she required: a place to sleep, cook food, and be alone. Her own private universe. She arranged her clothes in just half of the wardrobe and drawers. The remaining space was reserved for her husband.

She found work in the office at *Woolworths*, near to the sea front. It was undemanding and paid for the bills. Paul had asked her to get ready and make a life for them before his eventual return. Now, he would have somewhere to stay and a hard worker like him would never be unemployed for long. Then, they could move on to something bigger, more comfortable. Anything would be better than the single room they had used to share in Poland. She continued to miss him terribly, and Pam could only fall asleep when imagining that Paul lay beside her, holding her, underneath the covers. She remembered the dance in the school hall at Capel, so many years before, how she had noticed him gazing her way with those wonderful sea-green eyes. She knew then, immediately, that she would fall in love with him.

Pam remembered the words of his sister Anna, in Poland. *When we love, we love forever. You will see this, Pameli. I can see true love in Paul's eyes; he will not let you down.* She lay flat, curled up in the warmth of memory, hugging a pillow to her breast. Each day, Paul grew more beautiful through the fear she might never see him again. She recalled the silence of their final night together in Gdynia, at the home of his nephew, Bolek. She had never felt so close to him and no words had been necessary between them. Everything could be said with the eyes, with touch, with the body. Pam closed her eyes and dreamed of rising out from the bed, flying up and over the houses, above the jumble of chimneys. It was always the same. She floated slowly over the sea, through the thin blue air, to Poland. To Paul.

☉

One moment led to another until the pattern of her life was established. She woke early and left promptly for work, usually first to arrive in the morning. It provided a chance to plan for the day ahead, to savour the first cup of coffee. She never ate breakfast at home, possessing little appetite, impatient for the safe return of her husband.

During lunch hour, she walked along the Leas promenade if weather permitted. She had missed the proximity of the sea throughout her time in Pszow, in Poland, and how no two days it looked the same. The water could appear anything from calm, blue and flat, to wild grey, flecked with breakers: sometimes tranquil, relaxed, at peace, sometimes troubled and angry. Pam began to equate this appearance with her changing moods, staring transfixed for long moments at a time. Fellow strollers had to break stride and move out of the way. Traffic flinched past and behind her. She felt like a stranger in her own town, where she had grown up, recognising no one. It had become like living in a foreign country.

Evening came. Pam often visited her mother and sister in Capel. She continued to feel restless in the absence of her husband, unmoored, and it helped to seek refuge in the safe harbour of family. Again, she remembered the words of Paul's sister, how the only good family is in a photograph, but this was not true for her.

Pam's mother had definitely aged in the space of one year, the time spent abroad in Poland. Olive now appeared as a shrunken version of her former self, frailer, her lips drawn thin and tight. Her forehead seemed ploughed with fresh lines of concern each time Pam met her, but there was no mistaking the kindness retained within her gentle features. She always repeated the same words of greeting.

"Hello Pam, good to see you. Any news, my girl?" When Pam responded with a shake of the head, her answer remained unchanged. "Where there's life, there's hope. Don't you go giving up young lady. I didn't bring you up as a quitter. Things might all work out for the best, you'll see."

It was always good to see Olive. Peg, her sister, bustled from kitchen to living room, unable to sit still, bringing with her an endless succession of homemade cakes, biscuits and hot drinks. "Got to fatten you up, girl!" she said. Their company helped Pam to escape from her own world of silence and darkness and into the clutter of other people's lives.

The three women always sat in the living room sharing a sofa, chatting, discussing events of the day. Peg did not work but looked after her husband and son, Barry. The baby was growing quickly, beaming at all those who should free him from his crib and pick him up, inheriting the sociable character of both parents. Olive liked to talk about Joan, the daughter who had died tragically young, and Pam was glad about this. Joan had been her closest childhood companion and she would never forget about her. It was Joan who had first taken her to the old cobbled fish market and harbour, and to the boat hire in Radnor Park. It was Joan who had announced, prophetically, the importance of living in the present, not some intangible unknown future, but this was easier said than done.

The weekends were the hardest. Without the distraction of work, there was little to keep Pam from opening the trap door of memory. It disturbed her that Paul could not even be sure where she now was, how she was coping, his own situation unknown. She thought of his work at the mine, and how badly he had hated it. She tried not to consider his drinking, the never-ending supply of homemade vodka. She wondered constantly how he was doing, if he now felt as lost as she did, as lonely and unhappy despite the proximity of family. She was learning how to miss Paul, hurting with every thought of him. It remained easy to love from a distance, all bad times in Poland gradually disappearing from view. Forgetting was hard work, requiring much of her energy.

☾

Pam could never relax in her flat. She was not used to living alone and did not appreciate the empty rooms. She continued to visit the Warren as often as possible, remembering Joan, remembering her husband. She walked beyond the house of her sister in Capel, along the cliff tops, and then down the steep path that curved across the train lines to the water. She recalled the first time that Paul had accompanied her, how he had been followed by a white butterfly, and then raced her across the bridge before they had kissed. Life had been good and kind, simpler, without complication.

She sat on a promontory overlooking the rock pools and dark water. Always, there remained something very special about the lonely emptiness of this place. It suited her well, having the sea all to herself. Pam listened to the sound of waves gently caressing the shore. Cloud shadows hurried towards the distant horizon, towards France. The air was so clean, pure, and she breathed deeply. This was the only spot where Pam could feel calm, and she puzzled that more people did not venture from town to reach it. She was relieved they did not, that one place should exist where she could escape from her current concerns. It had always been the lake when living in Pszow.

Joan had never minded taking her out, and they had often rested on this very same headland. The sun always seemed to be shining whenever Pam recalled her childhood. Here, they had swum in the sea and collected an assortment of shellfish for supper. The other regular haunt had been Radnor Park and the boat hire. She remembered the boy who had helped out, collecting money, and assisting the girls in and out of the rowboats. Harry was his name – why did she remember that? He had appeared as a constant presence throughout her youth, and she had liked him. Joan had used to tease her about this first crush, and she wondered what had happened to him.

Time moved on. The sense of loss refused to disappear, and still there was no news from Paul. Pam wondered what she could do to regain contact – there was no phone number to ring, and only one letter had ever managed to breach the Iron Curtain and reach her. The Communist censors had seen to that, but she felt determined that she would have to write anyway, at least once a week, in the hope that something might find a way through. She would have to try. Pam needed to hear news of her husband; anything would do, to help take away her deep loneliness, to reduce the dull pain in her stomach that she now carried with her at all times.

When Pam received her first pay packet, she was able to send a package to Poland. She knew exactly what to send, remembering all too well what they could not obtain or afford. Aspirin, bandages and plasters were bought for the whole family, woollen scarves for Francek, Pawel and Paul, together with nylons for the ladies. She imagined Anna's delight at collecting such a parcel from Margaret in the village post office, and she allowed herself a rare smile. She remained impatient for any reply.

Next, Pam wrote a long letter to her husband, always careful with her words, fearful who might be checking it in Poland. She did not want to get any of them into trouble, and Pam went to great lengths explaining how she remained unwell, and how her doctor was doing all that he could. It was impossible for him to diagnose how long this recovery might take. She enclosed her new address for Paul, but did not mention the job at *Woolworths*. Pam had been allowed to leave the country solely on account of feigned poor health – if the authorities learned that she was working, they would realise this deception and Paul might never be allowed to join her.

Days became weeks became months. She wrote a letter each week and still there was no news from Poland. She sent all of the medicines and toiletries that she knew the family required, becoming more and more frantic to hear how they fared. How was Paul coping at the mine, without her? What was happening about his own departure? He had promised to follow her, after all, his words *it has only just begun* ringing in her head. Things could not be over between them, not like this. It was all so wrong. Pam continued to write, and prayed to God for strength and salvation, for the safe return of her husband. She struggled to sleep, battling insomnia, unable to avert her mind from Poland, from Paul. She grew to dread this ghost hour, when all thoughts remained fixed in the past.

Over time, her memories grew selective, remembering only the good things from Pszow. She missed the company of Paul's sister, Anna, and the many sayings she had used to come out with. She was so funny. There had been the time when Pam made trifles for everyone, using ingredients carried from England. Each one had been individually prepared in the best glasses and she had been extra careful when carrying these up the hill, past the coal mine, to Anna. She hoped they would enjoy them and had been shocked to discover later how Paul's sister had eaten them all. The rest of the family did not even see them.

"I couldn't help myself," Anna had smiled feebly, apologetic. "They were so nice Pameli, really delicious. Nearly as good as my own cooking! You know what we say here, Pameli? It is better to pay for good food than good medicine. I ate them all, for my health!"

"But," Pam had retorted, "you told me another thing, Anna. A hungry Polish man is an angry Polish man. What about the others? Pawel? Johan? What about their health?"

"Ah, Pameli," Anna had hugged her, and kissed her on both cheeks, "there you have me. But they really were delicious, thank you. And I do feel so much better." The ladies had laughed together.

Pam remembered Monika, the pretty lady who ran the only shop in the village. She had also become a close friend, and Pam felt glad that Monika had kept some of her clothes when she returned to England. Monika would not forget about her. She had told Pam about meeting her husband in Krakow, Henryk, where she had used to work on stage as an actress and dancer.

" My Henryk, he was persistent, I'll give him that." Monika smiled fondly in the centre of the store, where she moved from behind the wooden counter. The shelves were largely empty, as usual, and nothing was stocked from abroad. The Communists would never allow that – if it could not be produced or grown in Poland, it was not available.

"He saw me, driving through town, and he liked the look of me. You know, my womanly curves," Monika giggled, delighted at the recollection, running her hands absentmindedly along both sides with a slight sway of the hips. "He offered me a lift, and I thought why not?"

Pam had heard this story before, but she enjoyed it and was happy to hear it repeated. There was little to talk about in the village.

"Henryk asked 'Haven't I seen you before, maybe in Wisla?' It was a line but I didn't care. It's nice, sometimes, when a man makes an effort for you. Sweet. Don't you agree?" Pam nodded and Monika continued. "I made him stop three times, pretending to shop – it was a test. I wanted to know if he was patient. He didn't seem to mind, and then I didn't see him again for months."

The story was interrupted while an old lady tottered stiff-legged into the store in search of alcohol. "For my husband," she explained from the depths of her shawl. "You know what he said to me? If the illness isn't going to kill me, then vodka will be the cure. The old idiot! I couldn't bother to argue today, but give me the cheap stuff. That will cure him all right!"

She limped forward to the counter, before emptying an old purse of loose change for Monika to select the correct amount of zloty. "Good luck with that," her friend had said, while the woman edged back towards the door.

"Why do I need luck?" she cackled. "It's him who will need it after drinking this rubbish!" She banged the door shut quickly behind her, to keep in the warmth, while Monika again resumed her position in the middle of the store.

"Now where was I? Oh yes, I saw him at the box office, queuing for tickets for the latest show I was in. I tried to catch his eye, smiling, but he was away with the clouds, daydreaming. He didn't notice me until reaching the desk, and you know what he said, the monkey? 'Haven't I seen you before?' Must have tried it on everyone, but I got him that time. You should have seen his face when I beat him to the next line – maybe in Wisla? He was speechless, the daft goat." Monika smiled, her blue eyes distant and preoccupied while she scratched at her hair. She had obviously loved Henryk very much. "But he tried, after that, he tried. I'll give him that. Kept on chasing me until I gave in and the rest is history. He wasn't such a bad man," she sighed.

Pam smiled at the recollection, hoping that Paul would prove as persistent, feeling her own story deserved a similar happy ending. But then she remembered that Henryk was dead, Monika now lived alone. She worried about the health of her husband, again, and about the amount of his recent drinking. She hated the readily available vodka, and the effect it had upon him. Pam gazed up through the open curtains and watched raindrops tracing lines down the windowpane. Anna had told her that before their arrival in Pszow, the lake outside the village had actually been dry. It had been emptied by the authorities, searching for a man who had disappeared suddenly and not turned up for work. They found him dead – he had fallen in and drowned, drunk stupid on homemade liquor.

☾

The weeks crawled past. Still, there was no news from her husband and the Polish Embassy now requested her return to this far-off country. She did not leave. Her family were determined that she was going nowhere, and Paul's last words still sounded loud in her head. *It has only just begun.* He had promised to follow her to England. He would not let her down – even his sister had agreed on this. He would be doing all that he could to reach her, and she had to stay patient. They remained connected by silence. They remained connected by love.

Pam continued to reminisce about her time in Poland. She could not help it. She forgot about most of the hardships, the days when she doubted that she would ever feel warm again, the many lies promised to them on arrival. Only good thoughts now survived. She pictured the children who arrived in the village on market day, happy and inquisitive, faces stained scarlet with the blush of blueberries. They had followed her once, when she wore a pink summer dress, unsure who could exhibit such brightness in an otherwise colourless existence. Monika now kept this garment, and Pam wondered if she would attract similar attention.

There had been the big lake in the countryside, the fete. They had walked here after the procession through Pszow, both glad to escape from the oppression of village life. Lusty croaking of frogs and chirruping crickets had accompanied husband and wife, the sounds of people creating their own entertainment. Lush shadows of hills cut through the horizon, tall trees, a hazy blue sunset. New stars appeared in the sky. She recalled the absolute blackness of night, the piercing green eyes of her husband. She wrote again to the Polish authorities, stating how her health had not yet recovered. She was not up to the return journey alone, and needed Paul to come and collect her.

☾

Work at *Woolworths* continued to suit her. She spent much of the day alone, dealing with office administration and paperwork. Her colleagues appeared to be a jolly bunch, good sorts, and they often asked her out in the evenings. They never pushed her when she politely declined.

She liked her immediate boss, a serious young man with prematurely grey hair. She liked to watch him while he read during any available spare time, how his hands would hold the book cover delicately open as if in prayer, careful not to damage the spine. Pam liked him instinctively, recognising the gentle spirit within. Just once, he had also asked her out, for a bite to eat after work. She said no without hesitation. He was not Paul and she remained in love with her husband. How could she settle for anything less?

The chill of winter returned, although without the harshness of Poland. The first flakes of snow fell like white feathers. Shards of ice littered the pavements, late blossoming flowers bent heavy with stems of crystal. Pam noticed broken stone angel wings in the cemetery, how the breath once again vaporised on escape from her lips. She was alive and she spent her time waiting. Still, there was no news from her husband.

Pam visited her family in Capel as often as possible, to escape from the rut of constant anticipation. Peg bloomed in her new role as mother, taking everything in her stride as if she had been bringing up children her entire life, and Barry grew with incredible speed. Each time Pam saw him, he was bigger. Olive, on the other hand, shrunk. Pam's weight also fell sharply, anxiety for her husband ensuring the continued loss of any appetite. She ate because she had to, just enough and no more. She had written many times to Poland, sent as many packages as wages allowed, and still no response was forthcoming. She feared the work of the unseen censors, and that nothing might actually have reached Paul. He would be so worried about her.

Work alone made the long days bearable. It gave her purpose, a brief and welcome distraction from worry. It provided stability, and a reason to climb out of bed in the mornings. Pam prided herself on being professional. She was always dressed smart, never late, and only at work could she ignore the tidal wave of questions that flooded her waking mind. Where was Paul? Why hadn't he come yet? What had gone wrong? How long would she have to live without him?

It was during work, a busy morning sorting the wage slips, that Peg rang her in a panic. She never liked to disturb her sister at the office, and her breathless voice betrayed obvious concern.

"Pam! Thank goodness I've caught you. You've got to come now – there's a man here for you, a Polish man!"

Pam grabbed for her jacket and left the building in a hurry, for once losing her professional façade. The boss waved her away saying it was fine- he knew it had to be something important, but he puzzled as to her manic appearance. Pam was always so quiet and self-collected; he had never seen her exhibit such passion. Again, he rued the fact that she had turned him down.

Pam hailed a taxi from outside the bus station. A Polish man: he was home, he had made it at last. She could not stop herself from smiling – now things could return to normal and she could be happy again. Maybe they would be like Peg, and start their own family. The town unfurled before her and she looked back, out of the window, when they climbed the steep hill leading to Capel. The harbour glistened like a jewel in the distance. The sea shone like white glass about the curve of the bay. She would be able to take him to the Warren again, just like the old days; he would kiss her and everything would be all right. He was home, at last. He had come for her, as he had promised, and their lives could now move on like the seasons, no longer frozen in winter. They could move forward, allowing their relationship to follow its natural progression.

The taxi deposited her outside Peg's house and she felt stunned to see Bolek standing in the front garden. What was he doing there? It was Paul's nephew who had come for her, not Paul, and this was all wrong. Bolek turned and waved. He appeared both pleased and distracted to meet Pam again. The last time they had met was on the eve of her departure from Poland, when she and Paul had stayed in his Gdynia flat. He had later witnessed the devastating effect that her absence had upon his uncle, Paul.

"Czesc, Pameli." He managed to produce a weak smile,

holding his arms open in greeting. Bolek wore a smart blue uniform with matching cap. He carried no luggage.

"Czesc," she replied. Hello. It was only then that Peg moved out of the way and allowed Bolek to enter the house. He spoke no English and she had no idea who he actually was.

They sat in the small living room. Pam stared at his face for clues but Bolek carefully averted his gaze, staring determinedly at three ceramic blue and white swans that Peg had attached to the wall for decoration. Two birds were flying upwards, but the third had tilted down for some time, neglected. It had been like that for as long as Pam remembered. Barry gurgled quietly in his corner crib, asleep and unaware of the unfolding drama. It was Bolek who spoke first.

"My boat has moored for repairs at Dover, so I got permission to come and see you. I only had this address, from Paul. He didn't know where to find you."

Pam realised with dismay that none of her post could have been delivered. Paul should have known where she now lived, but the censor had seen to that. Who had kept hold of all the packages and letters that she had sent? Where were they now? It had cost Pam the bulk of her wages.

"Paul has been threatened," Bolek continued, his steady voice betraying the fact that he had rehearsed this speech many times. The message was so difficult to relate. "If he should leave Poland, his family will suffer. They will all be punished. He did try, but he was stopped. I also tried to help him Pameli, but it was no good. He has been told that if he tries again, we will all be in trouble. He is so sorry Pameli, but he cannot come."

And so it was over between them. Pam sat in shock, numb, disbelieving. Her head bowed down to the floor, shoulders slumped, while her eyes narrowed and she fought back tears. Poland had won, after all. She had escaped but what use was this if her husband could not reach her? What was the point of carrying on? All of her worst fears were now confirmed and Pam started to tremble. The tears ran and fell from her eyes, dripping freely onto the floor.

It was her sister who embraced her while Bolek stood up to leave. It was not his fault, she knew this, but she wanted him gone and out of sight. His presence only made things harder. Her love, the most important thing in life, had been left behind on a frozen quayside in Poland, then buried alive under the coal dust and ashes of Pszow. It had been extinguished by the cold fist of Communism. From that moment, it seemed to Pam that she had been living someone else's life, not the one God or nature intended, and there was nothing that she could do about it. She felt powerless, and could not allow herself to think of a future.

"Dowidzenia Pameli." Bolek began his retreat from the room. He felt awful, and dreaded explaining the details to Paul on his return.

"Dowidzenia."

Goodbye. It was the last Polish word that Pam spoke.

☾

Shapeless pale years were to follow. Pam retained the Brockman Road flat and carried on with the office work at *Woolworths*. She still waited for her husband's return, although she understood this to be in vain. Her mother and sister did all that they could for her, but it remained easier and simpler to live on her own. She visited all of their favourite places, not ready to let go of him yet. She continued to think in Polish, rather than English, whenever her memories were of Paul. She even dreamed in this foreign language.

Pam prayed in the local church, and in the cathedral at nearby Canterbury. She visited the little cottage in Gillingham, their first home together where they had been so happy. Another couple lived here now, but Pam's red curtains still hung in the windows. She wished they had never left, that Anna's letter had never been written and reached them. It had blown each of their lives off course. She wished that Peg had never delivered it, that she might have chosen to keep silent and destroy it in secret.

☾

It was only through the insistence of her sister that she eventually filed for divorce. Still, there was no news from her husband, not even a single card to help lessen the deep pain she felt to her core. Pam began to suffer cruel doubts – had he ever tried to communicate at all, had he actually planned to get out of the country? Was it all a pretence to get her away? She spread her belongings to fill both wardrobe and drawers. She was alone now. Poland had blown her apart.

The divorce was granted unchallenged. It felt so wrong. Nothing should have separated them, and only then she began to understand his sacrifice. Paul must have realized exactly what was at stake when he had vowed to get her out of the country. He had been prepared to risk everything, and he had lost. He could do no more than that, and she knew her love had not been misguided. Paul was a good man, and true to his word. He had in no way let her down, as Anna had promised, and he had not wanted the relationship to end. There was no mistaking the love in his eyes, his heart, and she wept for the pain he must now be feeling.

They had been robbed of everything by the Communists, by Poland. She recalled the ruined landscape of his country, which they had viewed from the slow train before her departure. Skeletons of houses and chapels had flitted past, jagged tips of trees visible against a faded grey sky. A sea of ruins. It now seemed to mirror the waste of their separate lives, a pale example of what might have been, and she could never forgive Poland for that.

☙

The years rolled over unbearably slow. Still, Pam never gave up on her vigil. She clung to the faint hope that he might yet surprise her in the end. Maybe the authorities would relent and let him escape. Maybe they would allow him to come and collect her. She saw him everywhere, when least expected: the face on the crowded bus, the man walking in the fields, the distant swimmer. Always, she was disappointed. It was never Paul. She thought about him every day, and continued her walks to the Warren, the Leas, and the old fish market. Nighttime was the hardest, in the gathering darkness, when she would have to sleep alone. The raw hurt from his absence remained undimmed, and Pam spent all of her life waiting for the man who never came back.

Family provided the greatest support, an anchor to her life unmoored and cast adrift. She went walking every Sunday with Olive, and Peg even treated her to a London shopping trip in an attempt to break her melancholy apart. It did not work. Nothing worked. Pam considered herself an experienced traveller compared with her housebound sister, and when Peg lost her composure while riding an escalator for the first time, Pam was in no way amused.

"I'm so sorry," Peg was terrified. She reached for the man standing above and in front of her, clutching hold of his trousers. Pam had turned away, aghast and embarrassed, while the serious looking city gentleman attempted to ignore her as his trousers were pulled steadily lower. "I'm so sorry," Peg had repeated.

The two women had returned home silent and grumpy, thin silhouettes against a blackening sky. Pam had lost her humour as well as her husband; Peg was simply fed up. Olive was deeply disappointed – the trip had actually been her own suggestion. She had been convinced of its certain success, and they were running out of ideas to release Pam from the straightjacket of her depression.

Sorrow and stress eventually reaped a rich human harvest, but it came as a shock to everyone when Olive collapsed while shopping with Peg and the baby. Her health had continued a steady decline, but neither sister appreciated how ill their mother had actually become.

"She dropped like a stone, Pam. No warning. I was so worried," Peg told her sister in the evening, while Olive recuperated in the upstairs bedroom.

"Where were you?" Pam asked, leaning forward. She tugged at the hem of her skirt, anxious, crossing one leg in front of the other. Her heel tapped rapidly onto the floor.

"Tontine Street, just down from the cinema. We were chatting away and then – bang – she hit the deck. It happened so quickly. It was a stranger who got us the ambulance. I think she must have worked in one of the shops."

" So what happened exactly?"

Peg took forever to get to the heart of a story, but she now explained how they had been rushed to the local hospital, breaking all traffic lights along the way. Olive had been quick to regain consciousness in the emergency ward, but the young doctors were unable to find out what was wrong. They fussed about her, taking blood samples, running tests, but no diagnosis had been reached.

"But why not?" Pam insisted, finally breaking out of her torpor. The family was at stake here. Her family – this was more important than anything, as Paul had always been quick to relate. Finally, she was done with sleepwalking through life. A time of action had arrived. Olive was ill, and they would have to do all that they could to help her. It was true – nothing was more important than that.

"I don't know, Pam, I'm not a doctor." Peg was tired. She fell back into the arms of the sofa, closing her eyes. "I wish I did. She seemed fine before, I couldn't believe it. She was just suggesting that we all go to the next dance on the pier, have some fun for a change. I asked her who would look after the baby and she said we could bring him along, too. A man needs to know how to dance!" She chuckled to herself. "I just hope she's all right. I couldn't believe it when she went down."

Olive appeared to make a speedy recovery. "I just hadn't eaten enough," she insisted. "Too much exercising my jaw! Don't you two go fretting about me. Where there's life, there's hope!"

But the sisters continued to worry. At last, Pam felt able to concentrate her attention on something other than her husband. She loved her mother dearly, and would do anything in her power to help. She would be ready for whenever she was needed. There were some days when she did not think about Paul.

It was while visiting a friend in Capel that Olive collapsed next. This time, she was taken to the general hospital in Ashford for x-rays and further tests. This time, a diagnosis was made. A doctor sat the two sisters down in a small room adjacent to the ward, where he informed that she had a large brain tumour. It had grown so advanced to be no longer operable. There was nothing that could be done to cure her. Now, the women had a new source of sorrow and upset.

Olive's health was quick to deteriorate. She became tired, forgetful, immobile, sometimes unable to remember the names of both daughters. The words ran tantalising out of her reach. She grew frustrated and impatient, not used to being so help-less. Olive's presence had always acted as the energetic centre of the family; the sun, radiating heat and love, which they all circled in different orbits. Now, she was reduced to the role of invalid and she hated it.

She had good days of lucidity, but these grew rare and unique, soon never to be repeated. With time, Olive became increasingly confused. She demanded pen and paper in order to write to her ex-husband in South Africa, Richard, and she said they were now going back. She had decided that the family would return, after all, oblivious to the divorce and his subse-quent remarriage. The daughters were heartbroken. It was awful to witness the decline of their mother, and Olive was now too ill to go anywhere. She could not even leave the house.

The sisters took it in turns with the nursing. Peg coped during the day, and Pam assumed charge in the evening. They fed and washed her, brushing and styling her hair, ensuring that she remained presentable, that she maintained her pride and dignity. Olive had always dressed beautifully. Her appearance had always been immaculate. They saved their tears for the sanctity of the living room, never once breaking down in front of their mother. It would only make things worse, while she maintained a delusion of cheerfulness. They were determined to keep her at home, that she would not see out her days in a hospital or hospice.

Olive became distant and preoccupied, living in the past and some indefinable future, separated from her children by an invisible divide. She did not always recognise the daughters, but one name remained fixed on her lips.

"Richard? Where's Richard? When's he coming?" She never stopped loving their father. There was never another man.

She shrunk away, birdlike and frail. She stopped eating and

muttered nonsense, asking for her own mother, saying that she had been a good girl. Pam imagined that Olive would soon disappear to nothing, that she would one day fly away on the wind and be gone forever, and this is what eventually happened.

"Richard."

Olive sighed, his name on her lips, a beatific smiling illuminating her gentle features for the final time. She closed her eyes and was no more, making a graceful departure from the recent suffering. Both daughters were devastated. It did not matter that they had time to prepare for the inevitable – they could not imagine a world deprived of the kind company of Mother.

Richard died four months later. His daughters were informed by distant relatives how he had never stopped asking for Olive and the girls, and his final wish had also been for reconciliation. Pam wondered when all of this sadness might come to an end. She had lost a husband and now both parents. She wondered if it might be possible to fly backwards through life, to reach a time of hope, before the emptiness had filled inside her.

She went to work early in the morning, always first to arrive at the office. She kept herself to herself, avoiding unnecessary contacts, preferring to keep it this way. Life was simpler, less complicated, keeping her distance from other people. It was less painful if she did not risk getting too close. She was late to return home in the evening.

She visited her sister in Capel. She walked alone to the Warren, the Leas, and the old cobbled fish market. She ate little, never regaining her appetite. She never went out in an evening.

At night, she prayed for departed loved ones. She read books. She avoided bed for as long as was possible, postponing the ghosts of her sleep. She dreamed the same cruel dreams. She closed her eyes and drifted high over the rooftops, gliding across the dark water to Poland. She dreamed of flying to her husband, to Paul. Alone, she withdrew into silence.

Part Three

HOPE

I FIRST saw the light of day in Park Street, Folkestone during the harsh winter of 1911. Born mid- January, one month overdue, the doctor thought I was waiting for the weather to improve. Our house stood opposite the main gates of the gas works in town, and we had to shut the doors and windows at all times to keep out the polluting blossom of coke dust. Mum hated it when we messed up her housecleaning. It wasn't so bad in the cold, but we were baked alive during summer. The street was named from its close proximity to Radnor Park, and it was here that my older brother Leslie ran the boat hire. He told me that he only did this because it was a good place for meeting girls.

Our house was the usual size – two bedrooms upstairs, small kitchen and living room downstairs, with outside toilet and water tap. Space was quickly made for me to sleep in one room with my father and two brothers, while Mother shared the second bedroom with my sister Doris.

Dad was a tall, imposing man, with a voice to match. You did not argue often with him. His name was Edward Horace, but everybody called him Ted or Molly. Even Mother. He was extremely shortsighted, and if Dad forgot to wear his tiny silver pince-nez spectacles he squinted in grotesque fashion. It scared us children, making sure that we kept out of the way in case he should be in one of his frequent bad tempers.

Dad took great pride in his appearance, spending more time in front of the hall mirror than our mother ever did. He told us boys that a real lady always appreciated proper grooming in a man. It was important to appear presentable, and there was never an excuse to be dirty. We watched fascinated as he trimmed the hair from nostrils, ears and then eyebrows, before cleaning his fingernails. He shaved once, sometimes twice, each day, and sported an extravagant wing-commander style moustache that was waxed meticulously.

Dad worked as a theatre attendant in the cinema at the top of High Street. His uniform consisted of baggy plus-four trousers, tweed hunting jacket, and a peacock feather stuffed in a bright blue cap. We thought he looked dashing, bringing much-needed colour to the worn out furnishings of the foyer. He tipped his hat to all of the prettiest women, causing many a blush and fetching giggle. Dad always seemed popular with the ladies, definitely at ease in female company.

He had done his time in the forces, serving in the Royal Army Medical Corps, until becoming one of many gas victims. It was then that the iron entered his soul, a bitterness, a hardness, affecting him, that was never too far from the surface. We loved him very much. We admired him, but he also made us nervous. We always knew when to keep out of his way.

At demobilisation, Dad had been offered the choice of a pension or lump sum of money. He selected the latter and promptly poured it all down his neck, for drink had become a close friend in the army. I learned to hide quickly during his many alcoholic rages, ending up with scarlet handprints on arms and backside from the occasions when he caught me. This drinking was a real shame – sober, he made for a fine friend and good company.

My mother, Lilian, was undeniably the first love of my life. She was tall like Dad, but slender and willowy, with hair the darkest shade of brown. She possessed perfect skin, rosy cheeks, and a smile to melt the hardest of hearts. I never saw her apply anything but soap and water to her face, and considered her the most beautiful woman in the world. Mother somehow managed to convince each of us that we were her special favourite, and in this way bonded the family together. Her kindness was responsible for any caring attributes that I might have inherited. It was because of her that I became a nurse.

If Mother was my island of security, then Dad was the sea, my passport to another world. He seemed to know just about everyone in town, and often let me accompany him on his wanderings. He knew most of the crews in the harbour, and it was my favourite adventure to be invited onboard the many visiting ships. There were always sailing brigs and fancy schooners in the harbour, and these nestled alongside dirty old colliers from Newcastle. Mum hated it when we ventured onboard, for we inevitably returned home black with coal dust. I was particularly fascinated with the big vessels that carried ice from Norway, and endlessly puzzled how this cargo could remain frozen and solid.

I always sat quietly in the corner while Dad chatted amiably with the crew. It was my first introduction to the secret world of men, and I liked it. It was exciting just to listen to the laughs, and take in the sense of camaraderie. I didn't understand everything that was discussed, but women were a frequent topic of conversation, as was the relative merit of various drinks. I got to eat pickles from Russia, gherkins from Prague, together with sausage and black rye bread from Poland.

Dad was a gifted musician. He had played flute and drum for his RAMC regiment, and he was now a member of both the St Johns Ambulance and Fishermen's bands in town. It was always good to watch him play, and if he spotted us he'd wink and deliver an extravagant series of inappropriate notes. We laughed our heads off. We felt so proud of him, and the music appeared to place him completely at ease. He steered clear of alcohol for days afterwards, and remained in the most genial of moods.

The Folkestone that dominates my memory is a happy, easygoing town, one of sunshine, clean beaches and bright painted bathing huts. The seafront Leas was then magnificent, a long promenade with smart bandstands standing to attention at either end. A third bandstand was found in nearby Marine Gardens, with military bands always proving a popular attraction. Three-wheeled bath chairs were lined up in ranks, together with horse drawn carriages. These were ever popular with Toffs and the elderly, who paid a princely sum to be transported along the esplanade while enjoying a view of the holiday sea. Us boys would sometimes attempt to cadge a sneaky ride, jumping silently onto the back rail, and earning a well-aimed crack of the whip from the cabby if detected. There were very few cars on the road.

When I was big enough to go exploring alone, my favourite spot became the old fish market and harbour at the bottom of Tontine Street. This was always crammed with fishermen and visitors, a range of intoxicating smells emanating from the many canvas food stalls dotted along the cobbles – if it came from out of the water, then this was the place you could buy it. Some of the cod on display were huge, far bigger than me, with mouths that could fit a human head. A penny bought a big tub of cockles or whelks. A carton of chips was cheaper.

I loved to be near the sea, and with my school friends we were in and out of the water most days from April until September. The Local Education Authority provided free weekly swimming lessons in the public pool, but I learned much more quickly through being pushed from the landing steps and quayside. This was much more fun, and we used to dare each other to jump, dive and somersault from ever increasing heights into the cool, still depths.

During summer months, holidaymakers descended on the town in large numbers. This was great for us boys, as they would throw coins into the water for us to fight and dive over. I was quite small at the time, rarely strong enough to win such bouts, but on one day this was all changed.

I noticed the pretty girl straight away. She was short, like me, with auburn hair and eyes a shade of green that I had never seen before. She was accompanied by an older girl, almost a woman, and I guessed they must be sisters. To my surprise, the pretty one appeared to be looking at me – I sucked in my belly, raised myself as tall as possible, then winked. If my brother Leslie had taught me one thing, it was how to behave in front of a lady.

The two sisters stood talking and laughing. I watched as the older girl reached into a pocket, before producing a shiny coin that was handed to the young one. I knew this was my moment, and vowed that if it should come anywhere near me it would have to be mine. My friends were too busy carrying on to observe what was happening.

Again, the pretty girl appeared to be looking straight at me. The coin was flicked high into the air, glinting with sunlight, and plopped just six feet in front of me. I was in that water like a shot, diving fast with both eyes open. I stretched out a hand and caught it before reaching the bottom, the shiny tuppence gliding gently into my palm. A firm kick and I was propelled back to the surface, erupting out of the water with one arm raised triumphant, brandishing the spoils of my victory. Through stinging salty eyes, I thought I saw the two girls clap and smile before they turned and disappeared. I wondered if I should ever see them again – they were new arrivals in town. We recognised and knew all of the locals like family.

I never felt the cold when swimming. We could remain in the sheltered harbour for many hours, waiting to search for all the coins that we had missed at low tide. The water became particularly muddy then, ensuring that further swimming was necessary to remove all of this grime. Mother hated it more than anything when I came home caked from head to toe in layers of grubby silt.

The owner of the harbour garage had a dog that often joined us in our games, a white bull terrier that answered to the name of Max. He had one special trick that we could never tire from – if a penny was dropped carefully into his mouth, Max would trot immediately to the Pent Wall ice cream stall, his short tail wagging in excited delight. He dropped the coin into the barrow to be fed an ice, guzzling the entire cone in two or three licks and gulps. We thought it hilarious, and kept the coins coming his way. Not once did Max decline such an offer. It was always us who quit first, not wanting to give away any more of our recently earned fortune. Max would then trot reluctantly back into the shade, where he slept soundly until the commencement of the next session.

Dad sometimes came down to watch us and feed the dog. He

thought it was funny, too. Afterwards, he would take me to the market square to listen to the town crier, a hairy walrus of a man by the name of Anderson, and we both enjoyed the colourful spectacle of this.

Oh yeh! Oh yeh! The words would be heard from a distance, echoing along the streets and announcing his imminent arrival. Three times a day, Anderson marched into the town centre to bark out the latest news. He was even bigger than Dad, twice as loud, and always appeared resplendent in gold braided uniform and black top hat. *Oh yeh! Oh yeh!* I am sure that Dad had a particular fondness for this outfit, perhaps fancying himself in similar attire. Anderson would shout out the news, which was largely unimportant, before signing off with the identical parting shot – *And remember, losing your temper shortens your life. Oh yeh! Oh yeh!*

Just once, my pals and I followed him home to Payers Park, the shantytown area between Old High Street and Dover Road. We watched him change into informal clothes and he appeared smaller in size, somehow diminished. He caught us scrumping his apples, and I was dunked headfirst into the water trough. In this way, I learned he did not practice what he preached about anger management, and it was a disappointment to notice this transformation. We hurried away before getting sidetracked by the nearest blacksmith – there were three in town, and we could watch them for ages. It was fascinating to see how they handled the horses so gently, whispering reassuring words of encouragement, never once causing any hurt or distress despite the bitter stench of burning that assaulted our nostrils.

Summer brought with it a regular migration of faces to the town, with some of these becoming familiar over time. There was a tall good-looking Negro in a slick brown suit, who claimed to be an African doctor. He was another good raconteur, like Anderson, and often drew a considerable crowd to the end of the pier. He had two wares to sell – a chalky powder that he claimed would produce sparkling white teeth such as his own, and a colourless liquid to be used as a remedy for all common ailments. *If the disease is not going to kill you, then this will provide the cure,* he said.

Dad always kept a small supply of the powder, as did my brother Leslie. He told me that real ladies always look for a good set of teeth in a man. This Negro must have found his visits to be profitable, for he lodged in the big hotel next to the seafront for the entire season, and his arrival always heralded the beginning of summer. I saw him fishing from the pier once, his rod a long piece of wood to which the line was crudely attached. He cast out further than I could see, and caught more fish than anyone. I used to see him in the same place nearly every day, but never spotted the girl and her sister again. This made me upset. I had managed to build up a stash of the powder, stolen from home, and wanted to see if it really did impress.

Folkestone was a good place to grow up. It was safe, I had friends, and as well as adventures with Dad my mother ensured that we never missed the pantomime at the Pleasure Gardens. There were always pennies for the rides and machines along the waterfront. We braved the switchback wooden roller coaster that ran from behind the old rowing boathouse to Victoria Pier, but best of all was the fantastic contraption on the right side of the pier itself.

ELECTRICITY IS LIFE. GIVE YOURSELF A TONE UP!

The words said it all. As many as twelve of us would link hands in a nervous, excited circle. The power was switched on and a tingling sensation experienced in fingers and toes. The current was increased and it resembled pins and needles, then our hair began to stand on end. We tried desperately to hold on, watching as the voltage grew higher, wanting more than anything to avoid being the weakling who broke the circle. All the hairs on my arms rose to attention, along with my neck and the back of my head; I gritted my teeth and was never the first to quit. We were cocky as a dog with two tails when the operator was eventually forced to return the handle to zero. We were invincible.

☾

My childhood was undoubtedly joyful, a spring of hope, but the recent war still haunted my memories. We had grown up with the First World War, and only lately had known anything different. It had been ever present, just another feature of normal day-to-day life.

My friends and I used to gather at the base of the Leas slope, near the water, where we could watch columns of troops march down and into a large transit camp. From here, they departed for Europe. These young men were our heroes; there was no grander sight to our eyes. The fact that they threw us scraps of food, loose change, and occasionally live bullets for souvenirs, merely enhanced the impression. We were converts already. It's a wonder that we never hurt ourselves when prising the bullet casings apart, but the smell of cordite certainly made our noses itch.

Once, we watched a soldier crumple and collapse heavily to the ground. He was not far in front of us, and we ran quickly to investigate. Another colleague stooped and bent low over his fallen comrade, who I could now see was not much older than Leslie.

"It's all right mate, the war is finished now. They won't send you back this time." He spoke in a coarse whisper that only us boys could overhear, and repeated the words three times before his fallen friend seemed to understand. "Good lad, you know it makes sense. Don't want to get yourself into trouble now."

The young soldier was breathing heavily and appeared to be crying. He sighed wearily before staggering to his feet. He needed help to lift and carry his pack. The pair trudged slowly forward to camp, and it was many years later on Malta that I finally understood this exchange.

We were open-mouthed spectators to the night zeppelin raids. These strange balloons appeared from over the channel, creeping towards us, silent and luminous with searchlights. They moved so slowly, cumbersome; I could never appreciate how we failed to hit them with our defence guns. We all knew they were heading for London.

Daylight raids became frequent and responsible for the strongest, most persistent memory from childhood. Still, I can see the bomb swooping majestic to earth against a blue sky littered with clouds. I can still hear and feel the force that nearly burst both eardrums from where I crouched underneath the archway leading into the fish market. I was so scared that I ran home straight away and hid beneath the kitchen table. It happened at a busy time, exploding right outside the greengrocers owned by the Stokes brothers in Tontine Street.

When the guns fell silent and the all clear sounded, I still recall the unstoppable pull to discover exactly what had happened. I knew it would be bad but this was no adequate deterrent. People were too preoccupied to worry about an unharmed boy and I was able to investigate freely. It is a sight I have never forgotten.

Dead bodies were strewn along the street, all over the place. There seemed to be a lot of injured folk who were being treated where they lay; I felt frightened by the cries and moans, but not enough to leave. Blood, flesh and bone was scattered onto the pavement and buildings. A sweet, cloying smell filled the air, and I gagged uncontrollably. I felt light-headed for a moment, but quickly recovered. There was nothing I could do to help the wounded, and wondered what would happen to them next. If I had been a nurse back then, I could have been useful.

Some of the shop owners were giving out damaged stock. I ran home again, this time clutching a bag of vegetables and confectionary. The stash included Spanish root, which you could chew for ages, tiger nuts and locust beans. I even had pomegranates, Mum's favourite treat. Everything was edible after a good wash, and Dad said that I had done well. There was a war on and we had to look after ourselves. We always seemed to be hungry and any contribution was gratefully received. I remember the feeling of complete surprise and some disappointment when later told that the fighting was over. A time of peace was now upon us, and we did not understand what this meant.

☾

The family never had much money, and our holiday consisted of two to three weeks spent working in the local hop fields. It started with the thrill of a train ride, our excitement increasing with each mile covered. The time was no less enjoyable for having to work, and it was the only way that we could afford to get away.

I knew a horse and cart would be waiting at the station, to carry us to the farm. How I loved the smell of that animal, together with the sudden jerk when we pulled away. The driver sometimes let me sit beside him, and if I was really lucky I got to hold the reins. It felt like I was doing the steering but there was absolutely no skill involved; that horse could have made the journey in its sleep, without any news from the straps.

Accommodation was basic. We shared with other families, sleeping on brushwood bales that were covered with hay or straw in enormous barns. It was warm enough in summer, and the smell was wonderful. I made several friends here, all from the east end of London, and these were happy hopeful days.

The hop stalks grew up an elaborate network of twines, and it was our job to strip off the fruit. We started as early as possible in the morning, my brothers and I competing with each other to collect the most while Dad stretched out in the sun. During the afternoon, a beer was never far from his side. He watched us, obviously content, while taking charge of the metal discs known as tallies that we were busy earning. At the end of a week, these tallies could be exchanged for money.

My favourite sight was the workmen who tottered about on high stilts, cutting down all vines that were ready for picking. The war was over and I didn't need to be a soldier any more. Now, I set my sights on this as an admirable job. I had a new set of heroes to worship. The pungent hop smell, and the bitter taste left on our hands, gave everyone an enormous appetite. We all slept soundly after an overdose of fresh air, returning to Folkestone refreshed and in high spirits.

I began to explore further out of town. Walking beyond the fish market and harbour, heading towards Dover, I quickly discovered a beautiful secluded area of coast known as the Warren. The walk seemed to deter most people, even though it did not take so long to reach, and I usually had the place to myself. Here, I could go swimming in my beloved sea, explore the many rock pools, and daydream to my hearts content – it became my favourite place in the world. All of my best memories come from the sea.

Sometimes, I managed to persuade Dad to accompany me.

While I ventured in and out of the water, he chose to sit on the rocks with his flask. He used to joke how the sea had grown up a boy – me. It was an idea that I liked, and he was not far wrong. The sea had crept a way into my heart, where it remains to this day.

I did all right at school, working just hard enough to avoid getting into bother from teachers and parents. I was an average academic, no more, good at sports, and I would gladly have spent all of my time at the Warren. I was happy to explore alone, undisturbed, and it was only when I started to help Leslie with the boat hire that I began to frequent it less often.

Leslie was determined to make a man of me. He was certain that I needed the discipline of work and, as he often repeated, I might just find myself a nice girl. Then, I'd need some money in my pocket to take her out. He was right about one thing, because the boat lake was undeniably popular amongst the young ladies in town. They used to arrive in groups of three to four, row sedately around the shallow water, and then chat idly on the benches near to our hut. They giggled and shrieked, taking it in turns to hire a boat, and accounted for the bulk of our business. I would have preferred a more manly pursuit, not yet interested in girls, but Leslie certainly appeared to be popular. They fluttered their eyelids and blushed in his direction, smiling coyly, often asking after his mother and sister, Doris.

I can't say that I enjoyed the work, preferring to spend time alone, but the extra pocket money certainly made me the envy of my friends. It seemed a price worth paying, it kept my brother off my back, and then it all suddenly improved. We had two new customers to serve – the girls who had thrown the coin in the harbour, the coin that I had collected.

There was no mistaking them. I would have recognised the younger one anywhere, her eyes a startling shade of green. Her hair was wavy and brown. She appeared to be embarrassed, unable to return my gaze, and somehow I understood even then that she liked me. This had never happened before.

She approached slowly with her older sister, her cheeks blazing red as a beetroot. She could barely allow herself to look at me, even when paying for the boat hire, although she managed an attempt at a smile. She was wearing a navy blue dress. Her sister was different again, all confident and sure of herself, and it was listening to her that I learned the name of my admirer. Pam. She was called Pam.

I must admit that I liked her too. This puzzled me and it scared me, a completely new sensation. Again, I was not sure what it meant or exactly what I should do – I wasn't going to ask Leslie, because he would then rib me mercilessly. Our paths crossed several times, each of us mute with embarrassment, and we never managed a conversation. I collected her money and steadied her boat. I smiled whenever she dared look towards me, but nothing more. I had no experience in such matters. I could not summon the necessary courage to act on these newfound emotions, and I feared I might be punching above my weight – Pam appeared much too pretty for the likes of me. And so I did nothing, but these encounters provided hope for the future. Who knew what surprises lay in store ahead? Anything might happen given time.

🕰

A close family provided a happy childhood, but it was Dad who brought about our one real storm cloud. He changed jobs and began working for the local brewery. This way, he was able to sample more than a fair share of the wares, accelerating his decline off the rails. Selling wine, beer and spirits all over the county, he met a young schoolteacher from London. They started to see each other regularly, making no attempt to hide this from the family. We all knew about it. He brought her to Folkestone on several occasions, although never to the house, and we were simply forbidden to approach them. We were too young to form opinions and, like the preceding war, simply accepted it as normal.

I couldn't believe it the first time I saw them together. He looked so happy and relaxed, so young, walking along the Leas like royalty with one arm wrapped tight about her waist. In that moment, I hated him. How could he do this to Mother? She was perfect, much better looking than this cheap Londoner, and even as a boy I knew it to be wrong. I could not understand Dad. I could not understand why Mother appeared to do nothing about it.

It went on for some time. Mother became quieter, although was otherwise apparently unchanged. She always made an effort to be cheerful for us children. Dad carried on as if nothing was different, and I remained unsure how to react. For once, Leslie was strangely reticent on the matter, keeping any opinion he might hold close to his chest.

It was actually some relief when Mother's patience finally ran out. One day, she surprised us all by packing her bags and leaving, taking my sister Doris with her. I felt glad on her behalf, pleased that she was at last standing up for herself, but for me it was an awful situation. Left alone with my brothers and Dad, we could not cope and simply fought our frustrations out between us, often resorting to violence. If Dad struck me, then I attempted to retaliate. The house was quickly dirty, no longer a home, and we became hungry with none of us able to cook. The only item in the kitchen that Dad recognised was a frying pan, and we quickly became bored of his tasteless offerings.

It was so desperate that he needed to employ a housekeeper. Dad had hoped to improve the situation, but the opposite occurred and things now grew even worse. The woman he employed was horrible. She could barely cook, her foul language was a disgrace, she was bad tempered and she stank. A mixture of onions, sweat and alcohol followed her every move. She had a big wart on the tip of her nose that convinced me of her witchcraft, and we all kept out of her way as much as possible. I stayed out of the house for as long as I could, growing wild and undisciplined without the loving care of Mother.

It was Leslie who came good and discovered her address from one of his admirers at the boat hire. She was living in Dover, a seven-mile hike away, but we managed to visit her more often than not. It provided us a new excuse to stay out, and she was obviously delighted to be reunited with her boys. Mother fed us up and made us feel good again. The walk to reach her was easy and we often ran, but the return journey inevitably felt twice as long.

We pestered her to make things up with Dad, and eventually wore her down. The storm cloud passed when he finally came to his senses, dismissing both mistress and housekeeper. He pleaded to Lilian, our mother, for weeks on end until she eventually agreed to come back. The house in Park Street was once again a home. Arthur and Phyllis were born soon afterwards, and this completed the family.

☾

I loved my mother so much. It had caused real pain to watch her unhappiness, and I now endeavoured to do everything possible that would make her life easier. Washing dishes, scrubbing floors, cleaning windows; nothing was too much for me. She sometimes protested that she enjoyed the housework, but I refused to listen. I was stubborn right from childhood and, through persistence, she began to allow me to do some of the shopping. Fruit and vegetables became my allotted responsibility.

I started to feel like a man and be useful. I chose to wear Dad's old army cap to enhance this illusion, despite the fact that it was several sizes too big and the peak obscured my vision. I always tried to get to town and back as quickly as possible, to better my record time and also show off to Mother how clever I was. I'd been walking this route my entire life, like the horse carrying us to the hop fields, and knew it better than the back of my hand. I knew all of the short cuts and this task never took me too long.

It was a sunny day when the queue was much bigger than usual. I always shopped at the same grocers where a boy similar to my own age, Terry, helped his mother when not at school. It was hard not to feel an allegiance to the lad, that we were both cut from the same cloth and decent people. I had been told that Terry's mother, Pat, had been unwell. She had disappeared for weeks on end, causing his absence from school, and this ensured that I admired him even more. Also, like me, he was keen on sport and in particular football. He was never seen without a shiny enamel Newcastle badge pinned to his jacket lapel.

I stood in the queue for what seemed ages but was probably minutes. Terry saw me and waved a hand. He grinned, shrugging his shoulders for the delay, apologetic. One old dear was taking an extremely long time deciding what to buy, and this held everyone else up. She insisted on feeling each piece of fruit individually, and tasting the selection of cherries. When my turn to be served eventually arrived, Terry worked quicker than usual. The order was simple, consisting largely of potatoes.

I was late and impatient to get home. I struggled up Tontine Street as fast as I could manage, swapping hands to carry the bags, arms stretched and feeling longer with each step taken. It was just after passing the Stokes brothers that I stepped out into the road.

The army cap was the real mistake. My head was turned to the ground and I didn't look up once. I couldn't see anything other than tarmac, and was half way across the street when I received a sharp push from the left. I twisted to find out who had knocked me, and why, when I was struck firmly to the ground. My hands never once let go of the shopping.

Screams and shouts implored me not to move, but I couldn't help it. Instinct alone ensured that I tried to stand up, and this was my second mistake. Immediately, I received a blow to the head that knocked me out cold, which was not surprising when fighting a double-decker bus.

The next thing I remember is being dragged by the legs. Still, I held onto the shopping. I would not let Mother down so easily. Warm liquid ran down my face, soaking into my clothing. Cuts to both scalp and forehead were oozing heavily. My head felt enormous and numb, I could not see for red, and all I could taste was blood. It was only when carried into *Gosnolds*, the drapery store, that pain cut through and into my senses. I would have screamed out loud, but did not want to show myself up in front of the shop girls who carefully dabbed at my wounds. In pain or not, I remember a sly pleasure from their close attention, and my first thought was how I could brag about it later to Leslie. Dad always said how women love scars – now I would carry some of my own, I wondered if Pam and her sister would look at me with newfound admiration.

A passing baker was soon flagged down and summoned to take me to the hospital. I recognised him from the Salvation Army band – he was actually the cornet player, a friend of my dad. His van smelled of fresh baked bread, and then I had saliva flowing to mix with the blood in my mouth. The now mashed potatoes were taken to Park Street, and I dreaded Mother's reaction when told the news about her Harry. The last thing I wanted was to cause her any more upset.

I had actually been very lucky, requiring nothing more serious than stitches. No bones had been broken, the doctor said, with no internal bleeding. I liked the atmosphere of the hospital, the quiet efficiency and calm authority of the nurses. It had an interesting smell. The doctor ordered that I spend one week in bed recuperating in a darkened room, and I was sent home within the hour. There, I lay still while fussed over by mother and sisters. A bout of slurred speech and double vision ensured their sympathy and attention, but this didn't last for long. Leslie, however, appeared suitably impressed, and congratulated me that I had not cried like a girl and made a show of myself. He attributed this maturity to my work experience.

In bed, I closed my eyes and dreamed of travel, of future riches, and glorious voyages sailing across the silk blue Mediterranean. I wore a scar on my left eyebrow with great pride, again impressing my friends. I think some of them were suitably envious that they secretly wished they had been knocked over. It was not long before I was back at school, back at the boat hire, and back at Terry's shop to do the chores. I walked to the Warren and swam in the sea, with or without my father. Life returned to normal, and it tasted as good as before.

☾

Passage through school was uneventful. I graduated each year without distinction, an average pupil, and continued escaping to the Warren whenever possible. We were not a wealthy family and, at the lofty age of fourteen, I decided it was about time that I should start earning some money. Then, I could help out more at home. I took on a part-time job with one of Dad's many drinking acquaintances, a gentleman by the name of Mr Hann.

Mr Hann had always been a source of fascination for me and my friends, looking as if he had stepped directly from the pages of a Dickens novel. A round face struggled to peep out through a forest of silver grey whiskers. He retained a good head of hair and possessed what my mother would call honest eyes; eyes that shone bright with the fervour of a Baptist preacher, as clear as spring water. He was short and very fat, never less than immaculate with his attire, and I knew that Dad would have approved of this.

Mr Hann walked with a peculiar rolling motion of his vast hips, reminiscent of fluid in a glass, or the brandy in Dad's hip flask. He could usually be seen wearing a long grey morning coat together with sharp pressed pinstripe trousers, and he always clutched a black top hat in stubby sausage fingers. I never saw this on his head, perhaps in fear of disturbing his elaborate flowing locks. Mr Hann spread smiles and goodwill wherever he ventured, his footsteps echoing with the sound of laughter long after his disappearance. He always shouted a greeting to us boys, and we liked him. There was nothing about him to cause offence.

Mr Hann owned three shops in town, and a farm in nearby Wye. My work began at six in the morning, when I sold and delivered newspapers. On a Saturday, I also delivered fresh meat. He shared the same gift as my mother of making you feel indispensable. Mr Hann addressed me as young man, always, in the most precise and correct manner. He was naturally, resolutely jolly, the work a genuine pleasure. He was a good man to be around at any time, but the highlight of the week was without doubt his lunchtime trip to the local bar.

He returned at two exactly, one chubby hand clutching onto a full jug of ale that was never spilled. The other hand was of course holding onto his top hat. He came storming into the Dover Road shop waving the hat, before dropping it onto his desk and depositing a sixpence into my hand.

"You're like one of the family, young man." He bellowed the same words every time. "We go together like gin and tonic, you and me, don't ever go forgetting that."

He plonked himself behind the desk, chuckled, sometimes

belched, and then promptly fell asleep for the next hour. His loud snores filled the room and I struggled to concentrate with the paperwork, but it was worth it. There was not a bad bone in Mr Hann's body.

I worked at the Dover Road shop until finishing school, when he offered me a full-time position at the main branch in Cheriton Road. Here, I would be under the direct supervision of his son Fred, who would teach me the art of butchery. The wage was set at ten shillings a week. Work was not plentiful back then, and my academic record did not allow me to be choosy. It was without hesitation that I agreed to this arrangement and, at last, became a proper working man. Now, I could really pull my weight in the family, and help out with paying some keep. The first task that Fred delegated was to pop to the chemist next door and buy a tin of *Gumption*, the latest brand of elbow grease.

Mr Hann remained a fair boss. It was good fun working with Fred and my life continued to prove enjoyable. The family remained together, Dad now making a great effort to look after Mother properly. He obviously realised the upset he had caused us all, and how much better things had become. I am pleased to report that he now cut back on his drinking.

I was allowed one week of holiday in the summer, on full pay. Mr Hann was not obliged to do this, but he was a generous man. The weather was fine and there was only one place I wanted to go – the Warren. The house seemed smaller now we were older, and it was always good to get away. My rucksack was packed, Leslie loaned me his tent, and I raced to acquisition my favourite spot overlooking the beach. To fall asleep listening to the waves, waking early with the dawn; I could think of nothing better.

The first day passed without incident. I swam, collected shrimps, lay in the sun and read a book while my skin grew dark with summer. Two novels had been carefully chosen for the week: *Island Nights' Entertainments* by Robert Louis Stevenson, and Jules Verne's *Around The World in Eighty Days*. Travel still dominated my thoughts and I dreamed of future adventures, exploring distant lands and meeting with sultry maidens.

Watery dusk flowed into the valley. I had one last swim, and then slept outside under a blanket of stars.

The second day was better. Much better. I lay beside the tent, flat on my stomach, and read some more. When I looked up, I could see the entire coastline stretching out into the hot blue distance and, as usual, the Warren was deserted. I took a swim and warmed up some beans for breakfast. There was not a cloud to be seen in the sky. The only sound was that of seabirds and the gentle lullaby of sea song. I drifted off to a comfortable nap.

It was voices that woke me. Female voices. My body prickled awake with anticipation, wondering who and where they were headed, and I did not have to wait long to identify the source of this disturbance. Two girls appeared on the path directly beneath me, before proceeding to pitch their tent in a lower hollow. I heard the occasional chuckle, a loud fit of explosive sneezing, and then watched them hurry into the cool water.

They both wore matching blue bathing costumes. I was able to study them undetected and could not believe my luck. Finally, I might get to meet some girls and right now I actually wanted this. Leslie had always been quick to remind me of my previous failings in that regard, of the total inaction over Pam, and I resolved that I might finally return home with something to talk about. These girls looked to be slightly older than me. One of them was undeniably beautiful.

I snuggled lower against the rock, pushing my book to one side. They swam out a little way, before returning to the safety of the shallows. They splashed each other, happy, gasping at the morning chill of the water. I laughed with them, wishing I could join in with their games, but it was too soon for that. Eventually, they retired to their camp. I rolled over and stared up at the vast expanse of sky, considering my options. I needed a plan of introduction, an innocent way of engineering our meeting, but my mind failed to come up with a single bright idea. The day was filled with dreaming and delicious anticipation.

The hours passed so quickly. I heard voices but did not see them again. I had a swim of my own, netted some flatfish for tea, and did not bump into anyone. Still, I had not come up with a suitable plan, but that night the angels were smiling upon me. The sound of water thundering on canvas made beautiful music to my ears. Darkness fell heavily into the sea.

I knew where they had pitched camp, and exactly what should follow. I had made this mistake myself, but only the once. The girls had made their home in a small hollow halfway down the slope. It was flat and sheltered, and looked to be the perfect site. This was actually true when the weather was good, but when it rained it flooded badly.

I bided my time, impatient, running through all of the things I should and should not do. I wished I had paid more attention to my brother, because he would have known just the right words to say. I tried to calm my nerves with a cigarette stolen from Dad, but it only made things worse. My heart beat so quick, I felt sick with anxiety. When sufficient time had passed to be certain of their fate, I edged a careful route out to the rescue. The water was now coming down in bucket loads, really unpleasant, and I cursed what it was doing to my appearance. I had tried to tidy myself first, smoothing my hair into place, and it had all been a waste of time.

"Hello. You all right in there?" I tapped gently onto the canvas. The base of their tent appeared to be submerged already.

One girl shrieked while the second was quick to reply. "Hello. Who is it?" A face appeared through the entrance flap. "Can you help us?"

"Yes, that's why I'm here." I was able to look at her properly. She had long brown hair, full lips, her dark eyes luminous with moonlight. She smiled, and inside I melted. I had never wanted to kiss a girl before, but now I wanted it badly. On her shoulder, above the strap of her bed shirt, I noticed a birthmark in the shape of a butterfly. "I'm pitched at the top of the slope, where it's dry. Follow me, and you can shelter up there."

"Thanks." She answered without hesitation and crawled forward immediately, towards me, while I tried not to look at her chest. Another voice spoke quickly from inside the flooded tarpaulin.

"What about our stuff? The tent?"

"It'll be fine," I insisted. "There's nobody else around and we can get it first thing in the morning." I led the way to my own camp feeling like a knight in shining armour. The girls were right behind me, and I thought that this must be the best holiday ever.

We huddled together for warmth. It was a squeeze to fit us all in, and I'd never been so close to any women other than immediate family. Everything was now different and they smelled so good. I expected to be nervous, but was far too attracted to the girl who sat squashed against my left side, our bare arms damp and touching. She had the most beautiful hands.

"I'm Harry," I grinned, trying to sound confident.

"I'm Dot." We shook hands. The girl who had emerged first from the tent appeared to be the more friendly of the two. "Dot Golding, and this is Julia. We've come down from London on holiday. Our friends told us about the Warren and said it was really nice. I thought the weather was always good here."

"It usually is," I laughed. "You must have brought the rain with you. Can I get you a cuppa? A cigarette?"

"I'd love a cup of tea, to warm us up. Didn't know what we were going to do back there – we thought we had the place to ourselves."

"I only just got here," I lied, not wanting them to know I had been watching.

A pot was brewed and I could not stop thinking how Dot was even more attractive close up. I could not stop looking at her eyes – they were amazing, filled with life, and I fought the urge to hold her and kiss her. Julia looked plain in comparison, the shy good sport who would always walk in her friends shadow. The wind howled outside, whistling along the strand, snapping at the poles of the tent. I hoped it would hold firmly in place and not let me down. I didn't want to appear an idiot, and hoped Dot would look at me as a man.

I couldn't stop asking her questions, while Julia lay quiet in the corner. Dot remained chatty and friendly, and I learned how she came from the east end of London. Her family also used to holiday in the hop fields, like mine, and she was one year older than me, making her even more desirable. One year more experienced, and refined from big city life. She laughed a lot, her whole face lighting up in delight, a warm hand reaching often to touch my arm. Julia watched us in silence, disappointed to have lost the exclusive attentions of her friend. She had obviously been in this situation before.

The torchlight was eventually extinguished and we lay together like sardines packed in a can. I had offered the girls use of my sleeping bag, but Dot would not hear of this. She insisted that it be unzipped fully, and the three of us huddled under the makeshift cover. One arm and leg remained in skin contact with Dot. I could not sleep, both heart and mind racing with possibilities. Could I tell Leslie that I had now spent the night with a woman? The holiday, on its second day, had already surpassed all expectation.

We woke to warm sunshine. The wind had dropped during the night and the sea appeared to be dozing gently after its recent exertions. It was a glorious day, but the waterlogged experience had depressed Julia so much that she was determined to leave and go home. I was devastated and tried to convince her to stay, fearing their departure just when things had looked so promising. She remained unconvinced, but to my surprise and delight Dot decided that she would stay on alone.

"I've only got two more days off, I don't want to lose them," she said. "You go, I'll be fine on my own, really. I can always ask Harry for help."

Dot turned and smiled in my direction. Again, I could not quite believe this good fortune and finally understood why Leslie had always gone on about girls. With Dot, it suddenly made sense. The girls left to pack Julia's things, and Dot escorted her friend on the long walk up to Folkestone Central station. I was so restless, unable to sit still, wondering what might happen next. I ran and swam in the sea, forcing great strokes through the water. I tried to fish but couldn't be patient, resorting to collecting shellfish from out of the rock pools. Time dripped so slowly and it was mid-afternoon when Dot finally returned. I felt so excited to see her alone, having the Warren all to ourselves.

I was able to show her my favourite bathing pools. We

explored the many rock pools left by the receding tide. We caught more shrimps and one big dab to eat for supper, and I showed her the hidden spring where we could fill up our bottles with water. Nothing tasted quite like it, and unlike Dad I had not yet discovered beer. Dot was stunning, a real honey. She was tall and slim, willowy like Mother, with long brown hair and an infectious laugh. She was fun to be around, easy company, and we never ran out of things to say. This was unusual for me. She was filled with warmth and energy, happy to get her hands dirty and help me prepare the food. I could not take my eyes off her. Leslie would be amazed when I told him.

We ate our meal under the glow of distant starlight, a full moon hanging low over the black water. Nothing tasted better than food you had caught yourself, and we were both in a good mood. At last, I took Dot's hand and she let me kiss her. She asked if it would be all right to stay with me, it would make her feel much safer. We ate wild strawberries for pudding and I said yes, of course, it would be just fine. My heart beat as violent as a runaway train.

We moved inside the tent and lay down without further conversation. Gently, softly, I kissed her neck and ears, which she appeared to enjoy. Leslie had once told me that this was a useful move. Having Dot by my side seemed too good to be true, a gift without match, and I kissed her again on the lips. Her breath smelled so sweet and she ran her fingers through my hair, grazing my cheek against her own. I felt the uncertain touch of her tongue.

Dot was wearing a white summer dress over her swimsuit, and I somehow managed to remove this. Next, I freed the straps of the bathing costume from her shoulders while she gazed up at me, expectant. The thin material was rolled down and over her breasts. It was a struggle to control my breathing and she smiled, reassuring. It was with pure delight that I was able to touch her smooth, taut skin, to feel her nipples tighten erect in my mouth. I gasped involuntarily, I could not help it, and Dot pulled me closer. She gave herself with such kindness that I was able to forget it was my first time.

Dot lowered herself slowly above me. I had imagined this so

many times, but it was better. Much better. She moved forward, brushing her breasts against my face, her long hair falling over and around me, surrounding me. Again, I was able to hold a nipple inside my mouth. I moved inside her, initially hesitant, before nature took over. After, I lay back grinning and speechless. My world had been changed forever; I was now exploring new unknown territory. From that moment, I believed in the power of love.

We slept wrapped tight about each other. I was afraid to let her go, that it might all prove unreal and she would disappear during the night. My last recollection was her smile, twilight filling both eyes. She felt so warm in my arms, so soft. When I woke in the morning, she remained holding onto me firmly. I felt safe. Comfortable. At home.

Those two days were glorious together, definitely the best of my life. We swam, talked, smoked, and loved. Dot appeared more beautiful each time I looked at her, those brown eyes revealing endless depths of joy and kindness. Wild poppies grew outside the tent, and on our last morning I sprinkled the petals over her naked body while she slept. She woke surprised and then laughing, admiring my handiwork. She sat upright, drawn-up knees touching bare breasts. A handful were gathered and thrown back at me. I emerged from the tent smiling to get us some fresh water, and for one awful moment believed I glimpsed Pam and her sister. I felt guilty, for some indefinable reason, but this emotion was swift to move on. I collected more petals, filled up the bottles, and returned to Dot with love on my mind.

She gave me a present before leaving, a small plaster of Paris teddy bear replete with blue bow tie that matched her bathing costume. He was moulded into a sitting position, arms and legs outspread, and smiling. I vowed that he would never leave my side and this bear became my lucky charm, looking after me during examinations and through the next war. I offered Dot my camping knife but she politely declined, saying there was little need for it in London. I was to keep it, but consider it as belonging to her. That way, I would never forget her. She did not need to worry about that – forgetting Dot would prove impossible.

The walk to the station was horrible. We put it off for as long as possible and I didn't know what to say to her, or whether we should meet again. Dot assured me that she would keep in touch and write a letter as soon as she was home. I made sure she had the address correct, checking it twice, and she laughed. She appeared so much more mature than me.

I waved her off from the station platform and trudged back to the Warren alone. It did not seem the same without her, for a moment losing all charm. I was resigned to the fact that I would never find love again, wallowing in the sweet sadness of it all. It was over. She wouldn't write, not a confident girl like that with everything going for her. She must have plenty of other admirers back in London. I found myself thinking about Pam.

☽

Monday morning arrived, and it was with a heavy heart that I dragged myself back to work. I felt lethargic and not in the mood for any company, but Mr Hann and Fred were just the right men to cheer me up. Mr Hann did not take long to extract the full story from me, and he had seen it all before with his own son.

"You'll soon forget her, young man," he said. "There's plenty more fish in the sea."

But not in my world, there wasn't. My ocean was empty without Dot, and I would not give her up so easily. I kept imagining her touch, the feel of her skin, and could almost detect her taste on my lips. Already, it resembled an impossible dream, a figment of imagination too good to have actually happened, and I felt determined to keep her memory alive. I was given to protracted daydreaming, oblivious to the taunts and joking of Fred. He even put salt in my morning cuppa, and was most disappointed that I drank it without noticing. To his great frustration, nothing he did could get a rise out of me.

Little by little, it was Mr Hann's good humour that worked its magic. Eventually, he had me laughing again. The lunchtime trips to the bar continued, and we still went together like gin and tonic. I still received my shiny sixpence, and it was impossible to remain miserable in his company.

Dot was as good as her word, and she did write to me as promised. She told me how much she had enjoyed the holiday, although Julia was not yet speaking to her. She had been furious to go home alone. Dot asked me to take good care of the bear – he had been with her since she was little, and she invited me to visit her in London. I would just need to find some accommodation, as their place was too small for a guest. Right now, I couldn't afford this. It seemed a foreign land, an impossible far away destination, but she had not rejected me as expected. Again, I carried hope for the future.

☾

Life in Folkestone continued as usual. I paid keep to my parents, and helped Mother with the housework whenever possible. The months piled up and I never made it to London, too scared to risk losing the perfect memories of my time spent with Dot. She had only written twice, and I guessed she now had a new boyfriend. I couldn't really blame her, although I had no love life of my own to mention.

I always enjoyed working with Mr Hann and his son. As part of my training, Fred now taught me about different types of knife, meat and butchery, regaling me with gruesome tales of injury and accident. He insisted that both his previous apprentices had lost fingers, with another nearly managing to disembowel himself. If I did not pay close attention, he said, there was no saying what I might chop off.

Fred and I did not spend all of our time in the shop. If we were lucky, we got to walk livestock from the Wye farm to the local slaughterhouse, an eight-mile round trip from town. These days were the best; I hated to be stuck inside, always glad to be out in the countryside. If I was shut indoors for too long, anywhere began to resemble a prison. I felt a need to escape, to get away, perhaps the earliest signs of later claustrophobia.

We always walked two bullocks at a time, their necks loosely tied to prevent them from managing to get away. Fred and I walked either side of them, occasionally tapping a rump for encouragement, while chatting happily or enjoying a smoke. The beasts became tired on hot days, and leaned against each other for support. They were usually as docile as anything.

Mr Hann arranged these outings for the afternoon. We were able to shut early and, if we were quick, the rest of the day was our own. It had been a warm week, and we were later than usual, when I was too slow to step aside at the gate of the slaughter-house. One of the bulls stamped on my right foot, breaking the bones in two places, and I fell to the ground in agony. Fred was instantly doubled up; when he laughed, his whole body joined in.

"Told you Harry," he spluttered. "You can lose anything with this job, but I didn't expect a butcher to lose his toes!"

More ill luck was soon to follow, when Leslie collapsed in Radnor Park. There were no witnesses and his body was discovered beside the lake at the tide of dusk. He was dead. I could not believe it, and we never found out how or why this had happened. He had always appeared in excellent health, complaining of nothing other than my inadequacies when dealing with women. He gave me a hard time, never letting up with this teasing, but he was my brother and I loved him dearly.

I could not believe he was gone. We would never share a bedroom again, and I would never hear his adult banter with Dad. I would never be on the receiving end of his sharp tongue again, his tips about the ladies – it was so wrong. I missed him terribly and I miss him now. I still have no idea how he was taken. The boat hire was closed never to reopen.

Mother was devastated, taking to bed for days on end. It was awful to watch the life drain out of her, and Dad's response was all too predictable – he returned to drinking with a vengeance. My happy childhood was definitely over. Half past autumn, I grew up and became a man. I had no choice. Someone had to look after our mother.

My job and financial contribution to the family became more important than ever. Mr Hann obviously knew what had happened and he gave me an immediate pay rise. No explanation was offered. He was a fine gentleman, one of that rare breed you only meet sporadically in a lifetime. He taught the importance of laughter and generosity, on some level to live each day as if it might be your last.

And then it was my own turn to fall ill, while the family still mourned the absence of Leslie. It had been a busy day at the shop; I was late and jogging home, keen to get back in time for tea. The sun shone low over the rooftops, casting long shadows, and I admired the deep ink blue of the sky. It reminded me of camping at the Warren, the calm sea first thing in the morning. The air was fresh and I planned to get away at the weekend, to escape from the recent oppression of Park Street.

It was the sudden onset of pain that caused me to cry out in shock, as if burning hot needles had been jammed into both kneecaps at the same time. I fell to the ground like a sack of potatoes, nauseous, faint, and sweating intensely. My breathing was staggered and laboured. I could not move for some time.

I struggled to raise myself and it took an age to reach home. Mother said I looked ghastly and raced to my assistance. She obviously feared another death in the family, and I was helped upstairs to the bedroom. I swallowed some soup and attempted to sleep, but the pain was not easing at all. Dad gave me some of his medicine bought from the Negro at the end of the pier, and this did not help either. I tried to reassure everyone that I would be fine in the morning, I had probably just been on my feet too long, nothing more, but I was wrong. The next day, after a sleepless night, I felt even worse than before.

The doctor was summoned immediately. My legs remained so stiff that they refused to bend – I could not move from the bed, and was now running a fever. My skin was blotchy and clammy. My head felt under great pressure, fit to explode, with sharp pain jabbing above and behind both eyes. Worse still was seeing my mother's concern – she was frantic with worry, and it was my entire fault. This made me feel even more wretched.

Doctor Mason arrived within the hour. A tall thin man with sallow complexion, he was yet another acquaintance of Dad's. The doctor possessed an air of genial authority, a relaxed demeanour, to help put you at ease straight away. He had always spoken to me like a grown-up and I liked him. His long overcoat was draped over the back of a chair, black case deposited at my bedside, and diagnosis reached quickly of an acute episode of rheumatism.

"Nothing to worry about," he patted me on the shoulder, reassuring. "You should be up on your feet in no time. It's pretty common in men of your age, Harry."

Mother was greatly relieved, although Dad still reached for his hip flask. The doctor departed leaving behind a white tub filled with aspirin, together with a certificate for two weeks sick leave.

Doctor Mason was actually wrong. The pain reduced over time but I was confined to bed for eight long miserable weeks, and it would be months before I was able to walk comfortably. In the beginning, I tried to close my eyes and rest as much as possible, but I kept on thinking about Leslie. Had he felt like this at all? Had he realised his health was troubled? Nothing in his recent behaviour provided any clues. And then I thought about Dot, feeling useless to be kept to my bed. She would never look twice at the man I had suddenly become.

I chose to spend my time reading anything and everything that I could get my hands upon. Robert Louis Stevenson, Jules Verne and Ryder Haggard remained firm favourites. I devoured Homer, *The Iliad* and *The Odyssey*, before moving on to *The Letters of Pliny*. It was Dad who always enjoyed an appreciation of classical literature, and he also told me that ladies liked a man to be well read. It was nearly as important as fine grooming. I lived in the world of these books, providing an escape from my mundane existence. I reached for Dickens again, particularly *Great Expectations* and *The Pickwick Papers*. I re-read *The Christmas Stories*, fearing I might still be in bed come December.

Mother bought me a present that she could ill afford now I was no longer at work – a towering bright red geranium in a ceramic sea blue pot. It was amazing to watch this plant flourish so well out of its normal season, and she positioned it on the windowsill to cheer up both me and the room. I drifted off gazing at its nodding head, with dreams of water invariably flooding my sleep. Always of water. I could be swimming through crystal clear depths of the body warm Indian Ocean; I could be listening to the mighty roar of the Pacific, or sailing across the perfect blue Mediterranean. I made a vow to explore these places in later life, to smell geraniums in their natural climate, never once considering four years under siege on Malta as a desirable option.

Throughout this illness, Mr Hann continued to visit and pay one half of my regular salary. It is a measure of the man that he had no legal obligation to do this, and it came as a terrible blow when Dr Mason later insisted that I would need to change employment. I was not to continue working outside, he said, unless I wanted to spend another few months in bed. It was with sad reluctance that I resigned from my current position, and in so doing removed one of the finest characters from my life.

"But who's going to be the tonic now?" Mr Hann insisted. "I can't be drinking gin on my own. Mrs Hann and Fred would never approve of that."

☾

I began the search for a new job as soon as my health allowed, and was lucky to be offered employment as shop assistant to Mr Charles Adams. He ran a clothing store in George Lane, near Tontine Street, retailing under the name of *Rutherfords*. This was actually the maiden name of his wife, Maud. Mr Adams was of short, wiry build, with a matching head of spiky grey hair. To me, he always looked surprised, or as if he had just stepped from the electricity machine along the pier.

The shop was small but well organised. It contained far more stock than I had originally imagined, making use of every available inch of free space. Suits were hung to the rear of the counter, out of reach of prying hands, and all underwear was kept flat in large drawers. Shirts and trousers formed a maze through the centre of the store. It did not take long to discover that Mr Adams shared two important qualities with Mr Hann; he was a fair man, paying a salary of ten shillings each week, and he was not averse to a drink. At the stroke of eleven each morning, he used to send me out on the quiet to fill a hip flask with *Bols* or *Booths* gin. This was kept hidden beneath the suit counter and, when empty, he would eat a raw onion in an attempt to disguise the smell on his breath. It was all too similar to Dad, and my silent complicity in the matter was assured.

It never worked. Mrs Adams saw right through him, a formidable bruiser of a woman who could drive any man to drink, given time. She bellowed at him most days and he certainly commanded my sympathy and cooperation, but it was Maud who was the real boss of *Rutherfords*.

Training began on the first day and I was keen and eager to do well. I had hated being so useless, and felt determined to prove that I was the right man for the job. Initial duties consisted of till work, keeping things tidy, and helping to measure clients for suits. We had a short-lived problem with shoplifters, and security became an extra responsibility. With the encouragement of Mr Adams, who was certainly no fighter himself, I started to attend a local gym and learned how to box. I began running again, now that the strength in my legs had returned sufficiently, and was pleased to notice the subsequent improvement in health – I had my energy back. My concentration returned to normal, and I lost what was the beginning of a potbelly. For the first time ever, I developed muscles – Dot would maybe look at me favourably again, should we ever meet up, and I vowed to maintain this physique throughout life. I also undertook classes in English, Mathematics and Shorthand, seeing as the large majority of our customers were gentlemen. I felt determined to prove their equal.

☾

Four years passed without noticing. I remained in the same employment with no further career ambitions, and continued to escape to the Warren whenever opportunity allowed. I continued to live with my family, helping Mother while Dad took refuge in alcohol. He had never got over losing Leslie.

I now had sufficient money to attend the many dances, theatres and bars prevalent in a busy seaside town. The best dance cost just one shilling at the end of Victoria Pier, and this was closely followed by Saturday night at the Leas Cliff Hall. I watched my friends talk turkey chasing girl after girl, tireless, with endless enthusiasm, while I thought only of Dot. I realised that she had been someone special, perhaps the second love of my life after Mother, and it was much easier to dream about her. I had no appetite for pointless flirtation – it had to be love. I was never keen to join my friends in their heavy drinking, deterred by Dad and a continued will to stay fit, and watched them begin to lose hair while stomachs grew fatter. This was not the future for me. I had a different pathway through life to follow, a different destination.

It was a world depression that changed things for everyone. Money became scarce and jobs were quick to be lost. I felt safe, cocooned secure in my own little world, until the morning when Mr Adams beckoned me silently into the stockroom. I guessed he was ready to deliver his drink order.

"Harry, I've some bad news." He wouldn't look me in the eye, preferring to study the ground. He rubbed his chin, nervous, while the other hand opened and closed into a fist. "I'm afraid that we've got to let you go."

"What?" I was stunned. It was true that business had been slack for a while, but I had not been expecting this.

"I'm sorry, Harry. I've discussed it with Maud a few times and I wanted to keep you on, but the wife says we just can't afford it. These are hard times, and she's probably right. We're just not making enough. We'll certainly miss having you around."

One week of notice, and I joined the ranks of the unemployed, obliged to visit the Labour Exchange. It did not seem so bad in the beginning – I was disappointed, yes, reluctant to be shaken from the torpor of my usual life, but it had been easy enough to find work after my stint with Mr Hann. Now, I quickly discovered that everything had changed, that there were no jobs waiting to be filled. In a depression, vacant work was as rare as hen's teeth.

It was those trips to the Labour Exchange that I soon hated more than anything. Every day, first thing, I left the comfort of Park Street to be witness to the indignity that took away all hope, self-respect and confidence. We queued in long snakes through the building and out of the door – hours could pass before reaching the front counter, only to be knocked back by the faceless clerks smug in the security of their own employment.

The jobless remained resolutely silent – there was no small talk to be heard inside these walls. I watched my associates shiver and shake, sweating, and some even wept openly. It was all so unreal – Dad had led me to believe that a real man never cries in public. It was horrible, and I had it better than most; both my parents worked for the brewery, we owned our own house and never went hungry. Some of these people had nothing, but I still fell into the black well of depression. Nobody was able to help me, not even Mother, and there appeared to be no good reason to get out of bed in the morning. All of my optimism quickly ran dry.

Family and friends were unable to reach me. Mother continued to try the hardest, her approach an endless variation on the same theme – try and be happy love, we're not here for long so you might as well enjoy it; think about Leslie. It was not that I refused to let them near; there was simply nothing that they could do. They were powerless. Those pals still working stood me drinks and supplied me with smokes. They paid my entrance to the local dances, but I now considered myself a burden to everyone. The bad penny. I had lost all pride, and it was a terrible frustration to waste these days away. I used to enjoy work, and even trips to the Warren had now been ruined. You had to keep an eye out for the Ministry of Labour men who searched for wasters such as myself. It didn't matter that there was no work available – if caught idle, dole money was invariably docked.

The ultimate in humiliation arrived after six long months, when receiving a summons to appear before the Court of Referees. You knew you were in big trouble then. It was an enormous room, cold and draughty. Four men sat in a row behind a long desk, barely acknowledging my presence with dismissive cursory glances. They all wore identical slate grey suits, an expensive double-breasted cut that I recognised from my time at *Rutherfords*. The moment you sat down, the questions shot out like gunfire.

"Why do you have no work, Fisher?" The man on the far left was first to speak.

"I've tried for lots of things, but…"

"Don't you want to work? Is that it?" I was interrupted. "Have you actually sought employment?"

"Yes, but…"

"What have you been doing all this time, Fisher?"

"What do your parents earn?"

"Are there any disposable assets? Any capital?"

There was never a chance to reply. The tone of questioning was both condescending and aggressive, and I struggled to keep hold of my temper. Losing this would only make matters worse, but it was difficult to remain civil and polite. I tried to wrestle with the discipline learned from boxing.

The Court knew well that for every meagre job advertised, a crowd of men had been sent to apply. To prove you had actually turned up for interview, a form had to be obtained from the Labour Exchange and signed by the prospective employer. This then had to be handed in on any subsequent visit to the Exchange. It was all so pointless. I had years of work experience, glowing references from both previous bosses, not forgetting the certificates collected from night school in Business Studies and French, and yet no job would ever materialise.

Their questions ground on, relentless, repetitive. I felt cold beads of sweat drip uncomfortably down the back and sides of my best shirt, while I tried hard to maintain my composure. The Court probed further and further into the total income and circumstances of the entire family, so ensuring that I felt a more worthless burden than ever. Dole money was inevitably reduced.

These interviews were repeated at three-month intervals. Still, I could find no work, not even the faintest encouraging sniff, and after nine months my allowance had been reduced to virtually nothing. I could see no end in sight, sick and tired of having to borrow from friends and family all this time. Depression weighed heavy as a coat of armour and now, on top of everything, I became plagued with a recurring nightmare.

In this dream, I walked home alone under the blackest of

skies, surrounded by absolute silence. It took hours. I was lost, but eventually arrived at Park Street and jogged up to the front door. It was only then that I discovered my keys were missing. The air was so bitter to breathe, as if the world was all dead around me.

I heard a noise and realised that I had been followed. An unknown person stood behind me, clearing his throat and then reaching cold hands to touch my neck. I froze, terrified, while the voice continued to mutter incoherently. It's Dad, I thought, a drunken joke, until *he* spoke to me clearly from the other side of the closed door. *Harry, is that you?* The hands tightened rapidly, suffocating; I tried to fight back but it was no good. He was too strong and, just as I lost consciousness, I woke in a panic. These were frightful, hopeless days. It was the worst time of my life.

☾

A good family and friends was not enough to prevent me from feeling like a parasite and sponger. Still, I had no pride to speak of and my energy ran low. It didn't seem worth the effort to rouse myself – I could see no golden future in front of me, there weren't any jobs to fill. Mother worried, Dad carried on drinking, and I considered myself a burden to everyone. It was only running that helped me to keep things together, feeling the blood pump hard through my body the one time that I felt truly alive.

I considered emigration, to Canada, Australia or New Zealand. Things had become so desperate that only a fresh start seemed to provide any solution, a move half way across the world to where the grass might possibly be greener, but at this point I had lost the necessary drive to undertake such drastic action. I didn't want to cause Mother any further upset, through the disappearance of another son, and one by one such dreams fell asleep to be forgotten. I carried with me the stink of bitterness and depression, so reducing any possibility of finding myself a girlfriend. Dot was resigned to the past – I was not worthy of her now. Life acquired a sense of desolation, a moribund numbness. I was lost at sea, drowning.

Against all odds, it was Dad's drinking that actually saved the day. Leslie's death continued to haunt him – he had never been the same after that, and this was not helped by my own decline and inability to find work. He tried to get me a job at the brewery on several occasions, but still there was nothing available. Useless, he took comfort in whisky and cider. He began to drink himself into such states that we needed to summon the doctor for assistance. Mother was mortified with shame and embarrassment, and we could ill afford the fees sustained, although Doctor Mason was always fair in that regard.

I grew to know the doctor well as I was the only one in the family strong enough to help position Dad into a recovery position, his head moved down to one side. I supported and restrained him during the administration of both purgatives and fluid drips. The doctor always retained his calm authority and never hurried or panicked, working as if time was of no importance. He even let us off certain payments, understanding of our circumstances, and it was during one of these visits that he expressed surprise I should continue to live with my parents.

"Still wasting your time, Harry? Have you ever considered becoming a nurse?" he asked.

"Isn't that for women?" I'd been out of work for over one year, emptied of drive and inspiration. The idea of employment had actually begun to scare me.

"No, no, not necessarily. And there's jobs out there, I know, I heard about one this morning. I've seen you could do it, and that's the most important qualification. Nurses are born, not made, and you can be certain the sick will always be with us."

"How would I start? Where? They never said anything at the Exchange."

"They wouldn't," he patted my arm. "These positions are never advertised."

Desperation will make a man try anything. The prospect of becoming a nurse filled me with fear and unease, and already I could imagine the colourful taunts of some friends. Leslie would have had a field day at my expense, but he was no longer with us. I had to do something with my life, and all the better if it was something good, that I might finally be of help to other people.

Doctor Mason wrote a letter of recommendation there and then, and this was to be delivered to a certain Mrs Simm. She was Matron at one of the largest private nursing homes in Folkestone, just ten minutes walk from home. I changed and hurried there immediately, letter gripped tightly in hand, wearing my best suit obtained from *Rutherfords*. It had not been out of the wardrobe for some time, and I hoped no one else would be able to detect the camphor smell of mothballs. I hoped to make a favourable impression, and the doctor had primed me methodically how to behave. I was to speak slowly, clearly, and maintain eye contact at all times. He said that Mrs Simm could be a hard judge of character, and if I appeared unconvincing I was finished. She would dismiss me straight away.

The nursing home transpired to be a big old house, double-fronted, with pristine white washed walls and shuttered windows. It appeared immaculate, the garden mowed and trimmed neatly, although I noticed how the porcelain doorbell was shiny with age. The enamelled black number had nearly vanished through constant use. I swallowed, took a deep breath, and then pressed firmly on the button to my immediate future. The chime had an ominous deep ring, although this was nothing compared with the gaze of the woman who stood behind it. *What do you want?* Her small eyes questioned, harsh, uncompromising.

"Mrs Simm?" I nearly stammered, balancing my weight from foot to foot. A slight nod indicated yes. "I'm here from Doctor Mason. He's a friend of the family and has written this, for you."

I handed her the letter quickly and attempted what I hoped was a winning smile. The doctor had insisted I appear confident, and I knew that Leslie would have approved of the tactic. She snatched hold of the envelope while her eyes never shifted from my face, staring at me icily over thin half-moon glasses. Her grey hair was pulled back severely, lending an expression of mild surprise, her forehead strangely free of wrinkles although she was not a young woman. Mrs Simm was big, like the house, and wore a starched white apron over a billowing blue tent of a uniform. She possessed in abundance the quality to induce fear that some women develop with age. Maud Rutherford certainly shared it, and I found myself picturing a slight, meek Mr Simm, perhaps another secret drinker. I felt glad that I didn't walk through life in his shoes.

It seemed an age before, at last, she diverted her attention to the envelope, releasing me from the steel of her gaze. The seal was ripped open without ceremony, the contents devoured in a rush, and only then she opened her mouth to speak.

"You'd better come in then." The voice was kinder than I'd anticipated, much kinder. It was the stench of garlic that nearly sent me reeling down the steps.

"Thank you." I offered my hand and she shook it, before leading the way along a well-lit corridor to her office. She moved with slow, deliberate steps, and I was able to admire the vast expanse of her backside – it reminded me of Melville's *Moby Dick*, read from my previous sick bed. I nearly chuckled out loud, but such thoughts were quickly banished when Mrs Simm turned suddenly to inspect me all over again.

Her eyes ran the entire length of me, from head to toes, missing nothing. I did not feel like laughing now, and my discomfort increased while this silent study continued. What was she thinking? What was she looking for? I tried not to fidget or cower, determined to stand my ground, and something must have worked because she nodded her head again, twice, in rapid succession. A decision had been reached.

"I'll take you on, Harold, but only on probation. I want no messing from you, but it is true we could do with a spare set of hands. Dr Mason would never have sent you if you were no good, so don't let any of us down. When can you start?"

"Today. Now, if you like."

I began work early in the morning and it was wonderful. For the first time in over a year, I rediscovered my energy and hope. I was filled with enthusiasm and determination to be good at this job; I'd show them. I had never let any employer down yet. Mother was delighted to witness this change, and Mrs Simm was the unlikely angel to come to my rescue. Dad carried on with his drinking.

☾

The nursing home was deceptively huge, consisting of multiple beautifully furnished rooms, dating back to the previous century. I had never seen such a magnificent building and agreed with Mrs Simm that it had been a real blessing for it to be spared during the recent war. Outside, well-kept gardens stretched back to a tiny stream, and I considered the presence of water to be a good sign. It could be my substitute for the sea, the Warren. I discovered that Mrs Simm was as impressive as her reputation, and training began in earnest. There would be no breaking you in gently under her guidance – here, it was sink or swim, and I'd always loved to ride on the waves.

We had twenty long-term residents, all very comfortably cared for. Consultant physicians and surgeons were in constant attendance, visiting their personal patients, and I saw Doctor Mason on several occasions. The home even boasted an operating theatre where most types of surgery could be performed. It was run with military precision, orchestrated by Mrs Simm, and I found myself immersed into a strange, exciting new world.

The correct lifting of patients was mastered quickly and I could see that Matron was impressed, but she did not know that I'd had plenty of practice with Dad. This was followed with instruction in bed baths and the relief of pressure areas. The recording of respiration, temperature and pulse came next, before commencing with more invasive techniques.

I was instructed in the delivery of enemas, a job I could never care for, and worse still was the placement of urethral catheters. One old man insisted on calling his wrinkled little penis the king, and that I was now shaking hands with royalty. Mrs Simm tried to keep him away from the girls, but I didn't want to go anywhere near him either. Intramuscular injections were better, and it was a pleasant surprise to discover that Doctor Mason had been right all along. I did possess an aptitude for this work. My responsibilities grew quickly.

Finally, I was able to repay all previous debts, a huge relief to a man as proud and stubborn as myself. At last, I was able to contribute again to household expenses. Mother was definitely happy, and I believe that Dad cut back on his drinking. Slightly.

I learned how to smile again, and to have fun with my friends. I might even have got myself a girlfriend, in honour of Leslie, but it seemed more important to concentrate on work now. The fewer the distractions, the better.

Probation was quickly over, and Mrs Simm employed me on a case-to-case basis. She said I was doing well, but that didn't mean I could relax. The nursing home went from strength to strength, and I realised that Dr Mason had done me a big favour. Our patients represented the top end of Folkestone society, and we even admitted the travelling King of Belgium for removal of his wisdom teeth. Mother was particularly impressed with this.

I became more and more busy through word of mouth and recommendation, treating patients in their homes, hotels and even other nursing establishments in town. Ours was definitely the best. Mrs Simm proved far nicer than I had initially imagined, taking a genuine interest in staff and patients alike. She gave herself wholly to work, and I learned that her husband had been a victim of cancer. She commanded our respect at all times, and was never a lady to cross. Her bad temper was legendary, ensuring that everyone strove to remain on her good side.

It was Mrs Simm who introduced me to many of the local doctors, providing her personal commendation and ensuring that I was never left idle. I was to stay with a case until recovery or death, and then allocated responsibility in arranging the funeral. I got to know the undertakers as well, building up a list of acquaintances to rival my father.

It was a private case that took me to Tunbridge Wells, where I had been assigned to nurse the Reverend Joseph Hocking. A popular novelist, he came from a large family of clergy and writers. Joseph's brother Silas was famous for his book *Her Benny*, as it was the first time a novel had sold over one million copies. His sister, Salome, and daughter, Anne, were also published. It was a real excitement as a book lover to meet with such a man.

I had read about his accident in the newspapers. The Reverend had been on his way to visit Anne during the autumn of 1934 when his car had skidded on wet leaves, causing it to overturn. He had broken his neck and it was a miracle that he survived. I had arranged to meet with the family in hospital.

Reverend Hocking possessed the palest blue eyes I had ever seen, radiating kindness, and he maintained good humour despite the terrible injury. He had a long, flowing white beard that reminded me of one of the prophets, and this effect was strengthened by his powerful voice. He carried an aura of calm serenity, wisdom and acceptance that this accident was his fate and he would deal with it in a positive manner. He was not allowed to move for fear of nerve damage and paralysis, and it was my task to keep him comfortable. He called me Harry right from the start, already a friend, and I grew to love this dear impressive old man.

His wife, Mrs Hocking, seemed everything a proper lady should be. She dressed beautifully, presenting herself with grace and decorum, speaking to everyone as her equal. She appeared simply delighted to be sharing their company, and I knew that Dad would have liked her. Leslie too. She retained something of the girl about her, tall and attractive with straight blonde hair cut into a bob. Mrs Hocking walked with a swing to her hips, a spring in her step, her blue eyes sparkling bright with vitality. It was a privilege to find myself in their employ.

I was assigned the day shifts, eight until eight, while a member of the resident staff covered nights. The Hockings paid for my accommodation in a nearby hotel, and this provided me with another new experience. It seemed so posh and extravagant that somebody actually cooked my meals and made my bed in the morning. They even tidied up after me. I felt important and spoiled, with life definitely improving after the long year unemployed.

In the evenings, I was able to mix with an assortment of visiting salesmen who were never short of a story to tell. They all had the gift of the gab and it was a social crowd, really funny. Just like my friends back in Folkestone, they never passed on an opportunity to chat up a woman regardless of age, size or looks. Most of these men were married and I didn't approve of this promiscuity – it reminded me of Dad and his affair with the

London schoolteacher, the unhappy mess that was left behind. I could never envisage a time when I might cheat on a partner, and still resolutely believed in the power of love. I hoped, one day, to meet another special girl like Dot.

The Reverend made slow progress with his recovery. When fitted with a supportive orthopaedic collar, he was particularly eager to leave the hospital. The family now chose to rent a private house for his recuperation, and this was Charnwood. I was offered the chance to lodge with them, change to night shift, and receive an excellent salary of four guineas per week. It was an easy decision to take.

Charnwood was a large white building of colonial style, green-shuttered, and perched on a rise overlooking parkland and a sizeable lake. It stood alone as a wonderful paradise, and for a short time this would now be home. I couldn't believe my luck, especially when discovering that my lodgings were actually a suite. Not only did I have my own bedroom and living space, I even had a private toilet and washroom.

Nursing the reverend always felt more like a pleasure than chore. He was one of the most influential people I'd ever meet, and while I officially tended to him he did a more than reciprocal role in strengthening my own self-esteem and confidence. I looked forward to our talks, keen to learn from his obvious intelligence, while he asked questions about my family and background.

I told him about Leslie and Dad's drinking, about my long-term unemployment and the effect it had upon me. The awful depression. He explained that if other people could like me, then I should be happy in myself. "You've got to have an appetite for life, Harry, not take it like a medicine," he often repeated. "If they can like you, are you saying that they are all wrong?"

His humility and respect for all aspects of life proved a source of constant wonder, and I admired his unflagging determination to help others. Not once did I hear him complain about his own injury and disability. If that was God's choice, he said, then it was the right one. He would adapt and continue with his preaching.

I admired his quick strong mind, his gentle good humour. He stressed the particular importance of family, and to be true to yourself at all times. When pressed, he told me about making the film of one of his books, *Prodigal Daughter*, in 1923. I was only twelve at the time but remembered Leslie going on and on about the lead actress, Gloria Swanson. He said she was actually very nice, constantly reading, and I was always sorry when my shift and our conversations came to an end.

At Charnwood, I was able to enjoy walking about the crystal lake while mulling over the Reverend's teachings. The dark shadows of large carp could be seen idling beneath the cut glass surface of water. I enjoyed sunsets of purple and gold, their beauty doubled through reflection, and how sometimes the sky became a tangle of red while the treetops appeared that they must surely catch alight. Sometimes, I was surrounded and followed by butterflies.

It was the reverend who made up my mind to move on. I would have been happy to stay longer, but he insisted that I should study in college and train to become qualified as a state registered nurse. He told me that I was gifted and should make the best of my abilities, to further my prospects. When I protested that I would not be able to look after him, he shrugged the argument away. "I'll be all right Harry," he said. "It will make me glad to see you do well. Go on and make me proud."

Mrs Hocking and Mrs Simm wrote glowing personal references, and these were posted with a carefully worded letter to London. The reverend had helped me with this. It was not long before a reply arrived on the doormat, and I received acceptance into The National Hospital for Diseases of the Nervous System, Guilford Square.

It was on August 11th, 1935, that I returned to Folkestone and packed my bag for London, now filled with excitement and high hopes for the future. Reverend Hocking had taught me well and I had listened, constant, diligent. I was on my way, at last, no longer wasting my time. It was my turn to discover the world outside the safety net of a small town. It was my turn to enter a landscape of nursing, Gwen, and then Nan.

Part Four

LONELINESS

IT WAS during the childhood voyage to England that Pam first fell in love with the ocean. She could not comprehend its enormous size, the perfect shade of aquamarine, and wanted more than anything to leap from the wooden deck and into the cool blue embrace. She wanted to feel herself weightless, unmoored, and free to be carried wherever the current should decide.

Arriving in England, she was pleased to discover that her new home would not be far from the water. The old fish market was just down the end of the road, two minutes walk away, and here she found a strange, exotic world of underwater creatures, new smells and sights. Peg was not so interested, but her older sister Joan was happy to accompany her whenever she asked. Her mother would never let her explore anywhere if unattended.

The two girls strolled hand in hand past stalls selling cockles, whelks and mussels. Laid out on slick icy slabs were cod that were larger than Pam, prawns as thick as a finger, and peculiar crustaceans that neither sister recognised. They were following their noses to the smokehouse at the end of the cobbles, where the mackerel melted delicious in the mouth. If Pam was lucky, Joan would treat her to an ice cream at the old Pent wall where she could stroke the little dog, Max, who always attempted to lick at her cone. She never let him get near – Pam enjoyed the ice cream too much.

They stood and watched the local lads showing off, diving into the harbour, fighting and snatching at any coins that passers by threw in from their loose change. The sun always seemed to be shining. The crowd walked slow and unhurried, each person wearing the familiar relaxed smile of summer.

Joan proved to be her constant companion, a kind gentle soul who had inherited their mother's grace and considerable height. She possessed large brown eyes, rosy cheeks and auburn hair. Pam resembled a smaller version of this and they were obvious to others as sisters. Joan was happy to assume responsibility while Mother battled hard against cancer. She had moved to England for an operation to remove a tumour of the bowel, and this was thankfully a success. She now recuperated slowly, steadily, and it was a real help not to worry about her girls. While the middle sister Peg was quick to get serious with a boy, it was Joan who took over the family. She made sure that the house ran smoothly and everyone remained content.

It was Joan who first took Pam to the Warren, not far from the centre of town. She had heard about it from the surgeon, Mr Molesworth, and was keen to explore this for herself. He had told her that it was beautiful, unspoiled, and usually deserted. If they enjoyed swimming, then this was the place to go. They could reach it from the cliff tops at Capel, or by continuing east out of the harbour and clambering over the rocks. This sounded the best option to Pam.

Mr Molesworth had not exaggerated – the Warren was simply stunning, a curtain of yellow sand found at the end of a network of tracks, enclosing a myriad of rock pools and little beaches. The water glistened silver blue and both girls were quick to plunge in. Nobody watched or listened to their screams of delight. Nobody heard the peals of bright laughter. Natural springs bubbled up the tastiest drinking water, and there was even a small pond bursting full with freshwater fish. It became Pam's favourite place in the world, even better than growing up with the freedom of Africa. The two sisters usually had the place to themselves, their own private universe, and they both loved it. The walk from town seemed to deter all casual visitors, and it was here that Pam first learned how to master the waves. They swam most days from April until September. She levered winkles and muscles from the clenched fists of the rocks. She netted little shrimps for supper, which Mother considered a real delicacy.

Joan also accompanied Pam to the cinema. There were several to attend in Folkestone, but they usually stayed closest to home at the old one near the top end of High Street. They were often late getting ready, Pam struggling on tip-toe to brush her unruly hair in the hall mirror that hung too high on the wall, and it was inevitably a race to climb the steps leading up to the foyer. It was worth it because a fine looking gentleman, resplendent in bright blue uniform and matching cap, always greeted them. He bowed his head as if they were royalty, and addressed them as the dearest of friends.

"Evening girls. You're both looking nice. You can slow down now, you're just in time. It's not standing room only tonight, and it hasn't started. The feature won't be on for a couple of minutes."

Joan blushed while Pam giggled with embarrassment. What must he think of them, she wondered, always the last to arrive? He reminded her of an exotic bird, maybe a parrot, in his outfit, so colourful compared with the normal people in town. Both sisters were fans of the movie star Robert Taylor, and they never missed one of his films.

☾

Olive's health improved with time, all girls taking turns with the household chores. Theirs was a happy home, filled with brightness, laughter and singing. A joke was never far distant. They all enjoyed this new life in Folkestone. There was little talk of returning to Africa.

Peg was now serious with Bill, spending much of her free time away from the house, but Joan continued to keep watch over Pam. They visited the fish market as often as usual, with Joan now encouraging her sister to throw coins to the diving lads. There was one fellow in particular who captured Pam's attention, for she had also noticed him at the Warren. They must share something in common, she thought, because so few people ventured out there. It was Joan who discovered his name through friends – Harry. Harry Fisher. His dad was the usher in the cinema and there was some quality about him that she liked. This had never happened before. His hair was jet black. He was slim and quick, brown as a berry, and he possessed the most startling green eyes. They reminded her of the sea.

The two girls continued to explore the town. Joan loved to investigate the ramshackle hotchpotch of shops that sloped down to the inner harbour. Here, she enjoyed a tuppence of hot salty chips, or sometimes a carton of whelks. These were too chewy for Pam, too ugly to be considered as food. Pam always preferred an ice cream, and to remain in sight of the water. Joan watched while she played dare with other children on the strand, trying to stand still until the last possible fearless moment, before rushing away from the incoming tide. If she got wet and her shoes were ruined, as was often the case, it always resulted in a slap from Mother before she calmed down and was eventually forgiven. Pam found being forgiven to be deeply unpleasant.

It came as a surprise to the sisters when a new location soon became firm favourite to them both, when it was possible to hire rowing boats in Radnor Park. Joan did not need much persuading to accompany her when it opened, and they ventured out early on Saturday morning. Pam was so excited, she had been awake since six, but they were still not the first to arrive. The area about the lake was noisy with groups of young girls, many present for the same reason as the sisters. The lad who ran the boat hire was a stunner and he knew it. He stood a strapping six feet tall, his white shirt tight and displaying an impressive physique. His hair was immaculate, swept back in thick waves from an unblemished complexion, and he looked as good as any film star. When he smiled, and he smiled often, a mischievous twinkle lit up his eyes causing many a young heart to flutter. Even the usually impassive Joan was not immune to his charms, for once losing her confident demeanour. She stuttered and averted her eyes, even dropping a couple of coins when paying for the boat.

Pam sat in the front like a princess. Joan rowed and she

smiled, glad to be returned to the water. It was not the sea but this was still good, and she was dry so avoiding any punishment from Mother. They slid through the silk green expanse and grinned at each other with simple enjoyment. Joan was good, steering the boat with considerable skill, and they now had a new pursuit to fill their days. Folkestone was looking after them, offering up entertainment like jewels. It was never dull to live in a town beside the sea.

Both girls were keen to return to the lake, and it was a surprise to discover a new helper on their next visit – Harry, Harry Fisher. Again. Pam could never seem to avoid him, and this time it was her turn to stammer and blush. She liked him, and she was still not sure exactly why. He never spoke more than necessary, a few words to ask for the money, but she sensed that he might like her too. His smile was embarrassed, his cheeks flushed red, and his manner was sheepish and uncertain. Joan was quick to catch on and ribbed her sister, merciless.

"So there you go Pam, you've got your first admirer. You'll soon be getting serious like Peg," she laughed. "I'll be the only old maid!"

Pam hated to feel so embarrassed, but she continued to enjoy her time on the water. Joan could never deter her from that.

She grew older and, sometimes, Pam was allowed to explore on her own. She liked riding her scooter along the long road by the sea, envious of any lone swimmers. Pam was only allowed in the water when accompanied. Occasionally, she was daring and ventured beyond the penny arcades and onto the pier. There could be dancing with a real band right at the end, and this always enthralled her. Pam longed to move with them, the men all smiling and handsome, the women beautiful, graceful, impossibly elegant. She felt her own curly hair, the ancient dress handed down from both sisters, and she almost felt like weeping. She would never look as good as they did. Nobody would ever ask her to the dance.

Summer was without doubt the best. The sun was hot and Folkestone exploded with brilliant new life. Visitors now came to the coast, flooding the streets and beaches. The air was filled with chatter and laughter, an infectious good mood spreading everywhere, affecting everyone. Olive decided that, seeing as they had plenty of space, the family should take in lodgers for the season. This would pay for any extras, or little luxuries as she called them: sweets for the weekend, luxury bath soaks, pennies for rides on the pier.

Pam had to give up her room and share with Peg, but this was only for the holiday and she didn't really mind. Peg was out most of the time, anyway. It was fun, and each girl was given a specific job to help with. Pam was allocated the shopping and she loved this; many happy hours were spent admiring the window displays of *Gosnolds* department store. There had not been anything like this in Africa, and the shop girls all looked so glamorous. She hoped that a little might rub off on her. Quickly, the family built up a list of repeat visitors, who began to resemble an extended family. The extra money was used on clothing, toiletries and, for Pam, boat hire and countless ice creams. Pam liked to be warm and summer was the best season of all.

Every Sunday morning, Olive and the girls dressed up in their smart new clothes for church. Pam enjoyed singing the hymns, belting out the words as loud as her mother, but she always remained impatient for the end of the service. Then, she was first to escape out of the side door, across the Leas promenade, and down the slope that led to the beach. Here, she played happily with her school friends until it was time for lunch, and *Dare* remained the best game of all. The challenge was to stay still for as long as possible, yet manage to avoid the incoming waves. Pam was often the winner, but this success came at a price. Still, she ruined her shoes. Still, she earned a smack from her mother. Being forgiven did not improve over time.

The family gathered around the wireless on Sunday evenings, and even Peg made sure she was present although they hardly saw her all week. The radio was in the sitting room, made of a bulky brown wood and shaped like a falling teardrop or flame. They arranged themselves into an excited half circle before listening to their favourite programmes. Speaking was definitely unwelcome – this was quality time, Olive insisted, they could chat about nonsense the rest of the time for all she cared, but not now.

Pam never missed *The Ovaltinies* on Radio Luxembourg. She had been a member of the fan club since their arrival in England, collecting every badge and picture card, memorising the words to each song. It had been the centrepiece of her childhood but now she was tiring of this. Peg and Joan preferred the music programmes and, after watching the dances at the end of the pier, Pam could now understand why this should be.

☾

Time passed. Olive's health continued its steady improvement and they remained a happy, close-knit family. A sea of love bound them together and Folkestone continued to suit them well, although Richard was never forgotten in Africa. The girls missed their father and he wrote often, never once forgetting a birthday. He asked Olive to bring them all back to him, for the family to be reunited, now that she was feeling better. She insisted that her health was not up to the repeat journey. The girls were amazed because Mother appeared well recovered, but they did not care to argue. Folkestone was definitely home. They did not question Mother's motives, and it was many years later that they finally learned of his womanising.

Pam continued to visit the boat hire, although never alone. It was only a short walk from the flat and she still loved to be on the water, the novelty not once wearing thin. She remained pleased to see Harry Fisher, the lad who helped out, although he never had much to say. He was always polite and smiled nicely, probably as embarrassed as she was. When it was her and not Joan who placed the money into his hand, she felt the colour race into her cheeks and needed to look away so that he would not notice her blush. Her stomach became a tangle of nerves. She began to save her favourite outfits for Radnor Park, no longer on tiptoe getting ready in the hall mirror, but this effort was apparently pointless. While other boys began to take notice, she appeared to remain invisible to Harry.

This went on for some time. Her mother frowned at the state of her best clothes, never once guessing why Pam would smarten up for the boat hire, but these events were brought to a sudden, unexpected conclusion. Joan continued to accompany

123

Pam to the Warren whenever her own work allowed, and it was during one such excursion that they nearly bumped into Harry. He was holding hands with a girl and did not even see them, so caught up in his new affection. This was bad enough, but the next time they saw him he was actually emerging from a small tent with the same girl. It broke Pam's heart and she set about forgetting him immediately. Joan was kind enough to at last desist from her teasing.

☾

Years passed. The family remained in Folkestone. Peg continued to step out with Bill, her boyfriend, Joan now worked full time in the air force, and Olive was fully recovered. The family still took in visitors during summer, and it was only the shadow of war that cast gloom over this prolonged happiness. Appearing at the twilight of summer, it loomed larger, darker, spreading indiscriminate ripples of anxiety and fear. Pam sat with her sisters perched on the edge of a chair in the sitting room, Olive stood facing the window, while they listened to the Prime Minister speak above the oppressive grey silence.

He sounded so old and tired, sad, using words that Pam did not fully understand. Something about the British Ambassador in Berlin, then Poland, an unanswered message and now they were in a state of war. When Peg and Joan left the flat directly afterwards, visibly worried, she felt her throat swell and chest tighten with dismay. What did it all mean? How could these distant places have any affect upon her? It was all so unreal. She had never even heard of the country of Poland.

She followed her mother into the kitchen, where Olive now sat at the table. A serious expression clouded her features and she smiled resignedly at her youngest daughter, offering a hand to clasp onto. Olive's lips were drawn tight as a cut.

"So there's going to be a war, Pam. Another one. England will fight Germany all over again and it will be us common folk who suffer." Her voice sounded exhausted, similar to after she had her operation, and Pam felt scared.

"But why, Mum? I don't understand."

"Me neither, my girl. Things will be difficult now, mark my

words, but we'll be all right. You know I'll make sure of that. Where there's life, there's hope!"

Olive jumped to her feet and reached for the kettle, before advancing to the sink. Pam turned her attention from the floorboards, where she had been studying a particular pattern in the wood grain (it resembled a monkey), in order to gaze out of the window. The sun continued to shine brightly. White gulls sped overhead in crazy formation, squawking loudly. There was not a cloud to be seen in the sky.

The first sign that things were different was the disappearance of all holidaymakers overnight. They were suddenly absent, leaving the town strangely empty and silent. The shops also appeared to empty as people took to stockpiling food; all products that would keep were bought up in bulk, and shortages quickly became evident. Pam was unable to find sugar and jam on her next shopping duty, but this was not so important as they had no guests left to feed. Richard persisted in his attempts to persuade Olive to return to Africa, but his efforts fell on deaf ears. The family was staying put and going nowhere.

The blackout came next. All lights had to be hidden after dark, to help prevent Jerry from locating his targets, and this affected everyone. Patrols now roamed the streets to ensure compliance, and Peg complained that it was ruining her love life. She had to be home early – all locals stayed in more, trapped within their own homes. Pam took to reading with a torchlight held under the covers, her main lamp extinguished, and this she found rather exciting. She did not understand the significance of war, but this part was certainly acceptable.

She was less keen on the gas masks that were issued at school. Horrible and rubbery to touch, they also smelt funny, reminding Pam of slippery stinging jellyfish and old socks. They had to be carried at all times for fear of enemy attack, strapped over the shoulder like some strange new growth, and Pam did not enjoy this at all.

Christmas was unusually quiet and joyless. The darkness of war hung heavy over town, and news on the wireless went from bad to worse. It sounded as if Hitler was romping unchallenged through Europe, heading ever closer, with all celebration now suitably muted. A strange sadness infected the town. For the first time since arrival from Africa, laughter ran dry from the streets of Folkestone, replaced with a lonely melancholic blue. The people were scared, afraid of an unknown future, and Pam was not immune from infection.

She walked with her mother through empty streets and onto the deserted cliff tops. It was a clear day and the long, flat shadow of France drew an ominous line along the horizon. It would not be long before Hitler reached the opposing shore, and then what would happen? Would they be safe at all? It appeared so terribly close. They returned home in silence and Olive sat her down in the kitchen.

"You've got to go, Pam. It's the only way we'll have you safe."

"Where?"

"To Wales, until the end of the war. You heard the news, and it shouldn't be long coming."

"But I don't want to, Mum," Pam protested.

"You have to, it's for your own good."

"What about Joan and Peg? If they're not going, I want to stay here with you."

"I'm sorry Pam, but you are going young lady, and that's the end of it."

No amount of tears or protestations could weaken Olive's resolve. It was no use for Pam to argue, and Mother insisted on her evacuation together with most of the local schoolchildren. The Government had decided that children who lived on the south east coast would be safer if evacuated until the end of the war, and a rumour now circulated that this would not be long coming. It remained Pam's one and only hope. She looked out of the window with tearful eyes, where black clouds piled high in the sky. She shut her eyelids, trembling, and took herself out of the world.

☾

2nd June, 1940. The day of departure arrived with terrible speed. Pam's leaving had tightened an already close family, ensuring that farewells with her sisters were suitably painful. Olive packed a brown leather suitcase for her youngest daughter, and made an enormous batch of her favourite ham and cucumber sandwiches. It was only when pinning a label onto her navy jacket, stating name and home address, that she finally gave in to her own tears.

"I'm sorry Pam, I don't want this either but you have to go. I would never forgive myself if something happened to you."

Pam stood frozen in the hallway, resigned to this fate. She clutched a white card tightly in her right hand, to be completed and posted on arrival. *Have arrived safely, my new address is . . .*

It was decided that only Olive should accompany her to the school, where a wheezing shuddery double-decker waited to transport the children to the station. Here, they said goodbye quickly, unlike some mothers who were reluctant to let go at the last minute. Pam was glad of this, keen to avoid the frightful shame of crying in public. She took one deep breath, her last of the salt sea air, then steeled herself to enter the open jaws of the vehicle. She sat alone, away from the other children who slumped in miserable silence.

The day was baking hot, so increasing the sense of discomfort. Everyone appeared to be heavily laden with cases, bundles and gas masks, and it was a great relief when the bus finally pulled away, leaving behind the last of the sobbing mothers. Pam sat staring at her feet, her newly polished shoes, reluctant to chat to anyone. It was easier this way, to keep herself strong, and it was not long before they were all streaming out and onto the platform at Folkestone Central. Teachers and policemen helped marshal the children into smaller groups.

"It's all right love, don't worry. I'll wait for you to come back!"

A smiling young copper attempted to cheer up one girl who looked particularly grim-faced. He was sweating in his uniform, face red and jowls slack, dark eyes heavy with lack of sleep. Pam watched as the girl grinned back, and the others around her also grinned. She kept herself alone, to the edge of the crowd, willing her feet to remain still rather than bolt for home. Already, she missed her sister Joan, with no idea when they might meet up again. It was an awful, lonely sensation.

The journey seemed endless. It was a peculiar, muted affair for such a large group of children, with the exception of one tiny black-haired girl who cried non-stop. A teacher attempted to calm her, walking her up and down the carriages repeatedly, but this only made things worse. It spread the feeling of imminent doom to everyone.

The hours passed so slowly, cruelly, all travellers becoming more and more upset. Sniffles and sobbing became louder, spreading through the carriages like water. Pam concentrated on staring out of the compartment window, tracing a single raindrop as it leaped and staggered across the dirty glass. She gazed blank at the swerve of a river, the distant towns and villages. She counted the tunnels, attempting to empty her mind and think of nothing, but Folkestone and family refused to disappear. She was determined not to cry – not on this train, not in front of the other children or adults. She made sure she was stronger than that.

It was late afternoon when they finally arrived, heads bowed and gas masks clutched grimly. Pam wanted her mother badly now, her own bedroom and her home. She was hot and tired; she felt dirty and sad. The ham sandwiches remained uneaten. She was not hungry and they were a taste of home, something to hold onto and savour later. Her stomach had worked itself into a tight knot of worry. The children were shepherded from the train and out of the station, emerging into a narrow street of terraced housing. Pam had never seen such dark, tiny buildings. It was her first view of Wales and it was not good. They were directed into an ugly grey building for brief medical examinations, and then loaded into buses for the remaining part of the journey.

It was not long before Pam found herself in a small village hall. It was cool inside, so welcome after the heat of the day, and several ladies were handing out milky cups of tea in unfamiliar singsong voices. They smiled often, kindly, and it was such a relief to finally stop moving. Pam stretched out her aches and pains from sitting too long. Thick sliced sandwiches and homemade scones with strawberry jam and cream had been arranged on a long wooden table, although food remained the last thing on her mind. The Head Mistress stood up to talk and everybody immediately fell silent.

"Well done children. You've all been very good today, a credit to the school, thank you. We have now reached our destination," she spoke in clipped, polished tones. "This is Abertridwr. Names will be called out and you will be allocated to your billets. These will be your new homes."

My home certainly isn't here, Pam's thoughts grew suddenly angry, it's Folkestone. What is she talking about? She doesn't know anything. This is only for a short time, nothing important. I'll be back before too long, Mum said so.

"Pam Aulsebrook."

Her name was called first and Pam scanned the room quickly, anxious, curious to see what happened next.

"And Wendy Coates. You will be taken to 66 High Street, where you will both be staying. Alison Doran . . ."

The names continued but Pam was no longer listening. She would have to share, and with a complete stranger; she felt her heart shrink further while her stomach tightened. The least that Pam had hoped for was some privacy, a room to herself, and now this had also been denied. She watched in dismay as a tall thin girl rose to her feet, moving uncertain to the back of the hall. She was pretty, with long brown hair flowing down her back, and appeared to be in a similar anguished state. It was not her fault that they were thrown together, and she seemed friendly enough when they were ushered into a waiting black car, although neither dared speak. A sympathetic nod would have to suffice for now.

"Hello," the driver twisted around in his seat to smile at the girls. He possessed a jovial red face, a twinkle in his eyes, and to Pam's amazement what appeared to be a complete absence of teeth. "I'll take you to your new home. How was the journey?"

"Fine, thank you." It was Wendy who replied, much to Pam's relief. Her mouth felt so dry, as if her tongue was glued stuck. The driver nodded and continued to speak.

"That's good. And I am sure you will be well looked after. Well, we'd better be on our way then."

The engine was started and the car moved smoothly away. The front windows had been left slightly open and Pam was pleased to feel the breeze on her face. The day was cooling down, at last. She could not shake the thought that she was leaving everything that she knew far behind. The people spoke funny here, and she had no idea where to find Abertridwr on the map. Would her mother know where she was? She didn't even recognise the girl who sat beside her, the one that she would be forced to share with. She gripped the handle of her bag as if her life depended upon it, hoping and praying with all her might that war would be over in the morning. This whole experience would then be over, reduced to an adventure that she could relate to Joan. She still did not understand how Poland, an unknown far away country, could have brought about this evacuation. Surely Great Britain would not take long to conquer Hitler and Germany?

It was a surprise to discover that the car had stopped moving. They had arrived at the billet, and Pam stared out of the window trying to take it all in. The light was now fading, but she could make out that they had parked outside a neat row of terraced houses, a blossom of hanging baskets breaking up the monotony of grey facades. They did not look so unpleasant, much better than the first streets she had seen. Maybe things would not be so bad, after all. The driver jumped out of the vehicle and bounded up to the nearest front door. Pam and Wendy exchanged nervous glances while he hammered energetically onto the knocker.

The girls watched lights appear inside the building. Neighbouring curtains twitched, and the door opened with a flourish. A short stocky man waved out to them from the hallway. He had a good head of tight wavy black curls, a white face, and Pam was pleased to notice the obvious kindness retained in his features. Deep laughter lines suggested that this was a man who smiled often.

"Ah, so you've arrived then, I see. I'm Mr Raymond. Welcome, come in." A melodic voice suited his features well.

"Here are your visitors Mon, safe and sound." The driver grinned, beckoning towards the car. "No queries have you?"

"No, no. None at all." Mr Raymond slapped him on the back. "Come on, we'd better give a hand with the bags."

"Right, then I'll be on my way, Mon. Got a few more deliveries to make."

Both men unloaded the luggage quickly. The driver smiled a goodbye before jumping back into the car and disappearing rapidly into the gloom. They were on their own now, completely alone. Mr Raymond picked up the remaining bags and ushered them forward.

"In you go, girls," he said. "Make yourselves at home now."

Still, neither had spoken. The front door was closed behind them and a slim lady emerged from the kitchen. She had short, neat black hair, a long face, and eyes that sparkled brightly. She walked towards them with outstretched arms, smiling with undisguised warmth.

"Hello girls, and welcome. You must be very tired. Across the road we have some friends who are getting a nice hot bath ready for you. We haven't got a proper bathroom in this house, you see."

At last, Pam found her voice. "But I did have a bath. Last night."

"Oh bless you, girl," Mrs Raymond laughed. She spoke with a strong unfamiliar accent that Pam found difficult to understand, and she felt the knot in her stomach work tighter. "It's not that we think you're dirty. We just thought that after such a long journey a nice hot bath would make you feel better, see? Come on, let's take you over and see if it doesn't. Now which one of you is Pam and which is Wendy?"

The girls raised their arms as each name was spoken.

"We have two girls of our own, see. They're sleeping now. Wanted to stay up and meet you, they did, but we told them it would be too late and you'd be tired tonight. There'll be plenty of time in the morning. Come on now, let's take you over for that bath."

Mrs Raymond had thought right; the hot bath relaxed both girls, a change of clothes making them feel more comfortable. On return, Mr and Mrs Raymond took them on a short tour of the billet which neither of them liked to consider as home. A small living room was situated to the front of the house, containing a faded brown sofa, two little bookcases and record player.

"All mine," Mr Raymond joked. "I love to listen to my music. No girls allowed in here."

One picture hung on the wall, depicting a blue vase and bunch of orange tulips. A carved wooden standard lamp, topped off with dirty cream shade, sloped in the corner.

The kitchen was larger, with a solid pine table commanding the centre of the room. Six chairs were arranged about this, a big window was located behind the sink, and Pam saw that Mrs Raymond enjoyed use of a large gas cooking range. Her mother would have been jealous, often complaining how her own kitchen was nowhere near big enough. A shiny silver cross was positioned upon the wall.

"The toilet is out back, girls," Mr Raymond explained. "And I have a shed to wash in, for when I come back from the pit. That's where I work, getting too dirty for the house so Mrs Raymond tells me. She never lets me inside until I'm clean!"

"There are three bedrooms upstairs, girls," Mrs Raymond chimed in, laughing with her husband. "Yours is a good size, you'll see. Our girls are sharing while you are here. They were very good about it, didn't complain at all."

She led the way up a steep, narrow staircase, Mr Raymond just managing to follow and manoeuvre the bags. It was late and both girls were now ready for sleep. They were pleased to finally be left on their own, after saying goodnight to the hosts.

The bedroom was a fair size, although smaller than Pam's room in Folkestone. She could not avert her eyes from the double bed – even that would have to be shared, she realised, and no one had warned them of this. It was much worse than doubling up with Peg. A large dark wood wardrobe, together with matching chest of drawers, completed the furniture. The floor was covered with polished boards, no carpet, and Mrs Raymond had left a yellow vase filled with white flowers on top of the drawers. A picture of a mountain scene was above the bed, the colours gaudy and bright, making it appear unreal.

"Wonder what my mum's doing?" Wendy spoke her thoughts aloud.

"Yes, hope my mum's all right, and my sisters. They say it won't be for long."

"I heard that too."

Both girls were quick to undress, standing with backs to each other. Their clothes were folded neatly and rested on top of the bags. Neither chose to unpack. Wendy had gravitated to the far side of the room, nearest the window, and she climbed onto the left side of the bed.

"I hope they are right," she said. "Goodnight Pam."

"Goodnight."

Pam turned her face to the wall. The sheets felt cold, almost slippery, and she did not want Wendy to notice the tears that slid slowly along her nose and soaked gently into the pillow.

☾

Pam struggled to fall asleep. She tossed and turned, restless, unable to stop herself from thinking about home, family, and all that she had left behind. There was the Warren, the old fish market: she might never get to see them again. What if something terrible were to happen? It felt awful to be so far removed from everything and everyone important. Already, she missed the boat hire and thought briefly of the helper, Harry Fisher. What changes had the war brought about for him? She thought of her mother, her parting tears, and wished again that it could all be over in the morning, that she might wake up to find everything returned to normal. She tried not to disturb Wendy who lay dozing beside her.

Both girls felt exhausted in the morning. They dressed quickly, silently putting on outfits worn from the previous day. Wendy led the way as they tiptoed down the stairs with trepidation – what would be expected of them next?

"Hello! How are you today?" Mrs Raymond spotted them first, calling out cheerfully from the kitchen. "Come in here and meet Barbara and Margaret. You'll all soon be friends, see."

The daughters were tiny, with pale faces, dark eyes and coal black hair that had grown too long for their bob cuts. They were very pretty, resembling miniature dolls in their best summer frocks, and appeared terrified at the prospect of meeting new people. It took awhile before anyone dared speak, Mrs Raymond chivvying away, but she would be proven correct once again. Quickly, the girls became friends. Mugs of tea were poured out, and then thick slabs of buttered toast passed around the table. Conversation was not long to follow, when Barbara asked what it was like back in Folkestone. Wendy said it was nice and warm, and Pam told them about swimming in the sea. There was no coast to be found near Abertridwr.

Mr Raymond appeared at the kitchen window, before opening the door with a broad smile on his face. "Look girls, look at the mountains," he said. "Seems like a yellow carpet, doesn't it? That's all buttercups. We'll take you for a walk there later. Our girls love it, and so do we. All the time we've lived here, I never grow tired of that view!"

Pam found herself admiring the scene from the painting in the bedroom. It was beautiful, and in real life the colours also appeared unreal. She had never seen such a vivid, luminous yellow. At the end of the garden, she noticed a small stream tumbling down the slope to join with a river. The grass on the banks was picture book green.

"You can drink from the stream," Mr Raymond continued. "It's clean water and ice cold, nothing quite like it. Better even than beer, although you wouldn't know about that I hope!" He laughed and Pam smiled with him, cheering up. Their hosts seemed to be good people and the scenery was undeniably lovely. Things could have been worse, much worse, in the billet.

The low branches of a willow tree bent arthritically and dangled into the curve of the river, where the water moved lazy and sluggish. This was to become a secret hiding place for Wendy and Pam, where they could talk openly about missing their home and families. It seemed ungrateful to mope in public, when the Raymonds did everything in their power to make both girls comfortable. Abertridwr was a nice town, but it could never be a substitute for the familiarity of Folkestone.

It was a long hot summer. Pam bought stamps from the local post office and sent letters to her mother every week. She lived in anticipation for the return mail, her strongest connection with the home she had left behind. Both girls went through spells of tears, but they also enjoyed happy times. Just once, Mrs Raymond took them all to the nearest swimming pool for a special treat. It was too warm and far too crowded. That night, Pam dreamed of the deep cool sea, the many rock pools and swimming at the Warren. For the first time in weeks, she woke up crying.

It helped Wendy and Pam to be able to discuss this homesick feeling, and to share their sorrow. When life seemed particularly hard, they sneaked off and made their way up into the mountains, or to the hiding place beneath the embrace of the willow. Undisturbed, they sat for hours, talking and sobbing until the tears ran dry, taking solace in the company of each other. It was a help and a comfort to be in this situation together. Only once, Mrs Raymond caught sight of their disappearance and subsequent red, swollen eyes. She understood immediately, and in her kindness remained silent. That evening, she baked a special cake and made cherry ice cream for pudding.

"Listen up girls, your local priest is coming to visit." It was Mr Raymond who broke the news after returning from his shift at the mine. "He'll have news from your families and, if you're lucky, some little presents!"

Pam and Wendy felt their excitement increase in the days leading up to his appearance. His trip provided a definite link with home, making Folkestone appear far less distant and more real. Maybe they would be able to return with him? Or not long after? They very nearly knocked him from his feet in greeting when he eventually showed up at the front door. Pam had long forgotten how bored she used to become in church, when she had been first to escape from the service and race down the slope to the beach.

"Hello you two. My, you look well!" He smiled, one arm reaching about both girls. "Must be all the fresh air."

"How's Mum?" they shouted in unison. "Have you any letters for us? Any news? Presents?"

"Well let me inside and we'll see, shall we?"

Mr and Mrs Raymond grinned from the foot of the stairs, beckoning the priest through to the kitchen for morning tea. He sat, apparently weary, than revealed that he did indeed possess letters for both girls, and small presents that were easily carried.

The poor man had been terribly laden for the long train journey from the south coast, and he had many evacuees to visit.

Olive had sent Pam a book of poetry and quotations, to help her through this prolonged departure. She wrote that she missed Pam dreadfully, but they would all be together as soon as God intended. Hopefully, this would not be too long to arrive. She signed off with her usual expression – *where there's life, there's hope*!

Joan had also written Pam a letter, and enclosed a wooden hairbrush carved in the shape of a fish. The fish was smiling. Apparently, all of the family remained in good spirits and health, Peg was dating as serious as ever, and they all looked forward to being reunited in the not too distant future. They sent Pam best wishes, and prayed that the war would soon be over.

The visit from the priest proved a great encouragement, and both girls were sorry to see him leave. His appearance had provided fresh hope, and they were able to dream of a safe return home again.

Autumn drew near, with no change in circumstance forthcoming. The girls walked high into the mountains with their host family, carrying large enamel jugs up to where the tall bracken grew. Pam loved the coconut smell of the gorse, which reminded her of posh chocolates, and she raced forward to inhale this sweet perfume, placing her nose as close to the flowers as the sharp thorns would allow. They enjoyed long games of hide and seek, crouched low and invisible in the tall grass, and Mrs Raymond always took with them a picnic. Pam thought that she made the tastiest ham and egg pie, even better than her own mum's.

They collected blueberries from under the bracken, filling all jugs with ease. Pam and Wendy ate nearly as much as they gathered, purple tongues providing ample evidence of this crime, and Mrs Raymond scolded them both while laughing. "How can I make flans if you eat them all?" she protested. "You'll be giving yourselves upset tummies."

The girls grew to accept this new life, although they continued to miss home. They never once stopped hoping for an end to the war, a return to the comfort of Folkestone, and for life to continue unchanged. Meanwhile, they were certainly not unhappy. Both realised that they had been fortunate to end up with the Raymonds and each other. Not all of their school friends had been so lucky.

☽

Pam continued to write letters each week, and to wait excited and impatient for any reply. It was the highlight of her day, and she always opened the post slowly, carefully, savouring the delicious moment of anticipation for what might be contained, and what news she might discover.

She sat at the kitchen table with Wendy, while Mrs Raymond scrubbed the front of the hob. Mr Raymond stood at the back door, breathing deeply, watching his daughters play in the garden. Pam always recognised the handwriting on envelopes, revealing the identity of the sender, but this morning she had received an unfamiliar package. The envelope was small, brown, with name and address typed in thick black ink. She decided to save this one until last.

Olive had written, and Joan. There was news about Peg but she never seemed to write a letter herself, too preoccupied with her boyfriend, Bill. Pam read news of the family greedily, the town and neighbours, before returning her attention to the final packet. Who could this be from, she wondered? She never received anything unusual.

The envelope was opened carefully, before she read the contents in a daze. She had to read it again, just to make sure she understood. When the words took shape in her head, she began to tremble. Next, big tears fell from her eyes, dripping onto her clean blouse. She burst into loud sobbing, not hiding on the mountain slope or under the willow tree, but right there in the kitchen, in front of everyone.

"What is it Pam?" Mrs Raymond spoke quietly, rapidly.

"This."

Pam shoved the letter away, for her host to read it. Maybe she had been mistaken, and it did not mean what she now feared. Maybe it was all a mistake.

Further to your successful scholarship examination for Folkestone Grammar School, you have been allocated a place at Merthyr Tydfil Grammar School with immediate effect.

"That's good news, isn't it?" Mrs Raymond enquired.

"No it's not!" Pam had forgotten all about the exam. "I don't want to leave you and go to live with strangers. I want to stay here until I can go home."

"My poor girl," Mrs Raymond moved to hug her. "It's not so very far away. If you want to do well when you grow up, and have a good job, then you'll be better off at Grammar School.

"You can come here at weekends and tell us how you're getting on," Mr Raymond now entered the conversation, stepping backwards into the kitchen. "But don't try walking, mind! You save your pocket money and come on the train."

He had obviously not forgotten Pam's talk of walking home to Folkestone during her first weeks in Wales, when she had been particularly homesick. Now, it seemed that Pam had love all about her and she had no desire to leave. It was a horrible thought. Wendy began to cry, the truth sinking in of how she would also be left on her own, and she hurried around the table to embrace her friend.

"I don't want you to go," she stammered.

"I don't want to go," Pam replied.

"I know, I know." It was Mrs Raymond who spoke. "But it looks as if you will have to."

☾

Pam waited once again at a railway station. She remained heavily laden with suitcase, sandwiches and bundles of books. The platform was empty except for her and Mrs Raymond. The sun again shone in an unbroken blue sky. The wind was warm and pleasant, carrying with it the smell of cooking. It should have been a good day, they could have ventured up into the mountains, but instead she cursed her bad luck repeatedly, wishing she had never sat for the stupid exam. It all seemed such a terrible, unfair mistake. Pam was never allowed to settle into a home, her life a restless path of travel and uncertain movement. She was leaving everything familiar behind once again, and this did not get any easier.

The train pulled into the platform. She climbed onboard, the whistle blew, and Mrs Raymond waved her off to another unknown future. It felt exactly like leaving home all over again, and she knew that there would be plenty more secret tears ahead. She stuck her head out of the window and waved in reply, her eyes fixed determined on her host until the train rounded a corner and she was gone. Disappeared. Pam was returned to her solitude.

"Merthyr Tydfil, dear. We're here now." The ticket inspector spoke kindly. He knew from Mrs Raymond that it was her stop, and helped to unload Pam's belongings while she remained reluctant to leave the seat. It was easier this way, to remain cocooned in the small compartment than have to start all over again. The inspector offered his hand, and she took it with a deep sigh. She stepped down to wait on the platform.

A tall lady with long blonde hair came jogging from out of the station office. She moved purposefully towards Pam, a radiant smile lighting up already attractive features. Her eyes were blue, her smile wide, and she wore a blue dress that displayed a shapely hourglass figure. She shimmied as she walked, graceful and elegant, as if dancing.

"You must be Pam Aulsebrook, by the look of the cases!" She laughed, a twinkling melodic laugh, the words all blending together. "I am Miss Price, come to meet you. Hello and welcome. I'll escort you to your new billet. Is this everything?" She gestured to the luggage and Pam nodded. "Good, good. Well hop along then, we don't want to keep them waiting."

She moved off at a fair pace. Pam needed to jog to keep pace with her while Miss Price continued to speak. "Your host and hostess are a young couple with no children of their own. They are looking forward to meeting you very much. A classmate lives nearby, and she will call for you before school on Monday. Be ready at eight forty-five. I am sure that you will be very happy here."

Miss Price seemed really nice and friendly, but Pam doubted her words very much. How could she be happy when forced to move on and start all over again? When she would have to face life on her own?

The luggage was loaded without ceremony into the boot of a waiting black taxi. Pam experienced the knot in her stomach grow larger, by now a familiar sensation, and it appeared to extend right to the back of her throat. She thought of herself as the girl with the loneliest eyes, wondering when all of this upheaval might end. When would she be allowed to return home? What did Poland and war have to do with her? Why wouldn't they leave her alone?

The taxi sped through what appeared to be another mining town. Pam spotted a pit wheel not far in the distance, turning slowly above the rooftops, while the vehicle moved beyond rows of smoke blackened terraces. The mountains of Abertridwr seemed a long way away and she wondered how much further she would have to travel, before the driver braked to a sudden halt. Pam felt herself thrown forwards, her shoulder hitting into the back of the passenger seat. Miss Price, apparently unaffected, jumped nimbly from the cab to rap sharply on the nearest front door. The driver began to unload her luggage, and Pam dragged herself out of the car.

A tall slender woman appeared in the doorway. She was almost pretty, but for the smallness of her eyes and pinched, nervous expression contorting her face. She had fine strawberry blonde hair and gazed at Pam intently. A brief look of disappointment darkened her features before she regained an even composure. Pam felt herself shrink under this close inspection.

"Good afternoon Mrs Evans." Miss Price was the first to speak. "This is Pam. June will call for her on Monday before school, at a quarter to nine. I hope that you will be happy together. Do let me know if there are any problems or questions. Goodbye now, and goodbye Pam. I'll see you on Monday."

She smiled and spun around, still elegant, before disappearing back into the waiting taxi. Pam continued to cower in front of Mrs Evans, unsure what she should do next. It had been easier when Wendy was with her.

"Come in then, I'll show you to your room." Mrs Evans spoke slowly, as if half asleep. Her accent was softer, clearer, than Mrs

Raymond's, but Pam instinctively liked her less. There was an absence of warmth about her; Mrs Evans seemed to be a particularly hard, cold woman. Pam had never seen such thin pale lips.

"Come on." She watched as Pam struggled to carry her luggage inside, before leading the way up a dark narrow staircase and into a small, single bedroom. The air felt musty and damp. The window was painted shut.

"Here you are then, I hope that you like it." Mrs Evans backed out of the door. "If you would like to unpack, I'll go and prepare us some lunch. Be as quiet as you can because Mr Evans is asleep. He works nights down the mine, you know. That's for you to wash." She pointed to a blue china bowl placed in the middle of a square table, a threadbare green towel folded beside this. "We have no bathroom here."

She glided silent down the stairs. Pam was quick to close the door before collapsing onto the bed, a handkerchief clutched over her face to muffle the sobs.

"Oh no, please God no. Please take me home."

She closed her eyes and prayed, but time refused to move backwards, neither to the Raymonds and especially not to Folkestone. She thought, again, of all the things she should really be doing: exploring with Joan, helping Mum with the shopping, and listening to the wireless on Sunday evening. How could the family be doing this without her? Just carrying on as normal? It was so difficult to imagine. So cruel.

Pam glanced about the room. It was small and dingy, in need of a fresh coat of paint. No pictures were hung on the wall. For furniture, a narrow chest of drawers was pushed into the corner, a spindly wooden chair tucked under the table. A white candle decorated with an effigy of Jesus rested on the windowsill. The curtains were brown. Outside, the hallway and stairs led only to more loneliness. She remained in the room for as long as she dared. She made no attempt to unpack.

☙

Mrs Evans sat in the kitchen resting a mug of tea on her stomach. She rose awkwardly when Pam approached, ill at ease, before mustering a smile for her visitor.

"There you go, Pam," she said, gesturing to the table where bread, jam and plain biscuits had been arranged on white plates. "I didn't think you'd want much now, so we'll have a bigger meal tonight."

"Thank you," Pam murmured.

"I hope you'll settle in all right, we're not used to having children about."

But I'm not a child, Pam thought, I'm nearly grown up. Events continued to strike her as impossibly unfair; her life spiralled out of control. She sat as far as possible from Mrs Evans, remembering the words of her mother. Germany had invaded Poland, and that was why she needed to move away. What did Poland matter to her?

After lunch, Pam returned to her room and wrote letters to Joan and Mrs Raymond. She told them about the train journey, the new billet and her host. At last, she had a plan, an idea to sound out on her sister: if Dad still wanted her to go back to South Africa, then surely this was the best course of action? She would be safe, away from the fighting, and also reunited with family. She would not be lonely anymore. It had to be worth a try – anything was preferable to remaining where she now found herself. She stood and walked to the window, gazing out into the gathering darkness. Row upon row of faceless tenements glared back.

When Pam ventured down to the kitchen, Mrs Evans busied herself preparing a vegetable stew. Moon white potatoes were peeled and washed, thick carrots chopped and onions shredded. Beetroot was boiled and peas shelled. Pam sat at the table and watched, all offers of help politely declined. It was early evening before Mr Evans surfaced, and Pam stiffened in weary anticipation on hearing his footsteps approach. Again, she would have to meet with another stranger. Introductions would have to be made and she was starting all over again. It was so hard and she wanted to hide, to put off this encounter for at least another day.

"Oh, hello Pam." He entered the room slowly, wearing a white vest and loose fitting black trousers. The straps of his braces dangled on both sides. "Something smells good. I nearly forgot you'd be here. It's nice to see you."

"Hello."

They shook hands. Pam noticed that his face was extremely pale, an unhealthy colour, and she wondered if this was due to lack of sunlight through working nights. He was tall, like Mrs Evans, and very thin, with thick black eyebrows and heavy stubble. He had a nice welcoming smile, unlike his wife.

"So did you get here in one piece? The train on time for once? Where are you from again? Folkestone, wasn't it? What's it like down there, I've never been?"

He was keen to hear of her background, and it was a relief for Pam to talk about something familiar. They chatted together while Mrs Evans stood stirring her stew, largely silent, until dinner plates were set on the table. Mr Evans hurried through grace, and the meal was consumed without interruption.

"Well, we're off out tonight," he was the first to finish. "It's the only chance we get, on a Saturday. You'll be all right on your own, won't you Pam? You know where everything is?"

"Yes, thanks, I'll be fine." Pam was glad to be alone, to gather her thoughts and regain some composure. She had to adapt to another life now, deprived of Wendy for company. She waited in her room while Mrs Evans boiled saucepans of water, and then poured these into a large tin tub in the kitchen. Her hosts left promptly and she was able to bathe in private. It was with tired legs that she climbed the stairs and lowered herself into bed. She closed her eyes. All was silent outside, a ghost town. She slept without dreams, exhausted, and woke to a room bright with sunlight.

Mr Evans was already awake and in the kitchen, making breakfast. "Hello Pam, did you sleep well? We didn't wake you, did we? I tried to be light on my feet, but the wife said I still managed to sound like an elephant." He grinned, stirring a large pan of porridge. Thick slices of white bread already toasted on the grill, and the butter dish was placed on the table. "Lovely morning, isn't it? I like a good feed on a Sunday, to start the day. Keeps me going until teatime, then. What are you going to do with yourself? Do you ever go to Chapel?"

"Sometimes. I used to go in Abertridwr." This had become a weekly occurrence after the visit from the priest, and Pam had

143

grown to enjoy it. It helped remind her of home, and she was glad of any opportunity to pray for war to be over, for life to return to normality. "Do you go?" she asked.

"Can't say we do, not often. Mrs Evans says it's not for her, and I'm always grateful to take it easy after the pit. We all need one day of rest, I think."

"Did you say that you go, Pam?" Mrs Evans walked into the room, pushing her hair behind her ears. She appeared less tense today, more relaxed and friendly. Her smile appeared far less forced.

"Yes, I like it."

"Well there is a Church of England two streets away. I'll show you the way, if you like. I checked before you got here, and the service doesn't start until eleven. You'll have plenty of time after breakfast. Sit down. Can I get you a cup of tea?"

Pam realised that her previous awkwardness was probably due to anxiety and natural shyness. It could not be easy for Mrs Evans to make room and take in a stranger, and she considered herself a burden to everyone. She longed for the day when she would be responsible for her own choices and actions, when she would not be a nuisance to anyone. She wanted to be out of the billet, to escape, to return to a life by the sea. She wanted her life to be without complication, to be shared with and not separated from her loved ones.

☾

Breakfast was good but church was better. The local priest fascinated Pam – he did not look, talk, or sound like any of the precise, immaculate religious men that she had previously encountered. He was scruffy and untidy, thickset, his accent course and rough as old sandpaper, and yet his words came alive with a rhythm as natural and honest as a heartbeat. He had used to work as a miner, down the same pit as Mr Evans, before experiencing a vision of God underground. This calling proved so strong that he had quit his job immediately and changed vocation.

Pam sat in the back pew and allowed his words to shine light and hope deep within her, filling her with newfound strength and optimism. It was exactly what she needed. She would survive this separation, she knew, and her life would improve. The family would one day be reunited. She learned that there were two further services on a Sunday, and she chose to attend all three. This quickly became her routine.

Monday duly arrived, and a loud knocking sounded on the front door at precisely one quarter to nine. June stood waiting expectant to accompany Pam to her new school. A plump girl with red cheeks and straight brown hair, she spoke rapidly with a slight lisp. By the time they had reached the school gates, Pam learned that June had three older sisters, a rabbit called Peter, and she quite liked the young projectionist at the cinema but this was a secret. He was a bit of a dish and all of the girls thought the same, so what chance did a girl like her have? Pam assured her that she had every chance; there was nothing about June not to like. She laughed often, the smile never once fully leaving her face, and she took it upon herself to look after Pam.

The school transpired to be a marvellous old castle, standing as a majestic island surrounded by a sea of beautiful gardens. Several paths led up to the main building, radiating out like sunbeams, each lined with colourful shrubs and pretty flowers. The air was scented with perfume, and Pam could not prevent a smile from appearing.

"June, it's wonderful!" she exclaimed.

"It's not so bad, Pam, but you soon get used to it. And some of the classes have to be held in the corridors now, because of the new English girls. The older girls can be a bit catty, but don't worry yourself about that. My mum says that we just have to rise above it." June did not appear to require any pause for breathing, her words racing out at incredible speed.

Pam was able to mingle into school life with relative ease, having done this once already in Abertridwr. She was happy to keep her head down and remain as anonymous as possible. It was good to know June, and one friend was quite sufficient for now. Life was simpler this way. It would make it much easier to leave.

The first week slipped past without incident. Mr and Mrs

Evans treated her well, and it was not so bad to have her own bedroom again, the privacy craved since initial departure. When a letter arrived from Mother, she was able to rush upstairs and slowly devour it, sentence-by-sentence, word-by-word. She read how Joan had mentioned the plan and Olive agreed – her mother agreed! It was brilliant news, and through Joan's perseverance she would now be able to return to South Africa. She would live with Richard again, her father – this was all too good to be true. She would no longer be shipwrecked alone in Wales. Her many prayers had at last been answered. Pam kept her bags packed and ready to go, but told nobody of this, her future. It felt safer this way, not tempting fate, and less likely for things to go wrong. Her hosts could not fail to notice the improvement in her demeanour, but attributed this solely to her settling in.

Weeks passed, and Pam continued to await news of departure. She wrote to her mother and Joan, requesting specific details of sailings, but nothing definite was forthcoming. Initial excitement congealed into worry, and she buried herself deeper and deeper into schoolwork, grateful for any distraction. Pam quickly established her position as top of the class in many subjects, with English, Latin and Mathematics firm favourites. Miss Price was lovely to her, and at home Mrs Evans became more chatty and friendly. She never returned to Wendy and the Raymonds in Abertridwr. She still wanted to leave Wales as soon as possible.

It was a surprise to everyone when siren warnings began to take place in Merthyr Tydfil. There had been no concrete evidence of war, no shellings or bombings, and yet safe houses were allocated in the event of an air raid. Pam felt nervous, and could see no real reason to delay her departure further. The decisive moment had finally arrived. Her bags remained packed, she wrote again to Folkestone, and then the reply arrived from Mother, the one that contained the future.

She sat rigid with shock. Mr Evans was asleep and his wife had popped out to the shops. Pam had the house to herself and she had actually ripped the envelope open in the kitchen. She read how ships sailing to and from England were now being

146

targeted and attacked. It was no longer a safe voyage, and she was not allowed to leave after all. She would have to remain in the billet, in Wales. It felt as if a strong, cold gust of wind had suddenly blown her from the direction she was supposed to be taking. *If* she had only suggested the idea to her sister sooner? *If* the bombing had not begun? *If* – it was the biggest word in Pam's world. Because of *if*, she was now living a different life, not the one intended. It was yet another mistake. Why did events never turn out as expected? How different would things have been in Africa? Once more, she was consigned to an uncertain future. Pam felt her hope diminish and then flicker out. Writing letters and the return post no longer offered any joy. Time slowed to a painful stumble and crawl. It was only June who seemed able to make her smile, to raise her out of this deep seam of loneliness.

☙

Pam continued to study hard and visit the church. Mr and Mrs Evans understood that she was unhappy, and made every possible effort to cheer her up. They had grown used to her presence and enjoyed having her around. Now, they offered to take her on walks, swimming, even to visit the Raymonds, but all to no avail. Nothing seemed of any interest to Pam. Miss Price noticed her slumped shoulders at school, the uncharacteristic frown, and she could do nothing but watch while Pam grew ever more silent, withdrawing further into herself. It was only when Christmas approached that her spirits lifted.

"I've got some good news for you, Pam," Mrs Evans explained. "You're allowed to go home for the holiday, to Folkestone, if your mother will agree to it."

Pam had now been away for eighteen months. She was beginning to forget details of the flat in Tontine Street. She wanted to see her mother and sisters so badly, to check if they had changed as much as she had. She longed for a return to the Warren, the sea, and maybe a trip to the boat hire if she was lucky.

"Miss Price popped by to tell me. She wanted you to be the first to know – that was good of her, wasn't it? We both think it would do you good. I know it's been a long time for you, Pam. Now you go and run upstairs. Write your mum a letter. I'll do a few lines myself, and we can post them later today."

Pam galloped up the staircase, but not before planting a kiss on the surprised cheek of her host – she had never done this before. She wrote in a hurry, untidy and impatient, determined to catch the last post of the day. Her mother would receive it more quickly, and then she could return home as soon as possible. It was only supposed to be for the holiday, but Pam had other ideas.

She ran fast to the collection box, checking twice that her eyes had not deceived her and the letter had indeed been dropped within the box. She tried not to consider the many ways how it might be lost in transit, or get delivered to the wrong address. What if Olive said no? What then? She fretted for days, with difficulty sleeping, until a reply promptly appeared, together with the appropriate train fare. At last, Pam was on her way home. She wanted to take everything with her, hoping that the trip might yet prove to be permanent, but Mrs Evans would not allow it.

"You're only away for two weeks, no need to take the lot. You leave what you don't need here Pam, and any washing that wants doing. I'll have it all clean for when you get back. And have a good time mind, send our love to your mother."

She gave Pam a letter to take with her, and insisted on treating her to a taxi ride to the station. Her host appeared to be genuinely upset for Pam to be leaving.

☽

The return journey seemed equally slow and laborious as the one that had originally carried Pam to Wales. Each mile covered brought her closer to home, each stop arriving as an unwanted interruption. They travelled without lights, all station names blacked out, for fear of German invasion. Pam saw that war had a definite presence the nearer they returned to the coast, but she felt no concern about this. The only thing that mattered was that she was returning home. At last, she would be back with her family and where she belonged.

She left early morning, through choice, and it was near dark when the train finally pulled to a stop at Folkestone Central. She unwound the window and breathed deeply – the sea was not far away, she could taste the salt on her tongue. She might even go paddling in the morning, if it was not too cold. She jumped onto the platform and began the search for her mother.

"My, you've grown! Look at you!" Olive stood right behind her, her face lit up in recognition, and she moved forward quickly. They embraced and kissed, before embracing again.

"It's so good to see you Mum. I thought I'd never get back."

"Come on dear, I promised. I'd never let that happen, you know better than that." Olive appeared to have aged and had lost considerable weight. Her forehead carried more wrinkles than Pam remembered, she looked smaller, but her voice was as sprightly and kind as ever. It was wonderful to be back in her arms and Pam was in no rush to let go. They departed the station together and Pam set off heading briskly in the direction of Tontine Street, pulling her mother along with her, beside her. It was Olive who forced them to stop.

"We're not there anymore, my girl."

"What? Why?"

"A landmine hit the fish market. Our home was shattered, love. We've been under attack, as they predicted."

"But when?" Pam did not understand. "You never said."

"Just last week, after I'd written. We've moved in with Peg and Bill now, they're married. Peg has put two beds in the spare room so we can share for the holidays. They moved outside the town, to be safer. Hopefully, this home will not be hit!"

Pam listened in disbelief. It had been easy to pretend that war did not exist, so far away in Wales. She had not realised the danger her family lived with, and she was quickly realising this mistake.

"Don't you worry too much, my girl," Olive continued, noticing her daughter's concern. "At least we escaped without injury, that's a miracle to be thankful for. Where there's life, there's hope!"

Pam appreciated that things would now be different; her old life no longer existed, but even this could not dampen her enthusiasm for long. She was reunited with family, at last. It was her own mother who held her hand. She had waited too long for this day to be ruined.

☽

They caught a bus from outside the station, travelling past a deserted Radnor Park and up the hill away from Folkestone. Peg now lived in the neighbouring village of Capel, which was good news to Pam – it was actually nearer the Warren. There was a short cut down from the top of the cliffs, and she hoped that Joan would walk this with her.

Mother and daughter disembarked on the main road, then turned into a small track where Olive led the way along a tree-lined street of semi-detached houses. They appeared huge to Pam, after the little terraces of Wales. It was with great delight that she realised the figure who approached them was her sister, Peg.

"Pam!" she called out. "How are you? We've missed you, girl."

"I'm fine." They fell into each other's arms, and Pam was quick to note that she had grown as tall as her sister. "It's so good to see you."

"You too, girl. Come in, come in. You've got to see the new place." Peg pulled her by the hand and up three steps into one of the nearest gardens. The house in front of them was a good size, with whitewashed walls and black door. The garden was immaculate. Peg was obviously proud and her whole face crinkled up with delight. Her body had filled out and she oozed contentment – marriage, Pam thought, and being in love, suited her sister well. She also looked smart, wearing a sky blue jumper and trousers. She would have no complaint if these were handed down to her in the future.

They walked to the right side of the house, and through another door that led into the kitchen. The first thing that Pam noticed was the strange contraption placed in the centre of the room, taking up much of the space. It resembled a low steel table, with wire netting fencing in all sides.

"What's that?" she asked, mystified. She had never seen anything like it.

"The Morrison Shelter," her sister explained. "When the siren sounds, we have to sit in there and wait until the all clear goes. Sometimes it can go on for hours."

"Blimey, is there room for everyone?"

"Just. Bill is often out on civilian patrol, so he's not usually with us. I'm only glad he's still around. Couldn't bear to have him away for long, but the farm work got him exclusion from the army."

"What about Joan? When will she be here?"

"You know she's in the air force now? She's managed to take leave, and thinks she'll get here in a couple of days."

Pam's happiness felt complete. The whole family would be reunited, in answer to her prayers. They had a good tea, and Bill was as nice as anything when he returned late from patrol. His whole face creased up, both eyes disappearing, as he grinned from ear to ear. He gave her the biggest hug of all, and it was with a light heart that she lay down next to her mother. She thought she would be too excited to nod off, but Pam was asleep within seconds of her head touching the pillow.

She dreamed of the sea. She was on an ocean liner, the whistle sounding as they steamed from the dock. People waved from the quayside and she waved back, standing proudly alongside her mother and clothed in their best Sunday outfits. They were on their way to Africa, to Father. The family would all be together, unbroken, for the first time in years. She spotted Mrs Evans waving frantically in the distance, then Mrs Raymond and Wendy. Her friend smiled at Pam, a white handkerchief brandished in the air, and Pam smiled back. The whistle continued to sound.

They left the harbour and Pam saw dolphins alongside the boat, diving and breaching. The sea became rough and they powered forward, untroubled. She was in her cabin, thrown violently from side to side. A hand grabbed onto her shoulder. She heard a voice and then she opened her eyes.

"What? What is it?"

"Pam, wake up." Olive shook her gently. "Come downstairs, quickly. There's a raid on."

Pam now recognised the scream of the siren – it was not a

ship's whistle at all. She struggled out of bed, eyelids heavy with sleep, and followed Mother down the stairs where Peg was already in the kitchen, crouched in one corner of the shelter. She looked pale in a white dressing gown, shrunken, nodding to mother and sister. Pam ducked in beside her, hunching herself forward to take up less space, while Olive assumed position next to the entrance. She was guarding over her girls, while Bill was out on another patrol.

"Here they come!" Her mother's voice spoke sharply. The background drone suddenly increased in intensity and Pam found herself trembling. She could not help it. There was a brief moment of silence, terror filling the room, and then a loud explosion was heard. A bomb had hit the ground – it sounded close. Pam glanced at her mother, wondering how much danger they faced, but Olive's features gave nothing away. If she was scared, then she was not going to reveal it in a hurry. It would take more than that before Jerry could get to her.

A second explosion shook the house almost immediately. The Morrison Shelter jumped from the ground; the walls groaned and shuddered as if from an earthquake. Pam fought back tears as white dust was raised into the air.

"That was close," Peg sounded breathless. "Hope Bill's all right." She had bent right over, hugging both knees, as pale as a ghost. Pam's lips began to quiver, her eyelids continued to flicker, but she refused to cry. Not here, not now, when she had only just arrived. She was going to be strong, just like Mother.

It was a long wait before the droning disappeared. There were no more near misses, but not one word was spoken while they listened to distant explosions. Peg closed her eyes and attempted to nap, while Olive sat upright, ever vigilant, alert to any danger. When the all clear finally sounded and it was possible to return to bed, Pam found it impossible to sleep. She wanted her old life back, those happy days in Folkestone by the sea. She realised with sadness that this could not happen. Nothing would ever be the same again.

☪

Joan actually arrived the next day, surprising everyone. She appeared in good health, as lovely as ever, her luminous eyes sparkling with joy. Peg quickly made space, and it was now possible to enjoy a family Christmas together. Despite the war, it was all that Pam could have wished for. She was delighted to spend time with Joan, and it was not long before they managed to set out for the Warren.

"Seems like a long time since we were there," Joan said, their footsteps quickening as they approached the edge of the cliffs.

"I know. I've missed it. We're nowhere near the sea in Wales. It's not the same."

"I've missed it, too. What about the boat hire, and the boy you used to fancy? Getting all dressed up for him! What was his name again?"

"Oh shush, Joan!"

Pam stopped walking abruptly. Where they had previously been able to follow the path down to the sea, huge rolls of barbed wire now prevented access. Olive had said that things were changed, but she had not been very specific. Pam was learning fast and disappointed again. The two sisters could no longer walk down to the water, sit on the rocks, or dip their feet in the sea. Even that had been taken away.

"Can we just stay here for awhile, anyway?" she asked, and Joan readily agreed. They sat on a low stonewall gazing out over the silvery expanse of water. It appeared unchanged, even if everything else was now different. A cool wind ruffled Pam's hair, and she struggled to tidy this. It remained good to be home, to see both her sisters again. The boy's name had been Harry, in the boat hire; she still remembered that. Seabirds whirled high in the air, twisting and riding the currents of air. Grey clouds raced overhead, revealing mere glimpses of blue. She breathed deeply and her mind slowly became peaceful, like the sea, without a ripple to disturb the surface.

When Joan and Pam explored the centre of town, they discovered a whole new Folkestone. It was impossible to reach the seafront anywhere, due to the proliferating rolls of barbed wire. Many shops were now damaged and boarded up. The streets ran quiet, but everybody they passed was quick to greet them, to ask how they coped with it all. There remained a definite palpable kindness, camaraderie, with everyone united against a common enemy. This was the only good aspect of war, Pam considered, and she was particularly upset to survey the ruins of their former home in Tontine Street.

The flat had been completely demolished, swallowed whole into the ground and reduced to a chaos of rubble. She imagined the terrible roar when it had crashed down, her old room suddenly vanished into dusty air. What if the family had actually been present? What then? Her mother was right, it was a miracle that they had escaped this devastation. It could have been so much worse, and she threw this thought from her mind immediately, for fear of giving it life.

"It's awful Joan," she said. "I always believed we'd still be here. It's what I'd been hoping for all this time."

"Let's go home, Pam. You know what Mum says – where there's life, there's hope. She's probably right. We've seen enough for one day."

☾

Christmas day proved a real joy. Rationing had struck hard, but this could not interfere with celebrations. If anything, it made things better. There were presents, singing and dancing. Olive roasted a small goose with most of the trimmings, and the girls declared it her finest dinner. Pam was given the first apple she had seen in months, and she shared it with Joan. The Germans were not going to ruin this family's entertainment.

The world turned once more, and it was time for Joan to depart. Her leave from the air force was over, and soon it would be Pam's turn to follow. She wanted to stay in Folkestone, war or no war, but both Olive and Peg refused to listen to her many protestations. They insisted evacuation was for the best.

"It's not called Hellfire Corner down here for nothing, you know," Olive repeated.

The date was set, her bags packed, and she was duly despatched back to Wales. Mrs Evans met her at the station and life was returned to a grim normality. Again, Pam experienced the sharp pang of loneliness bite deep.

She continued to work hard at school, although it seemed wrong to live so far away in comparative safety. She walked to the castle each day, loitering in the beautiful gardens, while Folkestone remained under daily attack. It was horrible to hear the reports on the news, and she wanted to stay with her family, where she belonged. She tried to explain all this to June, her friend, but it was difficult for her to understand. June had never lived anywhere but Merthyr Tydfil. She had never been separated from her parents.

Pam returned from school one day to find Mrs Evans pacing about the kitchen, unusually pale and anxious. The look of recognition on her face was one of relief, but this was swiftly confused with despair. She gestured for Pam to sit at the table, who did not know what to expect next. A telegram rested in the middle of the table, and she saw it carried her name. Mrs Evans nodded that she should read it.

"I'm sorry, Pam, so sorry." She had become very fond of her guest, and did not know how to do this. There was no easy way.

Pam leaned forward to skim through the message. It couldn't be true, could it? She glanced up at Mrs Evans whose own tears now provided confirmation. Joan was dead. Not yet thirty – it had been a thrombosis, another terrible mistake. She could not believe that those wonderful luminous eyes had closed forever, her life extinguished so abruptly. She had appeared so well over the holidays –there had been no warning of this. She looked again to Mrs Evans for confirmation who nodded her head and stood at the window.

"I couldn't believe it either, Pam," she said. "I've been sitting here for hours trying to take it in. You poor thing, I'm so sorry."

They would never be together again. Pam clenched her eyes shut, to take herself out of the world, a well-practised habit. She felt too stunned for tears, and hoped to wake up from this ugly dream. She opened her eyes and it was all in vain. The telegram was still on the table. Mrs Evans had not moved from her place at the window. Her sister remained dead, and an absence opened up in her heart. Life was savage and cruel. When she was actually denied permission to attend the funeral, Pam understood that she could not go on living like this.

Her mind was set after receiving a letter from Mother. There was no other course of action left to pursue. Richard, her father, was reported missing from the South African Army, feared dead. Peg and Bill had each other to care and look after. Mother had no one except her. She was going home now, embarked on a road leading only to Folkestone. Quite simply, there was no other choice in the matter.

Pam had been careful to save her pocket money, and the small amount received over Christmas. She set about discovering all relevant train times and connections, rehearsing each detail of the journey inside her head. She bided her time and continued to work hard at school, not wishing to arouse any suspicions. Another letter arrived from Mother – Richard was found alive and well, but this made no difference at all. She continued to pray in the chapel.

Pam hid and stored food for the journey; cheese sandwiches that quickly became soggy and limp. It was a cold Sunday morning when she finally set off. A letter of explanation was placed on the kitchen table, thanking her hosts for their kindness and hospitality, and she crept silent from the back door of the house. Mr and Mrs Evans had been out for their Saturday night. They were usually slow to appear in the morning, and this provided her with a decent head start. All essential belongings were reduced to a single white carrier, and she ran through the terraces while her heart skipped with nervous excitement. It felt so good to be coming home. Life was moving in a new direction, at last; the right direction.

The nice old man in the ticket office was a doddle. She sounded confident and sure of herself: he asked no questions. The journey itself was a blur, the one surprise a diversion through Reading that she supposed was due to bomb damage in London. It still appeared strange to witness the blackout of all station names, a precaution too far in her mind, but once she neared home the landmarks soon became more familiar. At last she could relax, no longer needing to count the tunnels as a distraction. When she saw the cathedral at Canterbury, she knew she was nearly there.

Pam arrived in Folkestone under a smouldering twilight. The clouds were stained peach, the sky a dark inky blue. She did not have enough money for a taxi or bus ride, and she had to walk up the steep hill to Capel. It did not matter. She had been sitting all day and adrenaline now powered her footsteps. There were no sirens or enemy attacks. She kept imagining her mother's reaction, and how happy she would be to have her youngest daughter returned.

Pam reached the top of the hill and started to run. She raced down the main street in Capel, before jogging along Peg's road to reach the house. She paused briefly at the side door, just time for one deep breath, then opened it and stepped into the kitchen.

"I'm home!" she shouted, triumphant.

"Pam, thank goodness you're here. We've been so worried about you." It was Peg who hurried through from the living room, her mother in close pursuit. "You've got some explaining to do, girl!"

"Oh Pam, there you are." Olive embraced her daughter fiercely. She was not smiling at all.

"I just wanted to come home and be with you, Mum. I'll get a job and work, I'm old enough now. Please don't send me back, I'll only run home again if you do."

"Have you any idea of the worry you have caused today?" Her mother stepped backwards to look at her properly, severely, keeping firm hold of Pam's arms. "The police have been looking for you everywhere, in Wales, London and here. Mrs Evans told them you had gone missing. That poor woman was apparently frantic, and we've been waiting for news all day. We thought something dreadful must have happened to you."

"I'm sorry," Pam sobbed. She had never once considered the possibility of causing any panic or concern, so determined to get away. "I just had to get home. Especially after hearing about Joan."

Olive and Peg were both so pleased to see her that they could not sustain any anger for long.

"Oh it will be a nine day wonder all right, mark my words, but we'll sort it out." Her mother managed at last to summon a smile. "Don't cry anymore, my girl. Let's find you something to eat, shall we? I bet you're starving."

Her mother had definitely lost more weight, when there was little enough to start with. She looked old and tired out. Peg also looked diminished, she realised, as war rationing and anxiety continued to make itself felt. There had also been the considerable upset of Joan's death, and all of the family felt this loss dearly.

Supper was thrown together, the kettle boiled, and the woman sat chatting about the table. When Bill arrived home from patrol, he exhibited a total lack of any surprise on spotting the visitor.

"Hello Pam. Told them you'd be back, I did, it was only a matter of time." He grinned. "Good to have you with us."

For two days, Pam stayed at home and helped Peg with the housework. She did not want to venture out of the house, to leave the family, not even for a short walk to look at the sea. There were further raids and more time was spent in the shelter. Business as usual, Olive called it, but she looked pleased to have the family together and under the same roof. To Pam's relief, she never discussed the details of her unexpected homecoming.

On the third day, a letter arrived from Miss Price and Merthyr Tydfil Grammar School. She requested Pam's immediate return, stating how she was one of their most promising girls. It was for the good of her future, she wrote, and contained a short postscript explaining how June and the Evans were missing her.

"I don't know, Pam." Olive was torn, indecisive. "I think that you'll have to go back. It's still not safe for you to be here, as you well know, my girl."

"I'll only come home again."

They sat in the living room. Pam gazed at the three ceramic swans on the wall then directly at her mother, defiant.

"But what if something happens? I'll never forgive myself. And what about your exams? They are important." Olive wrestled with her fingertips, her head shaking slowly from side to side. A deep frown pulled at both corners of her mouth.

"I'll get a job. I'm old enough now." She was nearly sixteen.

"But you're doing so well there, the teacher said so." Olive reached again for the letter. She must have read it one hundred times.

"I don't care." Pam was insistent. "I hate being there. I've been away for ages and I want to stay here with you. I've had enough, and I'm not going."

"I don't know, Pam."

"I'm staying Mum. I'll only come home again." She had saved her trump card for last, and now was the right time to use it. "I have to be here. We need to be together, now that Joan's gone. She would have wanted this, you know that."

It was the mention of her sister's name that exploded Olive's resistance. Tears ran from her eyes and she stood up to embrace her youngest daughter. She buried her face into her hair, and Pam knew then that she had won.

"All right, young lady, you can stay."

Pam was ecstatic. She would find a job and be of use, at last responsible for herself. She would not be a burden to anyone. The family would all be together, and what could be better than that? She knew that Joan would have agreed, and imagined her smiling in the background.

☾

In the morning, mother and daughter left the house early to see if they could find some new outfits for Pam. She had come back with nothing other than the clothes she wore, and she could not borrow from Peg forever. They had decided to catch the bus into Dover, because Olive thought that nothing suitable remained in the Folkestone shops.

They walked to the Old Dover Road, and did not have to wait long for a bus to arrive. Twenty minutes later, they were deposited in the centre of town and next to Pencester Gardens. It was a bright, warm day, and Pam was surprised by the lack of people to be seen. Dover had always used to be busy, and now it appeared deserted. A scorched smell hung low in the streets.

Pam had always enjoyed the sight of the castle perched high on the white chalk cliffs. She liked to see the big ships moored in the blue safety of harbour, and to walk along the pier to the lighthouse. The sea was never far distant, and there was a good promenade right along the waterfront. The only bad thing was the absence of sand – bathing here was strictly on pebbles. She remembered a fine old town, somewhat grand, but things were now very different. Nothing looked the same as before.

Again, many of the storefronts were boarded up, the elaborate displays no longer in evidence. All glass had long been blown out from previous attacks, and this would not be replaced until the fighting was over. Some stores were reduced to ruins, like their old home in Tontine Street, and there was now a familiarity to this rubble and destruction. A virulent weed of barbwire sprung up everywhere. The people walked with grim, set expressions. No laughter was heard anymore.

They walked slowly, hand in hand, and had nearly reached the market square when a loud siren burst into action, dissecting the air with a surgeon's precision.

"Hurry Pam, that's the shell warning," Olive explained, while guiding her daughter towards a large building where they joined a trickle of people flowing down the staircase and into an enormous brick cellar. It was cold inside, and the hairs on Pam's neck stood up. A damp, fusty smell polluted the atmosphere, and she felt her chest tighten. The space was filled with long wooden benches, where the locals took their seats as if sleepwalking. It was obviously a well-practised manoeuvre, and she was the only person who jumped when the outer door banged shut right behind them. An explosion was heard quickly after.

"That's the first one," Olive whispered. "They shell us from France now. Never know where they're going to land, or how long it will last. Sometimes it goes on for hours – we might not get to do any shopping!"

Her face appeared uncharacteristically stern, her forehead puckered with fresh wrinkles and lips pursed tight together. Her cheeks were sucked in, and when Pam glanced about the room she realised that everyone carried this same expression. It was the face of someone who knew and had lived through real fear and horror. She was looking at the face of war.

They sat in uncomfortable silence, simply waiting for the next explosion. Pam studied her fingernails and pulled at her

160

hair, until another hit shook the building. Then, she sat on her hands, afraid to move. It had sounded much closer, and they all wondered which building should be next. Breathless sobbing became audible from the opposite corner of the cellar, dripping outwards. One lady near to Pam began to recite prayers, the words made ugly with tension. The atmosphere darkened ominously, suddenly, and it was Olive who jumped to her feet.

"How about a sing-song everyone? Come on, let's have *John Brown's Body*." She started to sing, alone, using her beautiful rich voice. An old man at the far end joined in, a deep baritone, and he was followed by a couple of younger men. Pam found her own voice, and soon most of the people were singing loudly, drowning out all sounds of attack. Pam looked up to her mother, who still stood in the centre of the room. She smiled, nodding slightly, and Pam had never felt so proud of her.

Hours passed before the all clear rang out. They had covered a lot of songs, and it was a relief for everyone to be allowed outside. Pam and Olive trotted briskly up the stairs and into the afternoon sunlight. They both felt hungry and cold, no longer in the mood for shopping, and retraced their steps to the bus station. Half an hour later, they were back in Capel and home. The birds had only just started singing again.

"So what did you think of that, then? Still glad you came back?" her mother enquired, pouring out the first mug of tea.

"Yes, of course. I told you, I'm staying."

"But weren't you scared?"

"A little bit," Pam admitted. "Not like you."

"What makes you say that? Of course I was!" Olive sat down, and her daughter felt even more proud. "You should know that better than anyone."

They held hands and smiled. Peg would have to share her clothes for a little while longer, especially after she had found work. Pam was home, without doubt. It was a fact that counted for everything. As long as she remained with family, then things would be bearable. They would be good. The war, and Poland, would just have to forget about her. Her time as the girl with the loneliest eyes was over.

Part Five

NIGHT

I HAD A BABY daughter. My world should have been happy, filled with endless possibility, but this was not so. Gwen and I continued to fight. We continued to grow apart from each other. On every occasion when life had thrown up circumstances to push most normal people together, the opposite had happened to us. We had become more distant, each painfully aware of the differences that kept us separate.

I had returned to live in Folkestone, after originally leaving ten years earlier to study nursing, and now everything was changed. I had a baby daughter and a wife who did not love me. I had experienced and then lost the greatest happiness during my time on Malta with Nan. I had lived through a war and did not know how to cope with the subsequent peace. I would have benefited from a talk with Reverend Hocking, but he was now dead. They say there is a dark night of the soul for everyone – little did I realise it but, for me, this was only just beginning.

Demobilisation proceeded rapidly, my own release arriving in the spring of 1946. Jacqueline was now six months old and, if anything, relations with Gwen had grown even worse. I spent the bulk of my time at work and was due 113 days of paid leave – I chose to receive the money instead, rather than spend it with Gwen. We remained broke, and what had sounded a princely sum was all quickly used up on much-needed furniture, linen and clothes. The last thing I wanted was any free time to wallow in problems and suffocate at home.

Again, circumstances dictated that I would have to change direction. The Wampach transit camp was soon being disbanded. Again, I became afflicted with recurring dreams and nightmares, as had previously happened during periods of stress and depression. Army events were a frequent occurrence, and I watched open-mouthed as coffin bottoms opened to deposit corpses into shallow dusty graves. I saw the man shot down in the hospital gardens in Malta, his skull peeled back like a tin of sardines. I was followed to the family home in Park Street only to be attacked and strangled on the doorstep. I was under fire on an athletics track, my enemy an army of clones of Gwen. In one dream of drill parade, I actually kicked Gwen right out of the bed. I was down and sinking fast, shipwrecked on the rocks of depression. I needed to escape, one more time; I needed to get away.

London seemed to provide the solution – this city had always been good to me. It suited and nurtured me. I could get lost in the vast anonymity. It had made me grow up and become a man. Now, I craved to be alone, to be allowed to clear my head and regain some sense of equilibrium. If there was one place where this remained possible it had to be London, and I applied for an immediate return.

I wrote to the London County Council, and a reply was not long in coming. I was offered work at Lambeth Hospital on the general surgical ward, and accepted before daring to mention anything to Gwen. It is telling that she made no attempt to stop me, instead appearing almost relieved at the prospect of seeing the back of me.

"Well that's good news, Harold." I listened to the words she spoke, her mouth pinched thin, how she would look after Jacqueline and the house if I would send her my wages. Her quick, wary eyes avoided my gaze at all times – she could never inspire trust or confidence, unlike Nan. She said that I was to take as long as I needed; the change would do us all good. And so it was determined that I was going to London, to escape and be free. I was going to the city I loved and nothing else mattered. Nothing else mattered at all.

The train journey was good. I felt an instant lightening of spirit, an unburdening, with each mile that carried me from home. I was so glad to forget about everything, even if only for a short while, and almost excited about what the city would now deliver. Almost – I had forgotten how true excitement felt, no longer capable of immersing myself into its waters.

Boarding at the South Western Fever Hospital in Stockwell, it was deeply satisfying to return to work on the wards. I had missed this since Malta, and felt useful again. Eric remained abroad in Palestine, but I had the new crowd from *Out Of The Battle* to socialize with. Thankfully, I never saw Carol again, cringing involuntarily at all thoughts of our bedroom encounter. I had missed the camaraderie of hospital, the smell of disinfectant wafting along long corridors, the calm authority of Matron. I had missed the drinkers and cads who haunt all lodgings, and the endless supply of invites for a night out on the town. Now, it was all returned.

I continued to visit Gwen's father, Harry Fletcher, whenever possible, unchanged in my opinion of the infamous Ruby Lloyd, the supposed bane of Gwen's youth. They were undeniably a charming couple, never short of a good story, and a safe bet for the best meal of the week. We enjoyed lobster and champagne, the freshest fish, fine wine imported from France. I still hoped to engineer a reunion between father and daughter, and missed a father figure in my own life. Harry Fletcher spoke a lot of good sense, and made for an excellent replacement. Never in these visits to Harrow did I return to the house of Len and Marjory, where we had lodged at the start of the war.

Work was less enjoyable when transferred to night shift in the cancer unit, because the majority of our patients died young. Nursing care tended to be palliative only, and there was little that could be done as a cure. It brought back vivid memories of the polio outbreak on Malta, and the same haunting sensation from my iron lung days. Now, I had lost the support and protection offered by Nan. The safety net was removed and I could no longer distance myself from the patients, hiding behind the mask of the job. I was not capable of maintaining a professional detachment, and it broke my heart to witness this suffering.

I sent most of my wages to Gwen, as agreed, resigned to the fact that this would never be seen again. It was worth it – I remained glad that my mother did not have to put up with her moods and extravagances anymore, and her superior city manners. It was no real surprise when she also expressed a desire to return to London; it was Gwen's birthplace, after all, and she was currently marooned out in the sticks. I knew it was no use to argue, and set about the hopeless task of finding vacant accommodation.

The city was being rebuilt. Empty properties were terribly scarce, invariably taken before I had chance to view or pay a deposit. The County Council Housing Department were no use at all, despite the fact I remained in their employ. I approached them several times, but the girls in reception struggled not to laugh in my face, suggesting I would do better to spread my search outside the city.

The cancer wards wore me down. I couldn't separate myself from the patients, and was often scared of breaking down in front of them – it was the last thing that they needed, and I had never cracked before. Not once. Professional pride ensured that I did not want to make a start now. The property search continued to draw blanks and to my amazement I began to hanker for home, the wide-open spaces of my youth. The rush and noise of a recovering city made me crave for the calm of the coast, the lull of the sea, and I had to admit this change of heart to Gwen. I decided to do so in a letter- it was much easier this way, and I realised that I would have more chance of winning any subsequent argument.

Gwen professed to be stunned, but she agreed to stay in the area provided that we actually lived together. She was bringing up two children on her own, she wrote, and finding life difficult. She needed assistance, a man about the house. It was hard to shake the feeling that any man would do. I was in the wrong place at the wrong time. With the wrong woman.

I applied methodically to every hospital within travelling distance of Folkestone, because we could not comfortably afford to move again. Dot's bear sat on my desk while writing the applications, and I enclosed references collected from Mrs Simm, the

Hockings and Major Merryweather. Success was confirmed within weeks, and I began new employment at Dover County Hospital on September 1st 1946. Jacqueline approached her first birthday, and I was finally pulling myself together. From the day I had left Nan and then Malta, I constantly fought the sensation of living someone else's life, thrown off course from the path I should have trodden. At last, I was ready and able to take on my responsibilities. Finally, some semblance of order was returned to my life.

☙

Dover County Hospital had previously existed as the Union Workhouse to care for the poor. It had operated as a casualty hospital during the war, when I was often told that many of the patients could not speak a single word of English. The road name had since been changed from Union to Coombe Valley. Despite this, it continued to hold a stigma locally that it was second rate and a place to be avoided at all costs. It was only through the effort and commitment of all post-war staff that this gradually disappeared.

Matron was Miss Eales, another lady of indeterminate age who possessed the same calm authority and beautiful manners of Miss Perry on Malta. Verging on the plump, not one wrinkle creased her round face, and when she allowed herself a smile it was really quite lovely. She had light brown hair that was always neatly arranged under a white hat, and she was never less than immaculate in both appearance and demeanour.

Dr Knight was the resident civilian doctor. A tall athletic man, hailing from New Zealand, he possessed a laidback amiable character that made him a pleasure to work with. A young English nurse had caught his eye during active service, and it was because of her that he had not returned home. Dr Knight seemed to possess a limitless abundance of patience and energy, never once appearing on any ward without a smile gracing his aquiline features. He treated everybody as an equal, so earning the universal respect of patients and staff alike.

Initially assigned to Male Surgical and Children's Wards, twenty-four beds were placed under my direct supervision, a far cry from the large numbers looked after on Malta. I left home at seven and caught the bus at ten past, arriving early to work each day. There was always something of interest happening in the hospital, and the shifts sped past without my realising. I could look at my watch at ten in the morning, and the next thing I knew it was four thirty. The work proved time consuming yet fulfilling; many of the new staff were untrained auxiliaries, and I often went in on my free days to provide assistance. I felt a professional obligation to help as much as I could, and it also acted as a great excuse to get me out of the house and away from Gwen. I did not like to think of her as my wife – since the wedding, she had not even taken my second name.

We were able to provide a high standard of care, and I was determined to make a success of work if not my private life. This appeared out of my control, subject largely to Gwen's ever-changing moods and emotions. We tolerated each other, no more, but Jacqueline appeared to be growing up well. An inquisitive child, she thrived to live near the sea, quickly demonstrating a love of the water that must surely have been inherited from her father. Diana continued to run wild, as she had through the war years, but I saw little of her. I had my mother and family nearby, and it was a grand feeling to be serving a close-knit community. I could not walk through Dover or Folkestone without garnering several greetings and wishes for my own good health, and I liked this. At last, I felt needed and useful again.

Anticipating the act of parliament that would later launch the National Health Service, all three hospitals in Dover were now amalgamated. The County Hospital had yet another name change, and we became Buckland Hospital. This also led to meeting up with old acquaintances – a new doctor was assigned to help, recently returned from overseas military service. It was a real pleasure and joy to be reunited with Major Henry Merryweather, when he sneaked up on me during a ward inspection. I was in the middle of checking a pulse when I felt a tap on my shoulder and turned around to find him standing there, right behind me, like an apparition stepped out from the past.

"Hello Harry, thought I might catch you in here. I had a feeling our paths might cross again, remember? Your BEM party?"

It was true – the Major had mentioned this just after I was decorated on Malta, when I had absolutely no desire to leave the island. I had no intention of ever being parted from Nan.

He continued to speak. " So how are you doing? Keeping all right? I hear you now have a family – congratulations!"

"Major! It's so good to see you!" I could not believe it was really him, and shook his hand vigorously. He had put on some weight and looked much the better for it. His hair had grown out from army severity and this made him appear younger, more at ease with the world. The Major carried with him only positive recollections from my service abroad, where we had worked together in both Sliema and Mtarfa. We had made a good team, and I took it as a fair omen to see him again. Life continued to acquire some semblance of purpose.

"Henry," he said, "call me Henry now, and don't you forget it." He took off his glasses and allowed himself a smile, while rubbing the lenses against the sleeve of his jacket. Henry Merryweather was a true gentleman and a fine medic. We arranged to meet up for a beer, and I quickly discovered that he had lost none of his previous humility and generosity of spirit. He soon became extremely popular among both patients and staff and every Christmas morning, without fail, he turned up on the wards. He dished out presents from home, chatting to the patients for several hours before returning to his own family and dinner.

Common admissions included heart conditions, strokes, peptic ulcers and pneumonia. Cases of tuberculosis were nursed in separate huts within the hospital grounds, recently available antibiotics proving invaluable in their treatment. We picked up sporadic cases of meningitis, thankfully without the complication of anxiety neurosis witnessed on Malta. Polio was also rare, as was the practice of lumbar puncture. I was glad to consign that to the past.

Promotion came quickly, when I was placed in charge of Male Medical Wards looking after thirty-two beds and assisting in the operating theatre. Previous maladministration had affected these departments badly, causing particular worry to the hospital governors. It was my task to regain a sense of discipline and order, and I set about this with great relish.

Hospitals, like armies, are a great breeding ground for rumours, and it was at this time that I found myself the subject of several funny stories doing the rounds. There was the one that I had previously been a doctor until struck off for some unmentionable misdemeanour, another that I had been top of the class in medical school before running out of funds. The reasons for this varied depending on who was telling the story, ranging from drinking to looking after my sick mother. My favourite version included a predilection for high-class prostitutes, and I never confirmed or denied a thing.

It did not take long to kick the medical wards into shape. I was used to managing much bigger departments than this, and my responsibilities now spread to include Dermatology. Mr Edelston, the main specialist for chest diseases in South East Kent, offered to put me through medical training with a gratuity of twenty pounds per month. I could have claimed a similar amount from the army. The only downside was that it would involve a minimum of five years away from home. I had a young family to support and had recently promised Gwen that we should live together. I had to turn him down, and another path in life was closed to me forever. My choices had narrowed and bound me to Gwen.

☪

1948 witnessed birth of the National Health Service, new beginnings, but for me this was the year of death. First it was Dad, who died while I was off-duty from the hospital, slipping away through complications of alcoholism brought about by his previous war service. His lungs had never fully recovered from the gas attacks, and he did not help himself in any way. The drinking that had brought about my own nurse training finally got the better of him.

The night of his death was strange. I knew that he was in trouble, although we had never been close. I always had the feeling that he considered me useless, and that he disapproved of the decisions I had made, particularly with regard to Gwen. Now, from the comfort of my own house, I sensed that he was scared and I tried to comfort him. I lay awake in bed and I told him to relax, to let go and forget about his fear. His presence seemed to fill the room, struggling for breath and panic-stricken. Again, I told him not to worry, the words spoken silent inside my head – I did not want Gwen to believe I had finally cracked. This strange dialogue continued long throughout the night, developing a pattern to the exchanges; first his terror and then my own calm response. I told him that I loved him and that it was all right to say goodbye, that he should have nothing to worry about. It was twenty to six in the morning when I felt his silent release, and I lay trembling under the covers. Gwen lay beside me, but I might as well have been alone for all the support she provided. Dad was gone and, later, when I received confirmation from the hospital this was indeed the exact moment of his passing.

There was little time for grieving before something else happened, when Mother suffered a severe stroke at home in Park Street. She had risen early from bed and was on her way downstairs for the usual cup of tea when she began to feel dizzy. She felt heavy, she said, and her vision clouded over with white blindness. Reaching the bottom step, she sat down to rest and it was then that the blood clot sailing fast through her arteries took anchor in the brain. She blacked out, falling forwards, and only after regaining consciousness discovered she was unable to move. She had also lost the sight in her left eye.

It was my sister Doris who found her, late afternoon. By then, she had also become incontinent, so bruising her great pride. Mother was in trouble. She could cope with her sick husband and errant children, but this was something else. She had bound the family together, single handed, and now we all took it in turns to nurse and look after her.

She remained in good cheer for some time, despite confined to her bed, convinced that she would make a full recovery. Her lady friends still called to visit, and she insisted that we keep her appearance presentable. My sisters Doris and Phyl bathed her daily, trimming her hair and nails, and even applied a coating of rouge. It was the first time that I had known her to use this, but she complained the absence of a good walk and fresh air was making her pale. We all kept her as occupied as possible, each telling her of our respective days and asking for suitable advice. We were united in our determination that she should not lose position in the centre of our world, and from her lively conversation this appeared to be working.

"I'll soon be running around again," she said. "You mark my words."

Even Gwen was impressed by her fortitude and occasionally deigned to visit. Mother remained as polite as possible under the circumstances, but she had never grown fond of Gwen.

It was only when informed how she would never walk again, by a visiting locum doctor, that she gave up the fight to live. I was furious, prepared to do damage and punch out his lights, but the opportunity never presented itself. He never appeared again, moved on to damage other people's lives. I remembered what the men had used to tell each other in the RAMC, to stay away from doctors at all costs, and it now made horrible sense.

My mother, Lilian, sat alone in her room, refusing all offers of help. She refused to eat, consenting only to rare sips of water, withdrawing from the world and from us. She stared for long hours at a blank wall; she had the saddest eyes in the world. If we were lucky, she spoke, but these words soon became precious as gold dust. Her sentences became random and distracted.

I see your father now, watching me. Waiting. He knows it won't be long. There's a man in black wearing a top hat. He comes and sits in the corner of the room. I don't like him. Who are you?

It was awful. Nothing any of us could do managed to breach the impenetrable wall that she built around herself. We tried so hard but she was drifting away, out of reach. Both sisters were devastated, and my nursing skills now counted for nothing. Mother contracted pneumonia and declined all possible treatment. She died at the age of sixty-nine. She had been the strongest one in our family, and she left behind a gaping raw absence. An open wound. Without her, I missed my father all the more. The centre of my universe had disappeared and I would have to find another one. Losing mother and father in the same year was like cutting off both legs, a double amputation, and a terrible price to pay.

I had no parents and I missed them like never before. I wished that I had known Dad better, that we might have been friends and I could have understood his actions rather than fighting him. I wished that I might have been of more use to Mother, instead of dragging her into my own web of problems. Since childhood, I seemed to have brought her only more pain and trouble, even inflicting Gwen and Diana on her while Dad was unwell. I wished that I could have helped her. Saved her. Death had lost any strangeness on Malta, but it was dreadful to surrender both parents.

It was Gwen's stepmother next, Ruby Lloyd. We had kept in touch since my return from London, and I knew that she was unwell. The diagnosis was all too ominous: cancer of the breast, well advanced, sewing its germs throughout her body and beyond all scope of treatment. I spoke to Harry on the phone, wrote letters, and at last Gwen became interested. For the first time in years, father and daughter were able to have a relationship. Finally, Gwen appeared to forget her previous grievances and offered him comfort and support.

Ruby was a fine woman. She had been a primary school teacher until Harry encouraged her to turn professional as a singer, launching a successful career in broadcasting. She had an appetite for life that Reverend Hocking would have approved, and courage to carry her beyond illness. In her final month, Ruby existed solely on champagne and narcotics while visibly shrinking before our eyes. She never lost her sweet voice, to her considerable relief, and she saw out her days with unflagging determination and optimism. With Ruby, there was never danger of her losing any dignity. She died in Harrow, a great woman, and a devastated Harry now chose to move to Folkestone. He wanted to be near his daughter.

Harry Fletcher rented a small flat and we saw a lot of him after that. He became a devoted grandparent to Diana and Jacqueline, both girls dearly fond of him. Gwen and I were able to spend many hours listening to tales from his past, when he had worked for the Edison Bell Record Company and later as stage manager in both music halls and theatre. He had worked with some of the best, including Chaplin and Laurel and Hardy. A born storyteller, it quickly became apparent even to Gwen that her father was an exceptional man.

Harry Fletcher was busy exorcising all ghosts from his life. He told us how his first wife, Gwen's mother, had actually died during childbirth, a fact she had never fully appreciated. He had raised her on his own, and it was much later that he met Ruby. He had needed help and missed female company. He had actually sent Gwen away for her own good, believing it would make her a stronger, more resilient person. It had been entirely his own idea, and Ruby had argued against this – she was a far cry from the monster that I had been asked to believe in.

I now see that Harry was teaching us in his own subtle way, and reminding us of the precious nature of life – how important it is to love, and always be generous. You never knew when your own luck might turn. Never go to bed on an argument, he insisted; nobody can see into the future, and you did not want to deal with regrets. Live each day as if you mean it, he said; be happy, and laugh often. It doesn't cost anything to smile. He was such a delightful fellow, a proper old-fashioned gentleman cut from the same cloth as Mr Hann. I was prepared to listen to anything he had to tell me, and then Harry was also taken from us. He went to bed one night, alone in his flat, and never woke up. There had been no warning, no previous sign of ill health. He was simply gone, without fuss or ceremony, and my black tie required yet another airing. I had lost another dear friend and mentor.

Gwen could not bring herself to sort through her father's belongings, and this unpleasant task now fell on me. I had to do it as quickly as possible – it was the only way I could cope. His clothes were bagged up and discarded, but I kept all the books and record collection. These had been his pride and joy. I also kept his collection of signed memorabilia from stars of the stage and music halls. His toiletries were thrown out, and I bunched his letters together for incineration. They were private, not for prying eyes, but I stumbled across one note that he had written and dated on the day of Ruby's passing.

I love you with all my soul, sweetheart. I could not have asked anything more from life than to share it with you, to walk with you by my side. I will never forget you. I will never stop loving you. I will come soon after, my dearest Ruby.

He had known that he would die, and he wanted this. His final act had been to sort out the problems between Gwen and myself, and it appeared to have been successful. With yet another death to deal with, huge waves of grief at last threw us together. For a short while we were a couple in every sense of the word, but this all changed on settlement of his estate when it was Gwen who became the main beneficiary.

For the first time, we had money in the bank. We could look to buy our own house, rather than continue renting – our first real family home. It had been a terrible year, both sets of parents now gone, and circumstances could only improve. I remained determined to make things work out, but it was Gwen who had different ideas.

"Harold, this is my money," she stated, "not yours. You heard the will – I'll do what I want with it."

All of Harry's lessons were quickly forgotten, and she intimated that I would now have to dance to her tune. Instead of improvement, unhappiness returned. It was hard to know what to do next. The relationship continued to throw us around like a roller coaster, with far more downs than ups, and I could not see a way off the ride. Our sham of a wedding, hastily arranged after my sudden return from Malta, had actually signalled an ending. It had acted as a funeral wake for the fleeting happiness we had once enjoyed, long since forgotten, when we had not been able to keep our hands from each other. Now, I knew it to be pointless, an empty, futile gesture, and what is worse I did not care. I was down and sinking fast.

Gwen had inherited Harry's car, a new post-war vehicle that could easily be sold for twice the original list price, and she immediately set her mind on acquiring this extra money. It was over this that I finally rebelled.

"What about all the cash I sent you from Malta?" I

demanded, getting myself angry and red in the face. "Have you forgotten about that? My money? You never did tell me where that went."

"We've been over all this before," she sighed, shaking her head and already bored. "I told you, it went on Diana."

"I don't believe that, and I'm keeping the car whether you like it or not. God knows I've paid for it!"

There must have been something in my voice that finally made Gwen take notice. For once, she lacked the stomach for a fight and allowed me to keep possession of the vehicle. I felt so utterly alone. There was nobody that I could turn to, and I missed my mother badly. She would have known the right words to say, the advice to keep my spirits up and maintain a flicker of hope. Events had happened so quickly, falling over each other like dominoes, and there had been scant time available for grief. Now, I desperately wanted to talk with her, to see her once again, and this could never take place. Realisation struck like a tight clenched fist.

The nightmares returned and I struggled to sleep, tossing and turning through cruel, restless nights. There was so much I did not know about her, and I understood that I would never find out. What had her own childhood been like? Was she happy before meeting my father? How had she been able to forgive him after the affair? To come home, as if nothing had happened? More than anything, I wanted to thank her for her unswerving patience and kindness, her absolute generosity. I had no mother or father. Reverend Hocking was dead and my best friend far away. I was on my own, with Gwen, and this was not easy. I was lonely and numb inside, all actions and emotion stifled as if underwater. I had to keep it together for the sake of the children, and for the hospital. Broken hearts are sometimes mended by work: Harry Fletcher had said this and it remained my only hope.

☙

We looked at a number of houses in Dover. It would be more convenient for travelling to the hospital, and there were too many bad memories in Folkestone. That town was now swimming with ghosts and the language of the dead. It seemed essential to move away, but we could not find anything that we agreed upon and the search was subsequently extended.

I liked the pretty village of River, hanging on the coattails of Dover. It was small, quaint and quiet, with a sense of the open space that I craved. It was named after the River Dour that ran through it, and I thought it amazing how native trout flourished in the shallow, clear water. Gwen disagreed with me on principle, declaring a preference for nearby Temple Ewell. Two parks separated these locations, Kearsney Abbey and Russell Gardens, and it was walking through these that we discovered Kearsney Court.

Kearsney Abbey was nearest to River. We walked here from the village, and along a gravel path leading down to the lake. There were big trees all around us, and we paused on the blue-railed bridge. Large white swans floated indolently below, hoping for spare crusts of bread, and Gwen noticed a red squirrel jumping athletically from tree to tree. We moved on, beyond the remains of the abbey, and crossed the Alkham road to enter Russell Gardens. It was beautiful, reminding me of Charnwood and my time with the reverend.

Pergola bridges marked the boundaries of another lake, where fat trout could be seen swimming beneath the native ducks, a lazy ripple occasionally breaking the mirrored surface. Again, there were trees everywhere, so welcome after the grey confines of town. We headed towards the boathouse, to sit and enjoy a moment of silence, when Gwen noticed the old building. Gardens were terraced from the middle of the lake, incorporating flowerbeds, tennis courts and yet more trees, and these led up to a large manor house. It was grand in the old style, with huge windows, a red slate roof, but it was the right side that particularly captivated my attention. It had a tower, replete with pointed copper-green turret, and below this hung a sign. FOR SALE. We glanced at each other, then climbed swiftly to investigate. Gwen even allowed me to assist her, taking my hand over the steepest part of the track.

Kearsney Court stood before us. Originally a single residence, it had recently been converted into seven separate units and the tower section remained vacant. We were shown inside by a little old man and immediately fell in love with the place. The building wore an attractive coat of ivy, home to a swarm of wild bees, and we quickly realised that there would be ample room for the four of us. From the dining room, a cast iron spiral staircase twisted up to reveal a wonderful panorama of unspoiled countryside. In the distance, it was just possible to make out the sea and this fact decided it for me. We agreed a price, shook hands, and then rushed back to inform the children.

Both girls shared our enthusiasm. The move progressed quickly and smoothly, heralding yet another new start. I had nothing else remaining – if this did not work I was in big trouble, and I determined, yet again, to attempt to salvage something from out of the wreckage of the life I had created. I had made the bed, as Mum said, and now I had to lie in it.

The journey to work was considerably shorter, reduced to a mere ten minutes with use of a car. I went in early, as usual, but left as soon as duties allowed. In the evenings, I could enjoy walking through the gardens surrounding the lake. It was so peaceful here, and words of the reverend floated back to me through time. Sometimes, it seemed that my mother walked bedside me, watching over me, making sure I was doing all right. I still spoke to her, asking questions and anticipating her reply. In this quiet, relaxed environment, the relationship with Gwen began a gradual improvement. The girls were so happy, and I believe that she could see some good might yet become of us. The fights and chilly silences became less frequent.

☾

Time passed, bringing with it another tentative returning of hope. I was becoming more comfortable in my own skin, the nightmares disappearing, when woken in the deep of night by the hooting of an owl. It was with some surprise that I discovered Gwen trembling on a chair placed next to the open window.

"What's wrong?" I struggled to raise myself, leaning on an elbow for support.

"Bad news, Harold, I can feel it." The thin back silhouette of her naked body shivered in the moonlight. It had been some time since she had voiced any premonition and I forced myself upright, alert.

"How? What do you mean?"

"I'm not sure exactly, but I know something bad is going to happen. I just know it."

"It's only an owl, Gwen. Come back to bed."

I pulled back the covers and she climbed in, allowing me to hold her within my arms. Gwen continued to shake, crying without sound, the spasms shaking her whole body as cold tears dripped from her face and onto my chest. She swallowed noisily, gulping for breath, before continuing to speak.

"It's my fault Harold, I know. Didn't I tell you, right at the beginning, how people can be cursed? I should never have worn Ruby's wedding ring."

"Try to sleep, love. We'll talk in the morning." I stroked her hair and held her tight. Eventually, her body softened into sleep and I also nodded off. In the morning, I had forgotten all about this until Gwen returned to the subject.

"I told you it was a bad sign, last night." She had her back to me, doing the dishes after breakfast, while the girls dressed upstairs into school uniforms.

"How so? What?"

"The owl. It's a bad omen, I told you. I knew I shouldn't relax, bad luck always seems to find me."

"Gwen," I interrupted, "I don't know what you're talking about?"

She turned abruptly, her hands dripping soapy water onto the kitchen floor. "Harold, I sold your eternity ring, the one you bought me in Elsham Road. I felt guilty, but you know how things were between us. Anyway, then I started wearing Ruby's wedding ring. It's my fault. I shouldn't have done it."

"It's all right, you might be mistaken." I was still unsure exactly what Gwen was afraid of, and attempted to stand but she waved me back down. The ring did not bother me so much – I had not seen it for some time, and there had been much bigger disappointments than that.

"When have I ever been wrong Harold? When have my hunches ever been wrong?"

She was right. Our time together had been littered with Gwen's premonitions, and not once had I known these to be inaccurate. Nothing I could say or do seemed to help, and I watched her become increasingly fraught and nervous. She lost weight, her skin acquiring an unhealthy pallor and dryness. She slept poorly, and I often woke to find her out of the bed.

"What's wrong?" I asked. "Did I wake you? Was I snoring?"

"You did nothing, Harold. It's me." The reply was always the same.

☾

When shifts allowed, I liked to start my day by dropping the children off at school. I could then return home and snatch a quick breakfast in peace. It was an overcast morning, the streets grey with rain, when I hurried back through the door and up the stairs just in time to watch Gwen collapse heavily to the floor. She fell backwards as if in slow motion, groaning, both hands clutching at her stomach while her head cracked hard against the fridge. She had been filling the kettle with water and the tap continued to gush furiously. I raced to her side, reaching instinctively to check for her pulse.

"What's wrong? What happened?" I whispered, frantic with worry.

She remained conscious, frowning and baring her teeth. "It hurts. Inside, it hurts."

Gwen's breathing was shallow, her pulse rapid, and I knew she was in danger of passing out. We needed help. I held her as gently as possible, lifting and carrying her outside to the car, then laying her flat on the back seat. It crossed my mind, I am ashamed to admit, how lucky she was that we had not sold this as she originally intended, but such thoughts were too cruel to hold onto. It seemed so unreal to head for the hospital, my work, with Gwen in such desperate condition. I could scarcely comprehend the situation, moving as if sleepwalking, while I carried her into the emergency room.

Blood transfusions were performed immediately, and Gwen

was taken into theatre for an exploratory operation. She appeared so weak and defenceless; I vowed to look after her properly once she was over the worst and we had heard the diagnosis. It was a flushed Henry Merryweather who later told me the full case history, and I felt relief that she had been in such safe, capable hands.

Gwen had suffered an ectopic pregnancy that had brought about severe internal bleeding. It came as a tremendous boost to hear she would make a full recovery, and I was allowed to see her as soon as the anaesthetic wore off. They had allocated her a private room, and I hurried to this impatiently.

"Gwen, dear, how are you? I was so worried." I reached to take hold of her hand, closing the distance between us, before noticing a coldness in her eyes that was definitely unrelated to sickness.

"I'm pleased that happened." She spoke slowly. "You know how I never wanted another child of yours."

I stared up into the floating blue light of the room, crushed all over again. We had made another false start and, again, our relationship faltered. Gwen appeared to make a speedy recovery, without complication, and from that day onwards we never made love again.

☾

Buckland Hospital prospered, enjoying a well-deserved golden period. A considerable amount of time and effort was then devoted to redevelopment of services to fit in with the new National Health Service, and this brought about a dramatic increase in staff numbers. We had more consultants available, and I had more nurses to look after. The range of treatments performed grew exponentially and our reputation soared. We liked to think of ourselves as London hospital by the sea, with so many of our professionals trained in the city, and my name was put forward for further promotion. Once again it was work that saved me, with home life showing little sign of improvement.

Jacqueline did well at school, which brought with it some comfort, but this was in stark contrast to her stepsister. Diana's behaviour worsened terribly; she told the most outrageous lies, stealing from Gwen and me, and could be trusted with nothing. We had hoped that the move would help settle her, but this was not to be. She failed every examination at school, and when we found her a succession of jobs she managed to get dismissed from them all. At the age of sixteen, she ran away from Kearsney Court.

Gwen was extremely anxious about Diana's safety. I tried to reassure her that all would be well, but she did not want to listen. However, the police soon traced her route to London and she was returned in one piece. We sought the advice of child guidance officers, friends, even the clergy, on bringing her home, but nothing worked. Lionel and Grace, Gwen's friends in Essex who had been witness to our marriage, offered their assistance and she moved out to live with them. Again, she proved uncontrollable and absconded to London a second time. The next we heard came from the police again, who enquired if we should like her to be detained for collection. By this time, Gwen had tired sufficiently of trying and refused to take her back, insisting that she was old enough to manage her own life and obviously did not want our help. It would be dishonest not to admit that we both felt relief she should not be allowed to influence Jacqueline further, and a period of relative calm entered our lives. We shared an attractive home and agreed to tolerate each other. It could have been so much worse, but this peace did not last for long. It never did with Gwen and me.

Len and Marjory reappeared on the scene and began to visit for holidays. I didn't enjoy these occasions but it was Gwen's house, they were her friends, and there was little that I could do about it. She continued to disappear with Len, no explanation offered, as they had during the war in Harrow, leaving Marjory and me alone to unhappy silence. Neither of us dared voice our concern, for fear of any consequence. I hated this quiet acquiescence. For some reason, I remained paralysed to act, although the suspicions refused to go away. Gwen would never discuss their friendship, dismissing my worries as paranoia and petty jealousy. She said that it was beneath me, pure weakness and unattractive insecurity. When they eventually returned to Harrow, Gwen would be miserable for weeks on end. She took regular day trips to London, allegedly to shop and watch matinee shows at the theatre.

It was not long before Gwen again started to feel unwell, now complaining of tiredness and stomach pains, an inability to sleep through the night. I tried but could not convince her to seek any treatment – she invariably reminded me of my own army saying, to keep away from doctors. It was only when the symptoms became worse that I was able to change her mind, and she agreed to make an appointment. The local doctor was unable to reach a firm diagnosis, and Gwen was referred to a specialist gynaecologist.

The consultant was quick to recognise fibroids of the womb, and Gwen was readmitted into hospital for surgery. One of her wishes was then granted beyond any doubt; following hysterectomy, she would indeed never carry another child of mine. By this stage, I was past caring. Again, Gwen appeared to recover without complication.

I continued to devote my energies into work, and the Hospital Management Committee advised I should apply for a place on the Diploma Of Nursing course. If successful, I was promised the appointment of Head Tutor, the highest position I could reach without qualification as a doctor and a fine incentive to study. Gwen was actually enthusiastic for my prospects, providing uncharacteristic but welcome support, and I set about the bookwork with relish.

The examinations were held over one week at Battersea Polytechnic. It would have been good to meet up with the fellows from *Out From The Battle*, but I kept myself to myself and worked hard. I hadn't forgotten Dot's bear, and he sat with me through all of the revision. I took him to every exam and he had lost none of his good fortune. Results were announced immediately, and I had passed with distinction.

It was with newborn hope that I returned to the south coast. I couldn't wait to tell Gwen the good news, and hoped she would share this optimism. I raced from the station at Kearsney, through the abbey and into Russell Gardens, considering how my career was definitely moving in the right direction. For the first time since F Block on Malta, it was work that I loved. After struggling with my key in the lock, I crashed through the front door calling out to anyone who would listen.

"I've passed! Gwen, you were right! I did it." There was only one month to wait before the next diploma course began and I hurried upstairs to shout out the news. The house was empty.

When she eventually returned in the evening, Gwen appeared distant and more than a little troubled. I had only been away for a week and yet there was fresh awkwardness between us. She put on a show of joy at my success, granting me one quick kiss on the lips, but her eyes told another story. Her thoughts were anywhere but home, and she refused to divulge what bothered her. I found it so frustrating – whenever I endeavoured to try harder, our relationship inevitably ran into brick walls. I did my honest best, but it only ever met with more failure.

Examination results were presented to the hospital board and I was granted the necessary year of absence on full pay. Henry Merryweather was particularly supportive, offering his assistance in any way possible. I wanted to do well on the course so that I would not be letting anyone down, be it colleagues, family or myself. The staff at the hospital appeared to be genuinely delighted for me, and it was only Gwen who dampened this feeling. It was after one particularly long shift, when we had lost one of my favourite patients, that I could not prevent this frustration from boiling over. Gwen was always so distant; we remained more like strangers than man and wife.

"What's your problem?" I had not even bothered to take off my coat and sit down. "How can I help if you don't tell me anything? What have I done this time?"

"Nothing, Harold, you've done nothing." She turned slowly, lifting her head, twilight filling both eyes. Gwen appeared weak, her porcelain complexion impossibly fragile, and this was definitely not usual.

"Then what is it?" I stepped forward, suddenly unsure.

"It's not you, it's me." She did not turn away but stared at me, unblinking. "I've not been feeling well for some time, and now I've found a lump on my breast. It's getting bigger, Harold. You know what that means."

I cursed our lack of physical relations, afraid of the direction this conversation had taken. This was not what I had planned to argue about. Once again events appeared to be heading out of my control, and I found myself immersed in something I had not expected.

"It's cancer, I know." Gwen's voice sounded robotic, detached from her own body. She burst into tears and I pulled her against me, desperately trying to magic the right words.

"You don't know for sure. You could be wrong. We'll get it checked and …"

"I know." She cut me short. "I know. But thank you. And there's something else I've got to tell you, Harold. Now seems as good a time as any. It's about Len. You were right about us. You were right all along."

Her sobbing continued, but this time I released my grip. My whole world, constructed over many years, had decided to crash down for a second time. Gwen's words struck like hammer blows, destroying all recent optimism. Despite prolonged suspicion, I was unprepared for the shocking truth of my wife's adultery and had certainly not been expecting to hear it now. I sat down, unsure exactly what I felt, the sole realisation that I had at last emerged from a long tunnel of lies. The truth did not help. Nan's precious truth only made things worse. I watched as Gwen stood and moved slowly to the window, staring at the pale violet sky. I could not make out her expression.

"Don't leave me Harold. Everyone leaves me. I couldn't cope on my own, not now. I've finished with him – it's over for good. I told him about the cancer and the coward didn't want to know. The bastard."

A blizzard of emotions and thoughts erupted through my head, crashing down like a tsunami, a vision of waves all around. I felt angry. Unbearably hurt. I was free. I could now say goodbye to this stranger who had entered and ruined my life. My parents had been right all along – she was bad news. If Gwen could cheat on me with a pretentious little shit like Len, then I didn't need to beat myself up about her anymore. She wasn't worth it. I owed her nothing. She'd already had more than enough from me.

But Gwen said she had cancer. She was never wrong with her premonitions and this was awful. Nobody deserved that terrible disease. Not even her, after all she had done. A tender, softer emotion rose up through the storm. I wanted to crush and quieten it, to stamp it down. I was free. At last, I was free. Surely that was the most important thing?

"Are you madly disappointed? Harold?" She spoke my name and it felt like a kiss.

"I need some time to think."

She nodded and I left the house, the darkening sky fading as empty as our future, the moon as pale as ice. I have no idea how long I walked, nor which route I took. I wanted to be a night without stars, to feel nothing, for inside I had died another death. My world had shattered into tiny pieces and I knew it could not be glued together again. It was broken. Unrecognisable. Changed forever.

I found myself in Folkestone. The old fish market and harbour, and then the Warren. The sea appeared equally exhausted, tiny waves barely visible in the heavy silence. I sat on the promontory where I had first pitched tent and spotted Dot so many years before, allowing my thoughts to float upon the dark surface, willing my problems to drift away with the undertow.

I had never felt so alone in the world and admit that I cried. What would Mother have thought of me now? Dad? I remembered the reverend and Harry Fletcher. What would they tell me to do? No answers were forthcoming. I lay back on the cool, hard surface of stone and prayed to Nan's God in the heavens. He did not reply. I shut my eyes, contemplating throwing myself into the still, dark water. Would death be the easy solution? Was that the best course of action to take? I stood up later, much later, as the stars ran away from the sky.

I reached Kearsney Court just after dawn. Gwen was nowhere to be seen, but Jacqueline raced down the stairs and threw herself upon me, wrapping me tight.

"Don't leave, Dad. Please don't go." She had been listening

for my return, obviously unable to sleep. "Mum talked to me last night. She's so sorry, she really is, and she doesn't want you to leave us."

I lifted my daughter from the ground, holding her face in front of my own. Her eyes were red from crying and I kissed her cheek, somehow managing a smile. There had been too much fighting during her young life. "Don't worry young lady," I said, "I'm not going anywhere."

Jacqueline produced the most glorious smile and only then my tears began. Until this night, and this news, I had not appreciated how deeply I cared for Gwen. She was my wife, and my wife had cancer. Of course I would not abandon her. A previously undiscovered well of love and compassion poured out of me. I buried my face into my daughter's hair and failed to notice Gwen's approach. She held onto both of us and I heard the gentlest of whispers.

"Thank you, Harold. You are a good man."

☾

In the morning, I was able to plead compassionate leave and we went to see the doctor immediately. Gwen was promptly admitted and I was left to suffer the anguish of waiting alone. My world was closing in one me, and I experienced a claustrophobia not felt since the war years. I needed to be strong for everyone; I could not crack or feel sorry for myself now. The receptionist tried to attract my attention but I ignored her, avoiding eye contact. I shook my head and closed my eyes, wondering what was in store for us next.

Gwen emerged from the consulting room in a hurry, her face all bags and lines. I jumped up and hurried after her, to find out exactly what had happened.

"So what did he say, Gwen?"

"He thinks I'm right," she stopped, suddenly. She studied the ground, refusing to look at me, knotting her fingers together. "I've been referred to his old boss in London, at the Middlesex. He's called already, and they're expecting us. I've got to see them straight away."

It was the first time that I dreaded the journey to London.

The city brought with it no comfort or joy. London had always delivered me life, but now it led only to death. Gwen was admitted that same day and I returned home alone, to collect Jacqueline from school friends and explain the situation. And so began the longest eight years of my life. It pains me to remember them. I hope this is of use to you.

☪

Gwen's treatment commenced with local excision of the lump, which was sent to the lab for biopsy. Subsequent tests revealed that it was indeed malignant, as she had predicted, and it had already seared a path through her body. The prognosis was far from good.

She was transferred to the Mount Vernon Hospital, also in Middlesex, and it became eight years of repeated admissions, repeated operations, a black time of living hell. A world of pain. A straight jacket of fear bound us together, from which there could be no escape. Our lives were polluted with the brown stain of cancer, casting a shadow as hard as stone. It is difficult to remember everything that happened. Still, it brings pain to recall.

Cobalt therapy was used as the next line of attack, with increasing dosages of radiotherapy. It was a recent treatment introduced from Canada, not readily available, and there were very few machines in the UK. I didn't know anything about it, but there had apparently been some good initial reports. Gwen required five treatments a week for six weeks, and I watched her weaken visibly before my eyes. It happened so dreadfully quickly. Her complexion became sallow and yellow, her skin perspiring and clammy. She struggled to remain conscious throughout the following days, and her skin became suddenly darker, as if burnt by a giant sun. She suffered atrocious diarrhoea that she hated, but she expressed one constant desire through it all.

"I want to see Jacqueline pass her exams and go to university," she said. "That's all. See her get the chances we never had."

This wish kept Gwen alive. I watched her endure countless tests and treatments, her blood drained repeatedly leaving her weakened and listless, but she fought on. She never gave up.

Her mind was not going to crack, even if her body went first. The radiotherapy brought about depression of bone marrow that led to severe anaemia. Her immune system was depressed and she picked up one bug after another, a white handkerchief never far from her face. Her stomach never recovered from the initial irritation, and she bounced between diarrhoea and constipation. She declined any painkilling drugs that might have shortened her life. Everyone who works in the nursing profession knows that women are stronger than men, but Gwen's bravery exceeded anything that I'd witnessed on Malta.

She grew to exist on the other side of an invisible divide, like my mother before her, detached from normal life. She was not truly with us anymore, residing in a place where I could not follow, kept separate by the disease. Most of the time she was quiet, resigned to this fate. Any complaints were rare, but when they arrived they were devastating.

"Why me? Why am I the one to get this and not you? You deserve it as much as me!"

She howled like a banshee, clawing at me, trying to inflict pain. There were times when I felt that I must surely break, to snap into little pieces and wash away from the world. Nursing Gwen between hospital admissions slowly destroyed my heart, nibbling away one piece at a time, leaving me ragged and raw. Broken.

Gwen's voice was sometimes possessed by disease. Anything I said would be wilfully misunderstood and twisted out of context. I could not sleep at night. She rang a bell kept at her bedside to summon me at all times, to deliver whatever abuse she felt like dishing out at the time. I became frightened to laugh or smile, to display any emotion except misery. I crept back to my own bed in the spare room believing I had lost everything, through trying to help and be a *good man*.

All of my dreams, my plans and hopes had again been snatched away, through little fault of my own. I was angry and sad, unsure how it would all end. What would become of us then? I felt so scared, and so lonely. I wanted to punch noses and cry; I needed help. I remembered all of the previous lost opportunities and I wanted Nan. I wanted Mother. Pain worked

191

itself into a tight knot within my stomach, then beat a path upwards to the back of my throat. My heart worked itself into a regular frenzy, crashing like a bird in a cage. I felt nauseous and faint, exhausted, a permanent headache crouched behind both eyes. Still, I could not sleep.

I railed against Gwen in my head, and this was only natural. We desert those who desert us; it is simply human, an ugly manifestation of the will to survive. With Gwen ill or in hospital, there were spaces everywhere: inside the house and inside me. We were bleeding the years away through disease, draining their poison like leeches. I would not wish these events upon anyone.

❧

Jacqueline was amazing. She viewed the decline of her mother with a detached acceptance way beyond her years, taking everything in her stride as only the young are capable. She worked hard at school and did well. She understood the importance of this to her mother.

Colleagues at the hospital could not have shown greater support. I was always allowed to leave early to collect my daughter from school, and given time for visiting whenever Gwen was readmitted to London hospitals. My superiors knew that I would make up the hours whenever possible. I did all of the chores at Kearsney Court; cooking and cleaning, the laundry and gardening, while Jacqueline did her schoolwork. If able, I sometimes managed a walk around the adjacent park, and I imagined my mother beside me. Springtime was always the best, when yellow crocus flames lined the path to our front door, blue afternoons sliding gently into night. Autumn brought with it a purple blush to early twilight. The seasons passed, relentless, and Gwen survived, no more. Her condition grew steadily worse.

With exhaustion, the nightmares came back, knocking at the door of sleep like unwelcome old friends. There was the old town crier from my youth, Anderson, still wearing his gold braided uniform but now reduced to a skeleton. He would approach slowly, ringing his bell and announcing *she's gone, she's gone.*

Mother would sometimes appear, shaking her head and

frowning, while my father floated silent in the background. Their faces were pale, gaunt, and I knew that they did not approve of my life. Visions from Malta returned, of polio, Gregory's suicide, the creak and wheeze of the iron lung. I saw Nan on the beach at Dingli, laughing with other men. I was followed home in Folkestone, and then chased to my boyhood bedroom in Park Street, a terrifying banging sounding on the door from an unknown intruder. In the mornings, I woke alone. I slept in our double bed only when Gwen was in London, and stared at the undisturbed covers on her side. It struck me as the saddest sight in the world.

And yet there was a definite glory in Gwen's fight, a triumph of spirit in the way she fought on. She even insisted we take occasional family holidays, determined that we carry on as normal a life as possible for the sake of our daughter. We visited Grace and Lionel in Essex, the Lake District, even France, but never saw Len and Marjory. We discussed him briefly, of course, but not in any detail. It was pointless and I continued to find it too difficult, preferring to attempt blank the episode from memory. Gwen finally admitted how much of the money I'd sent from Malta had ended up in his pockets, covering gambling debts, so making me hate him all the more. She was as good as her word, however, and no further contact was established. I never told her the truth about Nan, preferring to keep this story for myself, to keep it pure.

☙

Seven years passed in this manner. Would any of us have broken, had we known how long it would continue? Would the weight of the future have proved too much to carry? Seven years, and Jacqueline was successful in her examinations. She gained a place to study languages at Cambridge University, and only then my wife gave up her fight. The radiotherapy had acted as a palliative, not a cure, helping only to prolong her life. She was tired, at last expressing a desire for an end to this suffering. Finally, she began to consume vast quantities of morphine. She wanted to die at home, she insisted. She wanted to see out her days at Kearsney Court.

The cancer reaped a rich human harvest inside and around her, covering and surrounding her. Hospital admissions became more and more frequent, necessary to remove the fluids that now accumulated in both stomach and lung cavities. Gwen could only manage to walk a few steps at a time before exhaustion set in. She could no longer lie flat through difficulties breathing. Again, I gave up my place in the bedroom so that she might rest better. I lay awake in the spare room listening for her calls, the ring of the bell, waiting to provide help at all times.

A new growth appeared in her breast. The doctor, who never gave up in his efforts, recommended a further biopsy. He never stopped trying to provide Gwen with a lifeboat of hope, suggesting that one day a breakthrough would occur and she could be cured. I think it was as much to please him that she acquiesced to this investigation, although I could be mistaken – she might have known already what was going to happen.

I packed Gwen's bag and assisted her into the car, careful that she would not knock herself. She bruised so easily now. Each smile looked as if it cost her, but she attempted to sound jolly.

"Thank you, Harold. You know, you're rather a good nurse."

"Thanks, I've heard that once or twice before." I closed the door behind her, and then climbed into my own seat. The handbrake was released and we set off slowly for the hospital. It was a cold, bright day, the pale blue sky sprinkled with a dusting of clouds. I always tried to drive sensibly, to prevent throwing Gwen around and causing her extra discomfort.

We moved around the outskirts of River, travelling past the *Dublin Man Of War* pub, when Gwen turned to face me, reaching for my hand on the gear stick.

"I won't be coming home this time," she said.

"What?"

"This is my time, Harold. I'm going to die now."

My eyes were fixed on the road and I braked to a sudden halt, switching off the ignition immediately. "Are you sure?"

She took a long time to reply, beyond me now, each word crossing an ocean to reach me. "Yes, quite sure. Everything tastes of lead. I'm tired, no fight left."

"Well we'd better turn around then." I started the engine, battling tears. "I'll take you home, like you wanted."

"No." The voice was strong. "Thank you, but I'm ready and want to die now." She closed her eyes, slowly, her life shrinking away from me like a falling teardrop. Silence fell over us like snow. I had no words for this. It was some time before I felt able to resume driving.

Gwen was admitted to her usual ward in Buckland Hospital. The staff were as friendly and courteous as ever, suspecting nothing, and reassured me that she would be well cared for. I was in some sort of delayed shock, not fully aware of proceedings. I bent and kissed her forehead, promising to see her as soon as the biopsy was over. She appeared shrunken, clad in a pale cream hospital gown, thin hair matted over her face: there was little of Garbo remaining about Gwen, but I found that I loved her more. Only her true essence was left, surrounded by a fragile husk of physical body. She appeared tiny against the faded white hospital sheets, defenceless, and I did not want to leave.

"How are you feeling, love?" The nurses waited discreetly to one side, ready to wheel Gwen into theatre. I didn't want to let her go, not like this, not in any way. I could not bring myself to release hold of her hand, those delicate fingers. Her wedding ring appeared enormous now, barely keeping from falling off.

"Not good." She spoke so slowly. "But thank you, Harold. You've been good to me. You never left. The only one. Thank you."

"Stop that. You'll be home tonight, you'll see." The words sounded hollow and empty, even to me, hopelessly inadequate. I could not bring myself to admit that this might really be the end of us, after everything. We had been through so much together, over so many years. Gwen. My wife. She was virtually unrecognisable from the woman I had met, and it was such a struggle to force any words out. "Are you still sure?"

"Yes."

The voice remained calm. Her eyelids closed slowly, imperceptibly, her breathing shallow and chest hardly moving. She had made her peace first with the world and now me, her husband.

195

"I'll see you later. I'll come down, after the biopsy. I won't be far away."

Tears filled my eyes. I couldn't help it, but I didn't want her or the nurses to see me like this. I stood up, stroking the back of her hand.

"Goodbye," she whispered, the final word.

☽

I left the ward in a daze, taking refuge in Henry Merryweather's office. I knew he was away on a course, and would not mind me grabbing some privacy. He would understand how I felt. An hour passed, the clock on the wall ticking impossibly slowly, nurses clip-clopping outside at regular intervals. I heard distant shouts, the murmur of conversation, the bark of a wireless followed with a shush to lower the volume. There was a squeaking trolley and someone asked if I wanted tea, but I gazed at the floor and out of the window. I said nothing. I felt bruised all over, so powerful was Gwen's hold over me.

The office telephone thundered into life and it took a moment to realise what it was. All other sounds disappeared and I reached to pick up the black Bakelite receiver as if in a dream. I knew the message already by the weight of the plastic, the ominous burden of dread.

"Mr Fisher? Harry?" A disembodied voice thundered down the line, speaking rapidly, anxious. "It's the theatre sister here, we've been trying to get hold of you. Can you come down, please? The surgeon would like to speak with you."

I nodded a reply, words again failing me, and then replaced the phone gently into its cradle. I remained in shock, throat tightening and heart racing, while making my way to theatre. A crushing, suffocating sensation weighed heavy on my chest and they ushered me into an empty side room. My body was drowning in its own blood.

"Harold? You're here." The surgeon entered the room quickly, shutting the door firmly behind him. He was new at the hospital, a man I recognised only in passing and could not remember his name. I wished it could have been Henry Merryweather when he touched my shoulder and shook my

196

hand, gesturing to a seat beside the desk. His tie was all wrong and he looked scruffy, dishevelled, not professional enough for my liking. He leaned back in the chair opposite, running fingers through his thinning gingery hair, before eventually starting to talk.

"Gwen is dead, Harold. I'm so sorry. We all are. We'd only given her the local anaesthetic and placed her recumbent, but she died immediately. There was nothing we could do. We've been trying to find you, to tell you what happened – Harold, are you all right?"

I nodded, as was expected of me. Gwen had always said that she would die if placed flat, that she could not breathe. She was beyond me now and she was right again, right about everything. I nodded when the surgeon advised I should go home and take the rest of the day off. I should take my time, he said, as long as I needed, and come back to work only when ready.

At Kearsney Court, Jacqueline feigned surprise to see me home so early. It took just one look at my face, my eyes, to understand the truth and we collapsed together. We embraced and wept, sharing our memories of Gwen. We saw the moon and then sun rise. My wife, Jacqueline's mother, was dead. There was nothing I could do to prevent it. Gwen was dead. Another absence, like Nan. Like my parents. She was dead. I was a nurse and I could not save her life. I had sunk lower and lower until reaching this moment. Now, at last, I had touched the bottom of the sea.

Part Six

A DREAM OF LOVE

PAM'S MOTHER and father were dead. Joan, her best friend and oldest sister, was also dead. It was only her sister Peg who remained, and Peg had her husband Bill and a baby to look after. It seemed to Pam that she was all alone again, as she had been in Wales and then Poland. Why hadn't Paul come to get her, as he had promised? Where was he now? She knew the answers to these questions from Bolek, his nephew, but this did not stop her from asking. Once more, she would need to start all over again. She would be the girl with the loneliest eyes.

She continued to work at the office for *Woolworths*, hoping the safety net and familiarity of a small town would allow her to gather her strength and consider a future. She kept the Brockman Road flat – it was basic and small, but provided all that she required; a roof over her head, privacy, and a space to think. It was not far from her sister in Capel, and she visited Peg often.

Each day was the same as before. She woke early, restless, her sleep disturbed by images of Mother, Joan, and then Paul. Always Paul. Breakfast was quick: a bowl of cereal or slice of toast, followed with a wash, and the short walk to work. On good days, she found time to visit the Leas promenade, to gaze at the limitless sea. She continued to equate her mood with its changing appearance; tranquil blue, calm grey, or sometimes an anguished turmoil. She looked up and watched cloud shadows race over her head. She listened to the sound of the surf, the rolling of pebbles along the shoreline.

Her colleagues were invariably nice and polite. They had heard about the recent loss of both parents but knew nothing about Paul, and she was glad of this. It was simpler, avoiding unnecessary explanation, remembering to try and forget about it all, to put a distance between her and the past. She knew that Peg was not wrong – she needed to move on now, to drop her history like discarded rubbish and move forwards. *You're a long time dead, girl,* her sister often remarked. *Live a little – it's not a crime. It won't hurt you.* Try as she might, the stomach for loneliness remained. She felt reluctant to change a thing, secure in her own little world.

Pam still thought about writing to Paul, but what was the point? He was not coming. He was not allowed to leave Poland or his family would suffer. He had tried and the Communists had threatened them; she knew all this from Bolek, but it did not help her. She remained in love with her husband.

She considered what she should do next. Should she stay in Folkestone, near Peg? There was little point in returning to South Africa now that their father was dead. She could go to night school and gain further qualifications to maybe better her prospects, but then she enjoyed the security of *Woolworths*, the comfort of familiar surroundings, and was not ready to let go of that yet. She attended church and prayed for guidance, but no answer was forthcoming. Her God remained strangely silent.

Pam found it difficult to conceive that she would never see Olive again, her mother. She thought of her often, remembering her fortitude and kindness, her sense of humour and unflagging optimism. She missed their conversations, the sound of her voice, the soft pad of her walk. She missed her company. Pam decided that the only way she could honour her memory was to attempt following her example – she would listen to Peg's advice and try to live a little. She would be of more use to others, rather than keeping herself locked away. It was with this in mind that she spoke to Joy, a new member of staff at work. Pam still received sporadic social invites from her colleagues, and it had become second nature for her to refuse.

"I run a dancing school with my husband, Tony," Joy explained. She was a plump lady with olive complexion and straight brown hair, who always appeared to be happy. Deep laughter lines creased her face, her brown eyes shining brightly. "It's great fun, why don't you come along?" she asked.

"I'm not sure that I can," Pam replied. She prepared to roll out the usual excuse of insufficient time, what with work and helping her sister with the baby.

"Why not? Come just the once then," Joy persisted. "We all need a break sometimes, and if you don't like it I won't be offended. I promise I won't ask you again."

"Well . . ." Pam had always loved dancing. She thought of Eileen Ward, those initial outings so long ago when they had both worked for the estate agent in Folkestone. It was during the dance at the school hall in Capel that she had first met the young Polish corporal, Paul. He had always been good on his feet, and she had loved to partner him.

"Go on," Joy interrupted her thoughts, "don't you enjoy it? I thought that everyone loves to dance." Her hands were fidgety and nervous, despite the wide smile on her face.

"All right, just the once." Pam gave in. It might be fun, and it would be nice to meet up with new people, people who knew nothing of her history.

When Pam told Peg in the evening, her sister nearly fell off her seat in surprise. "Good for you girl", she exclaimed. "And about time too. Wondered when I'd get through to you – there's nothing common about common sense, Mum was always right about that!"

Pam left work a little earlier than usual. She felt excitement for the first time in a long while – dancing! She was going to be of use, an extra pair of hands, or feet, to help with the tuition. She smiled, allowing the warm glow to suffuse her entire body. There was no time for dinner, but she managed a wash and tidy-up before hurrying back into town. Her outfit had been selected and ready for days – a sleek dress of blue silk that had not been out of the wardrobe for years. It was one of Paul's favourites, reserved only for special occasions. Pam had not dressed so smart for a long time, and this also felt good. She wore a pair of Joan's earrings that glistened a perfect aquamarine, reminding her of the sea.

At the school hall, Joy's face lit up when spotting her colleague. "Pam!" she shouted across the room, beckoning her forward. "I'm so glad you could make it, I wasn't sure if you would. Come here and meet Tony, he's really keen to meet you."

Tony was a thin, wiry little man, his mannerisms all hustle and bustle. Arms and legs moved rapidly and jerkily when he approached to shake her hand, before clasping it tight within his own. His black hair was greased back over a high forehead, his pale skin already glistening with sweat. Pam noticed how Tony's face was creased with laughter lines identical to those of his wife.

"Glad you could make it love," he said. "Hope you're a quick learner. We need all the help we can get."

"Oh ignore him," Joy moved to his side. "We all love taking the class. It gives us such great pleasure to teach the youngsters properly. It's such a lovely thing to be able to do."

"It gives them an interest," Tony continued, while Pam's head swivelled from side to side to keep up with the conversation. "Keeps them from roaming the streets. Instead of getting themselves into mischief, they worry about whether their heels are in the right position!"

A laugh erupted from his thin lips, a good hearty laugh, and Pam was able to join in. He seemed nice, and she felt herself begin to relax.

"You'll be all right, I'm sure," Joy chuckled. "I've seen you walking at work. You move like a dancer already."

Pam had nearly forgotten how much she enjoyed dancing. The old steps soon came back to her, first learned at grammar school in Wales and then under Eileen's expert tuition. Joy and Tony were extremely kind and good fun to be around. Their patience with the beginners was endless, and fresh bursts of laughter were never far away. The end of the class arrived all too soon and Pam was sorry to leave and go home.

"You're a natural Pam." Tony clapped one arm around her shoulders. "So will you be back next week? It would be a crime to hide talent like yours!"

"Of course, yes. Thank you." Pam smiled. "I'd love to."

❦

Pam did return the following week, and the week after that. It quickly became part of her routine, the undoubted highlight of the week.

"I feel useful again," she explained to Peg. "And it really is enjoyable. You should come along yourself, you'd like it."

"Not on your Nelly," her sister replied, but she was pleased to see her sister so happy.

For the first time in years, Pam's sleep was untroubled, no longer haunted with broken memories and ghosts from the past. She took more care with her appearance, even treating herself to shopping excursions to London. She always had her hair styled in the city, not trusting the local boutiques after a couple of upsetting disasters. Pam often asked whether Peg would like to accompany her, and at last she finally agreed. Her sister was equally bad when it came to excuses, reluctant to do anything that took her out of her comfort zone. The baby and shortage of money were the usual reasons given, but Pam had already thought of this. She had arranged for Bill to look after their son, and the trip was on her, a thank you for Peg's kindness over many years.

The day arrived and Peg cancelled, complaining of a terrible migraine. In truth, she was terrified at the prospect of riding another escalator, at maybe panicking and grabbing another man's trousers. She did not want to go to London, but she remained glad to witness the changes in Pam, the return of her smile and newborn confidence. At last, it seemed her younger sister was listening to advice, and in Peg's opinion she did not do this often enough.

The dance school became busier and busier. Pam was delegated charge of the advanced ballroom lessons, specialising in foxtrot and waltz, and she enjoyed this increased responsibility. She felt disappointment when another helper joined the teaching, and feared she might now have to relinquish some of her tuition. This anxiety was quickly removed when Don was appointed to be her assistant.

Don Sparks was an old college friend who had known Joy and Tony for years. A dapper man in his forties, he was undeniably charming. Don wore such exquisite suits, making the most of his slim figure, and was never seen without a fresh flower in his buttonhole, a clean white handkerchief protruding from his breast pocket. He loved to tease Pam, good-humoured, and said the same thing to her after every class that they taught.

"I've kept my hair, my stomach, so when will you go out with me?" He made sure that he always spoke in front of an audience.

"Not at the moment, thank you." Pam blushed.

"Why not? You know you want to."

"I'm busy," she stammered, while the students watched her discomfort and laughed.

"Ah go on with you," he smiled, rakish and winking. "I'll wear you down, you know it will happen in the end."

The same scenario unfolded week after week. Pam's answer remained unchanged, and it was a surprise to both of them when she finally agreed. The words had escaped from her lips before she realised what she had done. "But only as a friend," she quickly added.

Don had moved from London to open a small restaurant in Hythe, on the outskirts of Folkestone. *The Sombrero* specialised in local seafood and meats, and he ran it with great pride. He had not owned it for long and it was apparently doing very well.

"It's all about quality, Pam," he explained. "If people are going to pay hard earned money, then you've got to give them the good stuff. They're not stupid and they'll soon go elsewhere."

He invited her as his guest, to see what she thought of the place.

☽

They met on the Saturday evening. Pam made a special effort to dress nicely, although she did not want to give Don the wrong idea. She was happy to be his friend, but no more. There had never been another man since Paul, and she had no intention that this should ever change.

She wore her favourite new dress, a loose summer frock decorated with bright orange and red poppies, and hoped it would be appropriate. Peg had instructed her to have a good time and enjoy herself; it did not have to result in anything serious, and she would not be cheating on Paul. She always insisted that Pam had wasted enough time on that man, and should simply start to enjoy herself again. She understood her sister all too well, and wanted only for her to be happy. She had been delighted when told about this invite.

"At last!" she cackled, breaking into a throaty laugh. "Now don't you forget to be nice to him, I was beginning to give up on you as an old maid."

Pam was nervous. It seemed strange to go out and meet a man, any man, apart from Paul. She had been with him since she was sixteen, and he was her only love. She shuffled about the flat getting ready, fumbling to put on her jewellery, then treated herself to a taxi to the restaurant. She hoped the night would not prove difficult, that Don would not try to kiss her.

The Sombrero was located beside the canal in Hythe, close to the sea, and she found this reassuring. Pam always liked to be near the water, to gaze out at the clear blue expanse, dreaming of where it might take her. She tidied her hair one last time, took a deep breath to steady her nerves, and then pushed open the front door. The restaurant was filled with young people chatting happily and enjoying their meals. A delicious waft of aromatic coffee reached her and she smiled. She had missed real coffee in Poland, and never passed on the opportunity to drink some now that she was back. Don had told her that he imported all of his beverages from France.

"Pam." He appeared from the rear kitchen area, smiling, walking between the snug round tables to reach her side. "You look lovely, welcome to *The Sombrero*."

"Thank you." She allowed him to guide her to a reserved table placed next to the window, one hand on the small of her back, allowing an uninterrupted view of the sea.

"So what can I get you? How about prawn cocktail for starters? And then steamed cod – we've got a fish out back that came in today, nearly as big as you! So you're here then Pam, I knew you'd come in the end." He smiled again.

Pam's nerves grew worse, but Don remained the perfect

gentleman. His manners were impeccable and he was a born raconteur and joke teller, first telling her about his early childhood in Croydon. "You'd never want to go there, boring as anything," he laughed. Don had then moved to London, where he developed an enduring love of the theatre. He had been lucky to meet some of the stars: Joyce Grenfell was his favourite, a real lady, pure class, and he was keen to point out the merits of a lesser known singer by the name of Ruby Lloyd. "Could have been one of the greats," he insisted.

There was no such thing as an awkward silence with Don, and Pam was content simply to listen. She looked about the room, the happy faces, absorbing the continual murmur of conversation that twisted throughout the restaurant. Don had made a good job of it. It was nice to be out, she thought, not alone in the flat as usual. The sea glistened liquid silver in front of her, a full moon hanging low over the water.

The meal was excellent, as Don had promised, and after coffee he arranged a ride to take her home. "So can we do this again?" he asked, for once lacking his usual confidence, nervously tugging at the collar of his jacket.

"Yes, I'd like that," Pam acquiesced. She was relieved that he made no further demands upon her.

☾

They became close friends, to the delight of Peg, Joy and Tony. Pam continued to teach at the dance school with Don as her assistant, and shared evening meals became a regular occurrence. "To check out the competition, that's all," Don insisted. He took her to Hythe, Folkestone and Dover, before venturing further out into the countryside. They soon discovered the idyllic village of River, with its pretty pubs and nearby parkland. *The Dublin Man Of War* was always good for a meal, and then they could enter Kearsney Abbey and Russell Gardens where Pam liked to walk beside the lake. Big fish swam lazily towards them, and Don told her that they were trout. He'd love to have them served up in a pot and on the menu at *The Sombrero*, he said. She looked up at a house on the hill, which always captured her attention. It had a pointed green tower on the right side, reminding her of fairytale castles. She often wondered who the lucky inhabitants were.

Summer moved on. A coolness returned to the air, the nights drawing in with a curtain of blackness. They kept their trips closer to home now, sticking to Hythe and the centre of town. It was too dark to walk off their dinners. Don remained good company, apparently satisfied in his role as her chaperone. He asked for nothing more of her, and she remained grateful for this. He was a good friend and she did not want this to be ruined.

She noticed that he was putting on weight, but said nothing. Don took such pride in his appearance that she did not want to appear in any way critical. It was Don who actually mentioned it after one of their trips to *The Sombrero*. He always took her home, careful never to drink with his meal. Don was a fast but safel driver.

"Look at this!" he gestured to his stomach. "You're not dancing with me enough Pam, or it's all these big Kentish meals. I was always skinny back in London." He glanced towards her before suddenly slamming hard onto his brakes. A lone jogger crossed the road in front of them, near invisible in the gathering blackness. Pam was close enough to notice his eyes – they were distracted and absent, as if he had not even see the car. He continued on his way, regardless.

"Bleedin' 'ell mate, look where you're going!" Don wound down his window to shout, but his cries went ignored. "Excuse the French Pam," he apologised.

Pam spotted this figure again on later nights, always alone, head down, pounding along sea dark streets. He looked lost, in trouble, and she wished she might be able to help him. From her own past in Poland and Wales, she believed she knew exactly how he might be feeling.

Winter came, a Christmas spent with Peg and Bill in Capel, and then the welcome return of spring. Pam continued to enjoy her work at *Woolworths* and the dance school, together with meals at the weekend with Don. He continued to put on weight, while her own stomach for loneliness disappeared. Simple contentment had returned to her life.

☽

It was with total amazement that Pam listened to Joy at the office. Her evening class at the dance school was cancelled. Don was ill and had been rushed into Buckland Hospital in Dover. She asked permission from her boss and was allowed to leave early. She caught the first bus out of town and hurried to reach him.

"He's in Ward Two, Miss. That's down the corridor as far as it goes, then second door on the left." She walked quickly from reception, her footsteps echoing loud on the hard wooden floor. It had taken her longer than expected to find the hospital, and she was impatient to finally get to Don. In Pam's haste, she had been so preoccupied with the journey that she had not really considered what she might find. She was in no way prepared for the changes in his appearance.

"Hello love, thanks for coming." His skin had turned ashen grey overnight. His face seemed on the verge of collapse, like a deflated balloon, making him appear much older. The voice was also different, drained of all energy. Don had always looked so smart and immaculate; it felt intrusive and unfair to see him this way.

"How are you feeling?" She placed a hand upon his forearm, before sinking into an adjacent seat. His skin was clammy, and a strange chemical smell tainted the air. Don appeared to be sedated, his breathing laboured and deep, while his eyelids struggled to remain open.

"Not too great. Could you pass me a drink?" She helped him sip from a glass of water, before he continued to speak. "Doc tells me it's osteo- something or other. To do with the bone marrow. Don't know what that means or how I got it, but I've felt better and no kidding. How are you love? It's good of you to come."

"Me? I'm fine. But you – are you sure?" He looked awful despite attempting a smile, and it was hard for her not to fear the worst. From recent experience, death was no longer a stranger to Pam.

"I think so." He coughed, a harsh rattling sound, before struggling to reach for a box of tissues on the bedside table. Pam helped him take one and he dabbed at the dribble leaking from his mouth. "Excuse me. That's what they've told me, anyway. Be here for a while, I should think. So what about you love, what's new?"

"Nothing really." Pam fought back tears at the plight of her friend. "The dance class has been cancelled tonight, so you've got to get better quickly. We need you back as soon as possible, it's so busy these days. Joy and Tony send their love. I know they're planning to come and visit you later."

Don attempted to sit up in his bed, but lacked the necessary strength. He settled back against the raised pillows, before opening his eyes wide and clearing his throat, apparently preparing to speak.

" There's something I've been meaning to ask you for a long time, Pam." The words came so slowly, with great effort. He reached and sipped again at the glass of water. Pam watched him swallow with difficulty, suddenly nervous. "Will you marry me, love?" he said.

She gasped in shock. They had been friends, nothing more, and now this. She did not know what to say or do and jumped to her feet, fighting back tears. "I need some time to think," she said, reaching to take hold of his hand. "You take care of yourself. I'll come back and see you soon."

His eyes never moved from her figure as she retreated from the ward, watching as she bumped into a small table positioned next to the door. She stumbled forwards, aiming for a line of black plastic chairs placed in the corridor beneath a window. Thick swathes of late afternoon sunlight cut through the dry air. The chemical smell lingered everywhere, reminiscent of fresh mown hay. What should she do? It was terrible. She had believed that Don saw her as a friend, nothing more, and had always attempted to make that clear. Now, she prayed for strength and for guidance. What should she do? Tears began to slide down her face, dripping onto the floor beside her feet. She could not help it. It was with dismay that she realised somebody was talking to her.

"Hello. Can I help at all?"

The voice was kind and gentle. She wiped her eyes and looked up to see a tall, slim man. His hair was thick and dark, his eyes a familiar startling green. They reminded her of Paul, and she felt momentarily dissociated – where was she? Had he come back for her, after all? At last? She shook her head as realisation swiftly returned – the man was some sort of nurse. He wore a white tunic fastened on the left side, and Pam noticed that the top two buttons had come undone.

"No thank you. I'm sorry, I'll go." She felt embarrassed.

"That's all right. I was just passing." He looked as if he would walk away, and this fact somehow made Pam continue to speak.

"It's just my friend. He's not well, and I was upset."

"Can I help?" She watched as he touched her arm, feeling nothing. She understood that he meant well, a kind man.

"Really, I'll be all right. Thank you."

There was nothing else for Pam to say. She looked down, her thoughts returned to Don. What should she do next? What could she possibly do? When she eventually raised her head, the nurse had disappeared and she sat alone in the corridor. She hoped that he would not think of her as rude.

Pam caught a bus back to Capel, where she planned to visit her sister. Peg was always happy to offer advice, and she did not want to be by herself. Don had looked so ill; it was awful. She felt so sorry for him but did not want to marry him. She had never thought of him in a romantic way – he was her friend, more like a brother than anything else.

Pam found herself walking along the cliff tops, towards the Warren. The sky thickened and darkened, before tiny arrows of rain pinpricked the side of her face. An atlas of clouds raced over her head, heading over the water to France. She looked down at a sea of trees, watching the curved ripple of branches against the wind. What should she do about Don? She had absolutely no idea. Hard rain fell and flattened her hair. A new thought troubled her mind, unfamiliar through long years of absence. The man at the hospital, the nurse – he had seemed nice. She replayed their brief conversation, over and over, all the time wondering why she kept thinking about him.

☽

Pam could not bring herself to visit the hospital on the following day. Still, she had no idea how she should act, and her sister had been little help. Peg only wanted her sister to be happy, and she had been pleased about the friendship with Don. She had not seen her sister so animated for a long time, and did not want her to throw away any chance of a relationship so easily.

"But you might grow to love him," she insisted. "He's nice, and I know you enjoy his company. Don't make a hasty decision that you might come to regret."

Pam's thoughts returned to Paul. There had never been any doubt about his love, and she could not settle for anything less. She would rather stay single and live on her own than compromise on this. She remembered the nurse at the hospital – maybe he could help her, after all. He could surely find out exactly what was wrong with Don, and his advice would not be biased in any way. He knew nothing about her: not about Poland, or the long separation from Paul. She determined to visit straight from work the next day. She would search him out before she plucked up the courage to see Don.

☽

Pam worked through her lunch break and was allowed to leave early. She caught the bus to Dover and made her way up the hill to the hospital. She walked more slowly this time, still considering the right course of action to take. She hoped the nurse might be able to help, but then she knew nothing about him. Was she acting unfairly? Would he get himself into trouble? It was a large hospital. There were a lot of staff, and she probably would not see him anyway.

Pam hesitated at the main entrance, before willing herself forward and over the threshold. She had never liked these places, and recalled the worry of visiting her mother after the operation to remove a tumour. She was only a child at the time and had felt so scared; she still associated these emotions with hospitals. Pam had tried to avoid them whenever possible.

The same lady smiled at reception. Pam nodded but had no need to ask for directions. She remembered the way to the ward. She still had no idea what she might say to Don. Joy and Tony had been to see him and said that he did not appear to have made any improvement. He had been asking after her, but there was no mention of the proposal and Pam felt immensely grateful for that. It was easier to keep this to herself.

Pam moved slowly along the corridor, hesitating at every opportunity. She recognised the black seats beneath the window where she had sat before, and was happy to wait there awhile, to defer the inevitable. She stared at the ground, again, feeling lost and out of her depth. Life had been simpler alone. Dealing with other people seemed only to bring more hurt. She shook her head, sadly, wondering just what to do next.

"Hello again, how are you? Is your friend any better?"

She noticed the feet first, the well polished black leather shoes. The trousers were dark grey, patterned with the faintest of pinstripe. The tunic was white. It was the same nurse who stood in front of her – he had found her, as she had hoped. Maybe he would be able to help and Pam smiled, despite all previous misgivings.

"Oh hello," she said. "He's about the same, thank you. And thanks for the other day. It was good of you."

"It was nothing." The man had a kind face. He stood with his arms folded loosely, and again she noticed the vivid green of his eyes. "As I said, if I can be of any assistance, please let me know."

She felt determined to speak, to ask for help, but it was so hard. She looked back to the ground, swallowing hard. The words just would not appear. It was only when his feet shifted as if about to retreat that she finally found her voice.

"There's one thing." She looked directly into his eyes. "I could do with some advice."

When he moved to her side and sat down, it was all she could do not to hug him. When he smiled, this became even more difficult. She turned to face him, twisting in her seat and uncomfortable. She was not used to asking help from anyone, and especially not from strangers.

"It's my friend, Don," Pam explained, hesitant. "He looks terrible since he got here, and he's asked me to marry him. We're only friends and I don't know what to do. I don't even know what's wrong with him."

"Why do you think he asked?"

"I'm not sure. That's what I keep asking myself – I think he must be really ill. I'm sorry, but what do you think I should do? I'm at my wit's end." She wiped at her forehead, her skin prickling with tension. The man sighed and looked out of the window. He appeared to be deep in thought.

"That's a tough one!" He turned suddenly. "Who is your friend? I'll make enquiries and have a think about it. I'll talk to you next time you visit and tell you what I've found out. I'm Harry, by the way. What's your name?"

He was called Harry, just like the boy from her youth. Pam felt the past reel her in like a fish on a line, and she was relieved to have asked for his help. It gave her the extra strength that she so desperately needed, some support in her time of need.

They said goodbye and she walked immediately into Ward Two. If anything, Don's condition appeared to have deteriorated. He looked shrunken and frail, swamped in the white hospital sheets, and two of his front teeth were now missing. Pam was amazed to spot a denture lying haphazard on a piece of tissue paper beside the bed.

"Hello love, how are you?" he asked, slurring the words. "I missed you yesterday."

"I'm sorry." She sat down, resting one hand on his own, then retracting this and folding her arms. "I had to baby-sit for Peg, but I asked Joy and Tony to send my best wishes."

"I know, love, I know." He smiled, the pink of his gums white with crusted saliva. Don suddenly realised the denture was out, fumbling and replacing this into his mouth while Pam pretended not to have noticed. "So have you made a decision?" he asked.

"Not yet, I'm sorry. I need more time. But what about you? Are you feeling any better? Do they know what's wrong yet?"

Don still waited to hear the results of his tests. He was obviously exhausted and his eyes closed repeatedly. He forced himself to stay awake. When he briefly fell asleep and woke himself snoring, Pam decided it was time to leave. She promised to visit him the following day.

"I'll be waiting," he managed a smile. "I'm not going anywhere. Say hello to the old *Sombrero* from me, if you're passing."

☪

The next day was a Saturday. Pam did not have to go to work and she was able to arrive at the hospital earlier than planned. She wanted to get it out of the way, unable to concentrate on anything else, and hoped that Harry might have been able to discover some information that would help her reach a decision. She hoped he would be in on a weekend, and had deliberately kept out of Peg's way, knowing that her sister would instruct her to agree to Don's proposal. Peg had watched her single for such a long time that she believed only another man could make Pam happy.

Pam followed the signs to Ramsay Ward, where Harry had told her he usually worked. She had not wished to be a nuisance and disturb him, but he assured her that this was no problem. He had a decent number of colleagues and they would not miss him for a few minutes. She had made an effort to dress nicely, and this would be the first occasion that he saw her in anything other than work clothes. She always prided herself on being professional, and Harry struck her as someone with similar standards.

"Hello." She spotted him on the far side of the ward, where he beckoned her forwards. She walked quickly between the rows of beds while he tidied a desk and grabbed a nearby chair, making room for her to sit down.

"Hello again. How are you today?" He smiled with genuine warmth, apparently pleased to see her, and she felt her pulse quicken.

"Not bad, thank you. I'm glad I found you, Harry. I haven't been to the ward yet. I can't get my mind off Don and what to do. Sorry to ask but did you manage to find anything out?"

He did not hesitate with his reply. "I've had a good think, and I think you should agree to marry him."

She was stunned, and had not been expecting to hear this. She felt suddenly light-headed while her legs began to tremble beneath the desk. He continued to speak. "I know it sounds strange, but I've checked up on Don. Pam, I don't think he'll be leaving the hospital."

He did not allow her to break eye contact and, slowly, she understood. "I see," she whispered.

"It will make him happier." Harry reached to touch the back of her hand. He spoke so gently, and she realised the advice had not been easy to give. "You won't have to go through with it, but it will make his last days much easier. Can I get you anything, Pam? A tissue? Water?"

Pam did not know if she could do it. She had wanted to be Don's friend, but this was dreadful. "I see," she repeated, struggling to her feet. "Thank you. I need to collect my thoughts, then I'll go and visit him."

She walked quickly from the ward, hurrying outside to the hospital gardens where she paced restless, ill at ease, considering the advice. Don was going to die – Harry had made this clear. She wondered if Don realised this himself? He was never going to leave the hospital. She had wanted to help people, like her mother, and be of use. She understood how it would make Don happy if she agreed, and Peg would also approve, but it was so hard to do. When would Don discover the truth? How long did he have left?

She marched one loop around the gardens and then returned inside. Ward Two was strangely silent, several beds now empty of patients, but Don was in his usual position. He struggled to raise himself, resting his weight on both elbows as she approached, his eyes expectant.

"Yes," she hurried forward. "Yes, I'll marry you Don."

"Thanks, my girl. You'll see, I'll make you happy."

They embraced, and she kissed him on the cheek. The chemical smell had grown more powerful. Pam closed her eyes – she was strong, she told herself, she had been through worst heartache than this, and she was going to help a good friend. She opened her eyes, her gaze beyond the room. She remembered a frozen quayside in Poland, armed soldiers, a husband who had disappeared.

☽

Don was jubilant. His health improved, some colour returning to his face, but this did not last for long. He did not know the exact nature of his disease, and still believed that he had a chance of recovery. Pam visited him most evenings after she finished work. She was tired, but knew it had been the correct course of action to take. Don's predicament was sad enough without her making things harder. He was a good man, and he deserved better than this. If she could be of help and cheer him up, then she was happy to do it.

She met Harry on several occasions, in the corridor and outside the ward. He always appeared delighted to see her and enquired after her own well-being. His actions were those of a friend, and she grew to enjoy these meetings. He always had a suitable word of advice and encouragement, and seemed to anticipate exactly how she was feeling. He admitted to her repeated questioning that Don was afflicted with stomach cancer.

Time passed. Don's health deteriorated, requiring an operation, and he died while still in theatre. There was nothing that could be done for him; the cancer had advanced too far. When Pam arrived to visit in the evening, it was Harry who waited to break the news. He guided her into a side room and explained in detail what had happened.

"If I can take you out sometime, for a walk or drive in the country, please let me know," he concluded. "I do know what you're going through, believe me, and you can ring me anytime."

"Thank you," she stammered.

"It would be my pleasure."

Pam experienced a tangle of emotions. She was sad that her friend had died, yet relieved his suffering was over. It had been an awful way to go, the illness steadily robbing him of any dignity. She would not have to marry him, after all, and Harry had given her sound advice. She felt guilty that she would now miss her meetings with this kind nurse, and wondered if she should ring him. Don had always been a friend, no more –

Harry knew this, but she feared what other people might believe.

It did not take long to decide. Pam needed a shoulder to cry on, someone to talk with, and Harry had been there at the right time. She rang him at home. He was pleased to hear from her, and told Pam how he had once been married before. His first wife had also died of cancer. It had been awful, and that's how he knew what she was going through. Since then, he had chosen to remain single for years.

They met in Dover at the weekend. Pam wore her dress with the poppies and they walked along the seafront promenade. It was hot day, the sky pellucid blue. Harry explained how he loved to be close to the water, and it always drew him near. He could never live too far away from a coast, he said. His father had used to joke how the sea grew up a boy, and she understood this. He wore a smart white shirt and dark trousers. His black hair blew wild in the wind, reminding her of Johan, Paul's father in Poland. Still, she considered he possessed the same green eyes as her husband.

She learned how they had actually grown up in the same part of Folkestone. Harry had also spent much of his time at the Warren and old cobbled fish market. She wondered if they had ever bumped into each other, perhaps at the cinema or one of the dances. They had tea at a cafe, a slice of carrot cake, and then he drove her back to Brockman Road. She was sorry to watch his departure.

☾

They met again, in Folkestone, having decided to return to the Warren. Harry picked her up at the flat and they sped to the cliff tops at Capel. Pam told him that her sister lived in the village, pointing out the direction of Peg's house, and he said that he would be pleased to meet her.

They walked side by side down the long path to the sea, reliving old memories of childhood. The water glistened like a jewel in the distance, the sound of waves becoming louder as they descended. Yellow gorse lined the path, and Pam loved the coconut smell of the flowers. She inhaled the perfume and she

219

felt happy. Candyfloss-white clouds dotted a pale blue sky, and Pam remembered running with Paul along this same track, the white butterfly that had followed his every move. They had raced across the train bridge before he kissed her, and she still wondered where he was now. Was he glad to be back in Poland with his family? It had been ten years since her return from Pszow. Ten years of waiting and life on her own, of time she would never get back. She suddenly understood why Peg had encouraged her to get out of the house and enthused about the friendship with Don.

"This was my favourite spot." Harry spoke and interrupted her thinking. He pointed to a small rocky ledge jutting out above the water, allowing a clear view of the adjacent shoreline. He explained how he used to camp here as a youth, his voice animated with fond recollection.

"We used to come here, too," she replied. "Me and my sister, Joan. I liked it, but my favourite place was actually Radnor Park. I couldn't get enough of the boat hire, spending all of my pocket money there. You could paddle all afternoon for a sixpence."

Pam recalled the frequent outings with Joan. She had never forgotten, and still missed her company and friendship. Pam remembered how Joan used to tease her and she chuckled to herself. "I don't suppose it matters to tell you," she said, "but I always fancied the boy there. He worked with his older brother, who Joan liked. My first crush!" She laughed again, not noticing the incredulous look on Harry's face.

"Pam," he spluttered, "that was me! The boy you liked was me!"

She gasped. The sun threw down a confetti of diamonds and they embraced for the first time. The water was blue green below, lapping at the many rock pools. Seabirds spiralled up in the warm air. She pulled Harry against her and Pam felt the past fall from her like loosened chains. At last, she might finally be safe. She shut her eyes and took herself into his world.

☙

The relationship blossomed and flowered. Pam began to feel warm inside for the first time in years, the cold of Poland all thawing away. The knot of worry inside her stomach unravelled and disappeared. She felt alive. Truly alive, not going through the motions as before. Pam had always believed a part of her had died after the separation from Paul, but now she was not so sure. Weeks and months passed. Her heart remained open, still. It re-grew, after all of the hurt and the pain. She understood this and she was happy. She was surprised to discover that she was ready to risk love one more time.

They met often, each growing dependent upon the other. Harry picked her up from the office straight from work, when they were able to walk or go out for a meal. They shared many interests: a love of the outdoors, cinema and theatre, books, a passion for music. He was a keen runner but could never persuade her to join him in this. He told her about his marriage, the war, his time on Malta. She told him about evacuation to Wales, a skeleton of detail about Poland.

Harry helped her cope with Don's death, sharing his previous experience of cancer, removing all guilt from her choice of decisions. It was not long before she took him to visit her sister in Capel. They had first ventured out for a walk to the Warren, where the water had been unusually clear. Harry wanted Pam to join him for a swim, but she insisted the sea was much too cold. "You're mad," she had laughed. "It will have to be much warmer than that before I go in." Pam always loved to be warm.

Peg was curious to meet the man who had reawakened her sister, cautious that he might prove the source of yet more pain. She continued to feel protective over her younger sister, and wanted to check for herself that his intentions were good.

"Come in here, Harry. Give me a hand with the tea, please." She called through from the kitchen, and he was quick to jump to his feet. Harry was very fond of Pam already, and keen to make a favourable impression. He understood the importance of family approval, and had never forgotten how his parents had taken an immediate dislike to Gwen. Pam sat alone in the living room, listening carefully to their conversation. She did not want Peg to give him a hard time and scare him away.

"No, no," her sister admonished. "You have to put the milk in last, or it will burn and be ruined."

Pam rolled her eyes – Peg was incorrigible, bossing him around straight away. She hoped that he would not mind, and was pleased to watch him reappear through the doorway smiling.

"Your sister has been showing me how to make a proper cuppa," he grinned, resuming his place at her side.

"Quite right too!" Peg followed him into the room, balancing a tray of drinks and plate of biscuits. "A man's got to learn sometime, but I'm glad you're here Harry. It was about time Pam got herself a man before it's too late. I'd just about given up on the girl, I had. But you'd better be good to her mind, or you'll have me to deal with. The girl has been through enough already."

Pam cringed in horror. She wanted her sister to shut up before she said anything more embarrassing, and stood quickly to straighten a ceramic swan on the wall. It had hung crooked for many years, but Pam had never dared touch it. She did not want to appear critical of her sister, the homemaker. "Remember that time I took you to London?" she said. "On the escalator, Peg? When you pulled down the man's trousers?"

Peg took the hint and fell silent, with the visit later pronounced a resounding success. "He's very nice," her sister agreed. "I like to see politeness in a man, and he seems a good listener, too."

☾

The relationship continued to flourish. Pam was no longer haunted with ghosts from the past. Now, she dreamed of love. The more she grew to know Harry, the more they appeared to share in common. They had both been married before, both hurt, and they knew what it was like to live alone. Despite everything, they had not lost the capacity for love. They continued to visit the fish market and Warren, the seafront at Dover, and Pam learned it was Harry who lived in the house with the pointed tower above Russell Gardens, the house she had often admired. They had known and liked each other as children, even then. Harry had been her first crush and first admirer. Soon, they were meeting every day.

The sky shone as blue as a swirling ocean when they walked hand in hand along Folkestone pier. It was a warm day and Pam leaned her head against his shoulder. She had not felt so content, so secure, since the childhood outings with Joan. Harry made her feel very special. He looked after her. She carried no doubts about his love.

The end of the pier was deserted. Seabirds whirled high in gusting eddies of air, the only sound a kiss of waves upon the concrete supports below.

"Come on, let's dance." It was Pam's suggestion. She remembered the dances here from her youth, and how she had always wanted to join in. Harry gathered her into his arms and they began a simple waltz, the dream of her childhood, to an audience of seagulls, to the music of the sea.

They moved in time, slowly, carefully. Pam was pleased to note that Harry was a respectable dancer, and she raised her eyes to the sky. She gazed at clouds that resembled human faces – first there was Joan, then Paul, and then her mother. Olive appeared to be smiling and she smiled in reply, nodding slightly. Finally, Pam was safe, the future no longer uncertain.

She closed her eyes and rested her head on Harry's shoulder. Together, they made a perfect fit. She was aware of his hand on the small of her back, the touch gentle. She smiled again and, later, when he asked her to marry him she said yes. Of course, yes. At last, Pam had found home.

Part Seven

SWIMMING
WITH GHOSTS

I SAW DIANA for the last time at her mother's funeral. She appeared suitably upset, dabbing ostentatiously at her face with a black silk handkerchief, but at this stage I knew her too well. Clutching onto the arm of some random fellow who accompanied her for the day, she was only present to find out what was in it for her. I was ready to argue and give her a piece of my mind, but Jacqueline was genuinely pleased to see her. I kept silent for her sake, to avoid another unpleasant scene.

I barely got through the day, recalling mere fragments now. It was cold and damp, dark clouds brooding ominously from over the channel, reminding me of childhood zeppelins. I said few words to anyone, just enough, and this was all I could manage. Sharp splinters of conversation. Friends hugged me and colleagues shook hands. My daughter cried, huge gulping sobs racking her young body. It was a difficult service. Len had actually got in touch, asking permission to attend, but this I refused outright. Things were hard enough already, and I never wished to set eyes on that bastard again. He'd had more than enough from me.

I could not bear to answer the telephone at home, preferring to let it sound uninterrupted. Each call determined confirmation of Gwen's death, making me relive it with every ring. I did not want to talk about her passing, to share this raw sorrow, but hugged my grief close, welcoming the grey loneliness. I could not sleep and I lost all appetite. Gwen, my wife, was dead. Everyone I loved disappeared. My heart exploded with grief.

Over the course of the following weeks, it soon became clear that Gwen had been in no doubt uncertain as to her fate. Everything was sorted into its rightful place and all affairs were settled, despite her lack of mobility. Her courage at the end had been staggering. It had taken me this long to understand that I loved her and now she was gone. I had not realised how much I still wanted and needed to say to her, and now it was all too late – I cursed myself, a fool, again and again, for letting stubborn pride get in the way of the truth.

I could not bear to look at my wife's possessions. Kearsney Court was now bloated with memories and I collected everything that my daughter did not want; clothes, books, toiletries, even jewellery. I burned the lot – just knowing that they were present was too much. I needed to remove all traces of Gwen, for these to vanish along with my hopes and my future. But what would I do now? Her nursing care had become the sole purpose of my existence. I should have moved away, made a fresh start, but lacked the necessary energy and drive.

At night, I lay awake reliving our time together, hoping that she'd forgiven me for the many hurts we had inflicted upon each other, for all the long fighting and arguments. There was so much that I wished to do differently, and I continued to live with this guilt. Now, I saw my mistakes all too clearly, repeatedly considering what I should have done to make things better between us. I was falling apart at the seams, useless to everyone, and it was only the presence of Jacqueline that kept me from going under. I had to look after her, for the sake of Gwen's memory. It had been the sole reason to keep my wife alive, and now I had to assume full responsibility for our daughter.

I saw few friends. It was easier this way, and I kept myself to myself as much as possible. It was preferable to appear cold and distant, keeping people from getting too close, and nobody should have wanted anything to do with me. But they tried. They really did try. Unfamiliar neighbours turned up with an assortment of casseroles. Colleagues at work never stopped enquiring as to my well being, offering help. The hospital superiors allowed me to keep my own hours of duty as much as possible. All this, and yet it was not enough.

I could be in the company of friends when they would unwittingly resurrect memories of Gwen. I found this so painful, so overwhelming, that I had to run away, to escape, but I had nowhere left to go. Kearsney Court gaped open like a wound, her absence felt keenly. There were spaces everywhere, a terrible silence, and it had begun to resemble a body missing the most essential part, a heart.

I took to running alone, preferably at night. It was the only time that I could feel the blood pumping through my own body, shaking me out of this torpor. I pushed myself to the point of exhaustion, welcoming all physical pain while charging along the Alkham Valley to Folkestone, through the streets of my youth, and ending up at the banks of the canal at Hythe. I could be out of the house for hours, knowing that tiredness would lead to oblivion, an eventual sleep without dreams. Just once, I was nearly run over, aware of the passing car at the very last moment and only then through the shouts of the driver. This was easy to ignore – such words meant nothing to me, and could not cause any more pain. It was probably just some loudmouth out to impress his girlfriend. I pounded forwards without breaking my stride, one foot moving fast in front of the other, always trying to out run my guilt.

The nightmares started again. I was living from day to day, a turbulent sea of emotion, and it was no real surprise that these should now come back and torment me. I half expected it, usually dreaming of old friends and dead colleagues from Malta. I would be on duty in F Block and they took it in turns to sidle up to me, whispering sinister unintelligible gibberish. I saw the squinting eyes of dead soldiers filled with hatred. I saw Nan floating face down in the sea, arms and legs in the shape of a cross, black stars awash in her hair.

I saw Gwen, always young, in her prime, and wondering the haunts of my childhood. She could be walking in the old fish market, turning heads and dazzling in her Garbo finery. She could be on the cliff tops above the Warren, at the local dance hall, the boat hire in Radnor Park. I even saw her smooching with my dead brother, Leslie. Sometimes, she was accompanied with an unknown man in a dark suit. She never spoke, and avoided me at all costs: she would change direction, shut doors in my face, and even get her man to stand in the way to prevent me from reaching her side. The most I could expect was a glance filled with hatred and disdain before she would turn and disappear. These visions were awful, and I grew to hate sleep. Running became my sole escape.

☽

The only constant was work. Jacqueline went away to university, fulfilling her mother's ambitions, and it was the hospital that kept me breathing. It became my entire life. I went in early and worked hard, keeping a distance from both colleagues and patients alike. I pontificated to the junior staff that they could work with me or for me, and I put in extra long hours to make up for my previous absence. I pushed myself and everyone around me. If standards slipped in any way, for instance regarding ward hygiene, I pursued the matter vigorously until the perpetrator had been identified and chastised, no matter how trivial the crime. I must have been a horror to these colleagues, but at the end of each shift they returned home to normal lives. I returned to Kearsney Court and had nothing.

These were shapeless, pale years. I remained lost, going through the motions, living in a world that was peopled with ghosts. The years were wasted and discarded cheaply. Thrown away. Jacqueline now chose to go travelling during her holidays, preferring to stay away from her dull father, while I continued to mine this rich seam of loneliness. I wallowed and soaked in misery and guilt. I remained the most stubborn of fools.

I became ill. First I was tired all of the time, no wonder considering how little I slept, but then my body developed widespread atopic eczema. Legs, arms and torso all came out in a strange landscape of inflammation that no doctor could diagnose. I burned a constant fever, the glands in my neck becoming swollen, tender and lumpy. Alopecia followed, taking with it much of the sides of my hair in great ragged chunks. Each morning, my pillow and bathtub was covered in black clumps while my hairline retreated at speed.

I knew what was wrong. It was obvious – all of the bad inside me, the selfishness and stubborn pride, was twisting and gouging its way out. I did not care and wanted to look ugly, undesirable. It was all that I deserved. Life was simpler alone, and after the experiences with Nan and Gwen I did not want to ruin things for anyone else. I was bad luck, end of story. I gave up shaving – there was little need, with the continuing hair loss, and ran a fever for weeks on end. Like Gwen, everything now tasted of lead. I felt contaminated and tainted by the past.

Somehow, a letter reached me at the hospital from my old pal Eric Reynolds. The address on the envelope revealed that he currently lived in Kenya, and I have no idea how he managed to track me down one more time. He had always been good company, and it was actually with something approaching excitement that I tore it open to read what he had to say. Events had never been dull when Eric was around in my life.

My Dear Harry,

How are you doing, my man? An old friend told me your news – sorry to hear about that business, and I haven't forgotten I introduced you to Gwen, too. No idea of the future mate, just like the rest of us – if only! We could have had some fun with that, before the war. I still remember those days – they were the best. Wonder how Margaret is doing now?

But look after yourself, mate. That's what I wanted to say. I know you can take life seriously. Just remember from your old pal that all women are beautiful but some are better. Get yourself back out there Harry – a good woman will put you right!

And keep in touch!

Yours,

Eric.

I was pleased to hear from him, folding the letter carefully and placing it into my breast pocket for later perusal. I would definitely reply, but was in no real shape to follow this advice.

It was work and the hospital that saved me. I continued to fight a strong urge to withdraw from contact with other people, but colleagues and patients refused to allow this. They did not let my bad mood or cold manner deter them – they remembered I had not always been like this. It was a sense of duty, of being needed, that kept me going, that prevented me from drowning and eventually brought me back up to the surface.

It was a constant relief to get up in the morning after those interminable nights without sleep. I threw on my clothes and was always first to arrive on the ward, where it gave me a chance to catch up on any paperwork and plan for the long day ahead. I could work out when I might run late, and where I could make up the time. I had a cup of tea and, sometimes, even managed to read a chapter of a book.

My colleagues arrived and I tried not to take any breaks. This involved making small talk, an enforced bonhomie, and I was not ready for this just yet. A quick cup of tea was easy to snatch on the ward, between seeing patients. I set about my duties with a misguided passion, submerging myself deep into every case, seeking refuge in the work. There was something of interest in each medical history if you were prepared to look, and I gained a reputation for meticulous thoroughness. When not on the wards, I studied my books, together with any old journals left around by the resident doctors.

I was always reluctant to leave the hospital, returning home late in the evening to prepare the simplest of meals: scrambled eggs, a tin of soup, or maybe beans on toast. I ate only because I had to, with little appetite or enjoyment. Sometimes, I bothered to look at a newspaper, but more often ran my mind over the day's nursing, considering the specifics of each case and intricacies of all patients treated. I met some interesting people, and wanted their care to be the best possible we could provide. Some were admitted for long periods and it was impossible to maintain an impersonal detachment. A connection was sometimes established, a tentative friendship begun.

Harry Teetsov was a case in point, in for a routine prostate operation. Complications after surgery ensured that I got to know him rather well, learning of his history as a displaced and proud Estonian. Many of his family had been shipped off to Siberia during and after the war, yet he bore his lot with a calm acceptance, an innate wisdom that reminded me of Reverend Hocking. I loved to hear him talk about an exotic Eastern Europe, eyes twinkling while he spoke about castles and kingdoms before war scarred the land and its people. He was a large man who enjoyed a drink, pleading that we should allow him his holy water, vodka, to ensure a speedy recovery. *If the problem isn't terminal, Harry,* he insisted, *then this will provide the cure.* A beatific smile of recollection graced his features, while he rubbed his hands together in anticipation of this favourite drink.

Nigel Robinson was another runner, like myself, and I tried to help him as much as possible because of the affliction he suffered – a nasty anal fistula, an exquisitely painful complaint. This reminded me of the horrors of the terrible rectal sigmoidoscope I'd endured on Malta so long before. It seemed a lifetime ago, as if it had happened to another person, but I hadn't forgotten the pain. I still sometimes wondered how differently things might have turned out had Nan lived. Would the future have been any better? Would I have stayed in the Mediterranean? Become a practising Catholic and learned to believe in her God?

I began to specialise in cases of dermatology, spending the majority of my time assigned to Ramsay Ward. Here, the consultant Dennis Sharvill persisted in telling colleagues and patients that I was in fact the best dermatologist in South East Kent. He was a big man with a big voice, his hair nicotine yellow with a long fringe that swept over his forehead. He was a good teacher, listening carefully and examining all patients thoroughly while dipping his head and gazing at them over the top of his spectacles, nodding periodically. If I carried out my duties satisfactorily, it was largely down to his fine instruction.

It was on Ramsay Ward that I met my favourite patient, Patrick Tyrrell. A dapper chap with a fuzz of sticky-up light brown hair, he never let me escape without first hearing a joke. Soon, I looked forward to our encounters, even seeking them out during quieter times on duty. He possessed a great infectious laugh, afflicting anyone who should hear it, and he was a top character to have around for raising the spirits of everyone. Pat was constantly making plans about what he would do after recovery, his lust for life an inspiration. He was a kind man, raining gifts and compliments on everybody who cared for him, and the female staff grew to love him. He always addressed them as princess or angel, something I could never have got away with, and he had an appetite for life that no illness could diminish or destroy.

My own health improved over time. I continued to run in the evenings, no longer at night because the nightmares had steadily reduced. I listened to music alone in the house: Grieg, Dvorak, and Debussy concertos. I read books. Dickens remained a firm favourite, but Steinbeck was my new idol. His compassion and understanding of the common man struck a deep chord within me, and he could also be funny. I longed to see the places that he described – Doc's lab in Cannery Row, the lighthouse at Pacific Grove, the long valley enclosing Salinas. The dreams of my boyhood began to return; a desire for travel, and to see more of the world.

In this way, I started to overcome the agony of always being the one left behind. Sometimes, I was able to stop carrying the guilt that weighed me down like a tight coat of armour. At work, some colleagues provided shoulders to cry on, others breathing space, and the rest hard facts about life. This combination, each part essential, allowed healing to slowly take place. A sliver of hope was returned. My future was at the hospital, yes, but at least I now had a future. I was serving a community and appreciated; my life was of use again, no longer wasted. A level of contentment returned to my daily existence.

Work continued to provide satisfaction, and at last I was inspired through meeting the rich assortment of characters who passed through our doors. Once more, I enjoyed the surroundings of Kearsney Court, especially a brisk walk through Russell Gardens or nearby Bushy Ruff that I'd recently discovered. This was a private nursing home that boasted the most spectacular gardens. The main house was built in colonial style, a magnificence of white washed porticos and tall green shutters. It stood perched on a rise overlooking its own lake, where fat trout swam in wide lazy circles gulping greedily at any food that should come their way. Never a keen fisherman, for once I imagined myself with rod in hand throwing graceful casts across the silky water to catch dinner. It reminded me so much of Charnwood and nursing the reverend. I hoped his last days had been kind to him; it was the least that he deserved.

Finally, I loosened up a little on duty and found time to be nice to the staff. It brought real pleasure to watch them relax in my presence, and not hurry to escape from my unpredictable moods. I found time to get out at lunchtime, to have a walk through town or even make it to the harbour. Still, I loved to be near the water. The sea remained in my blood.

It was on a bright day and after an early finish from the wards that I decided to head for the water. It was possible to walk right along the promenade and onto the *Prince of Wales Pier*, the sea visibly raging through the cast iron slats beneath my feet. Sometimes, it was possible to make out the long flat shadow of France in the distance. Ferries chugged their way tirelessly between the two countries, and people stood waving excitedly at the lucky travellers. There was a small café on the end, always busy, and I liked it.

It had been a good day on Ramsay Ward. Pat Tyrrell had been back in for observation, bringing with him a particularly fine collection of jokes together with chocolates for the girls. He'd been given the all clear. I felt delighted about the improvement in his health, but sorry to see him discharged – he would be a real miss. It was with this in mind that I raced down the corridor towards the car park.

The sun continued to shine with strength. I admired shadow patterns that were scattered along the pale green hospital walls, while my footsteps echoed satisfyingly loud throughout the narrow passageway. I was only vaguely aware of the figure seated on a black plastic chair beneath one of the windows. It would never have been allowed on Malta, when everybody was instructed to keep away from all remaining glass surfaces, and this was my only thought. Striding purposefully forward, it was movement outside the window that caught my eye.

Through the clear surface, about head height, a halo of brilliant white butterflies danced in the sunlight. They so captivated my attention that I stopped abruptly. It was only then that I realised the figure was sobbing quietly. I heard the familiar gulped breaths, the tremble, and watched the hand dab tentatively at moist reddened eyes.

"Hello. Can I help at all?" It was all I could think to say. On some days I would have continued walking, well aware that a person may prefer to be left alone, but on this day some other force made me stop in my tracks.

She looked up, surprised, and I found myself staring at a most attractive lady. She was small, like my mother, with hair the rich colour of autumn. Her eyes were green, the tears making her even more lovely. I was amazed to experience immediate attraction, having avoided any chance of a relationship since Gwen. I was well prepared for a life long loneliness, expecting and accepting it, but this all changed in an instant. Hearing her voice changed everything. Life had stopped after Gwen's death but now, completely out of the blue, it began again.

"No, thank you. I'm sorry, I'll go. It's just my friend. He's not well and I was upset."

I recognised the innate kindness, the compassion, from Nan. I felt reluctant to leave and move on while she sat hunched so tight and defenceless, alone with her grief.

"Are you sure?" I took a chance and reached out to touch her arm briefly, painfully briefly. My heart raced like the waves and I stood awkward before her, wondering what was happening to me. I didn't usually act like this – I preferred not to get involved, to keep my distance, and had long since buried the desire to love.

"Really, I'll be all right. Thank you."

She looked down, away from me. The butterflies remained outside the glass, behind her, as if they too were reluctant to fly away. I walked slowly forward, turning back twice to check where she sat unmoved, hoping I might see her again. When I walked along the promenade and onto the pier, returning home much later, I could think of nothing else.

Two days passed before I saw her again. I had found every possible excuse to loiter along the corridor during visiting hours, but she did not reappear. I couldn't help wondering why this should be, and hoped that I had not been in any way responsible. I hoped she had not seen through my thoughts and been scared away – it was the last thing that she needed right now. I wondered who her friend was, making tentative enquiries with my colleagues that led to nothing.

In the evenings, after work, I ran along the back streets to Capel, enjoying the pounding of legs upon tarmac, taking in huge gulps of fresh air that flooded my lungs. I jogged through parkland and into River, then Dover, avoiding the Warren and its resident ghosts, my old haunts in Folkestone, craving that I might at last be able to put the past behind me.

Two days passed and it felt like a lifetime. Still, I puzzled as to my condition. It made no sense; we had hardly met, but I knew that I desperately wanted to see her again, and to help in any way possible. It was with unfathomable relief that I spotted her perched on the edge of the same seat as before. She wore a brown jacket and skirt, a white blouse. She looked smart. Professional. I hurried forward, brushing one hand to tidy my hair, determined not to waste this opportunity.

"Hello again, how are you? Is your friend any better?" The words all blurred together in their race to escape from my mouth. She was not crying this time, to my relief, and she smiled in recognition.

"Oh, hello. He's about the same, thank you, and thanks for the other day. It was good of you." She wiped one hand across her brow and I thought she looked tired. Troubled.

"It was nothing." I studied her closely. "As I said, if I can be of any assistance please let me know."

I spoke too quickly. She did not reply and looked down to her feet, apparently studying the black handbag that sat on the ground. I waited, but she remained silent. It was with heavy reluctance that I began to edge away.

"There's one thing." Quickly, she looked up, sensing my departure. "I could do with some advice."

It was a delight to return to her side, plonking myself firmly into the seat next to her, careful to avoid any contact. I smiled, reassuring her to continue.

"It's my friend, Don," she explained. "He looks terrible since he got here, and he's asked me to marry him. We're only friends, and I don't know what to do. I don't even know what's wrong with him."

"Why do you think he asked?" I felt jealous of this unknown rival, and also concerned for her well-being.

"I'm not sure. I think he must be really ill." She wiped at her forehead, a nervous reflex, taking several deep breaths before starting to speak again. "What do you think I should do? I'm at my wits end."

Finally recognising the quiet desperation in her voice, I was jolted out of selfish thoughts. I knew it could not have been easy to ask for help from me, a stranger, and I started thinking beyond my own desire. I tried to put myself in her shoes, imagining how she might feel.

"That's a tough one. Who is your friend? What's his name? I'll make enquiries and have a think about it. I'll talk to you next time you visit, and tell you what I've found out. I'm Harry, by the way. What's your name?"

Pam. Her name was Pam.

☽

We arranged to meet on the following evening. In the meantime, I was able to discover all about Pam's friend and the news was not good. Don Sparks was terminally ill with cancer. His was a particularly nasty tumour, and that is why it had affected him so suddenly. I knew all about this disease through my long experience with Gwen, and I determined to help Pam in every possible way. I would be a friend, a good friend, like those who had carried me back to sanity. My experience could prove useful, at last.

☽

It was Pam who spotted me first, this time, earlier than I had expected. I beckoned her to my desk on Ramsay Ward, frantically clearing a space for her to sit down, where we would be able to talk with relative privacy. As she approached, I shuffled all paperwork into order, tidied my hair, and emptied a half drunk mug of tea into the sink behind my seat. I was determined to make a favourable impression.

"Hello again. How are you today?" I spoke too quickly again, too keen. She seemed to have that effect upon me, and I concentrated on slowing myself down.

"Not bad, thank you." She attempted a smile. "I'm glad I found you, Harry. I haven't been to the ward yet. I can't take my mind off Don and what to do. Sorry to ask but did you manage to find anything out?"

I was ready for this, having rehearsed in my head many times what I was going to say. It had been a tough decision, but cancer offers no easy solutions. "I've had a good think, and think you should agree to marry him."

She stared at me aghast, her mouth open, and I continued to speak more slowly, willing myself to remain calm.

"I know it sounds strange, but I've checked up on Don. I don't think he'll be leaving the hospital, Pam."

Understanding dawned in her eyes, and then sorrow. It was awful to be a cause of her pain.

"I see," she spoke so softly and, quickly, I touched the back of her hand where it rested on the desk.

"It will make him much happier," I continued. "You won't have to go through with it, but it will make his last days much easier. Can I get you anything, Pam? A tissue? Water?" I thought she was going to cry, but I was wrong. Pam was stronger than that.

"I see," she spoke more firmly. "Thank you. I need to collect my thoughts and then I'll go and visit him."

She stood up and hurried away. I hoped that I had said the right thing, and that my advice would prove correct. It was some time before I felt able to resume inspection of the ward.

☽

We were to meet on several occasions during Pam's subsequent visits to the hospital. Don had apparently been jubilant at Pam's acceptance of his proposal, bringing with it an unexpected improvement in his health. This was to prove short lived and the cancer soon regained the upper hand, going about its business with a ruthless efficiency. It was a much quicker illness than that of my wife, and his death was not long in coming. I remained determined to be there for Pam. Don's sickness brought back many painful memories, but this was the one chance to put my experience to good use. It fell on me to break the news of his death.

"If I can take you out sometime, Pam, for a walk or a drive in the country, please let me know. Here's my number. I've got some idea what you're going through, just give me a ring. Anytime."

"Thank you."

"It would be my pleasure."

She had taken the news well, although obviously upset. I simply wanted to be her friend, after going through every conceivable emotion with Gwen. I wanted to be her shoulder to cry on, her support if she needed someone, and it was not long before she called me at home. We met after work the following Saturday.

We walked along the cliff tops at Dover. It was a bright day, the sky silver, and Pam wore a summer dress decorated with orange and red poppies. She was more collected than I had expected, and I realised that she must have had her own previous experiences, her own personal heartaches in life. Don's passing was not the only sadness she had encountered. I detected a background similar to my own, a depth of emotion hidden within this pretty lady.

It was still warm, and the only butterflies present were those dancing inside my stomach. I learned with interest how Pam had grown up in Tontine Street, not far from my own childhood house in Park Street. We had enjoyed all the same places; the Victoria Pier, the fish market, and regular bathing trips to the Warren.

We met again, the next weekend. This time, I picked Pam up in Folkestone and we made our way to Capel. We walked down the path to the sea and Pam told me how she had been born in South Africa, sailing to England with her sisters as a young girl. She had actually been on the Atlantic while I lay ill in bed with acute rheumatism dreaming about life on the ocean. She also shared a great love of the sea. It flowed in her veins as well as my own. I thought about Mr Hann, who had granted me my first holiday so many years ago. Here, at the Warren, I had met Dot Golding from London. I pointed the spot out to Pam, where I had used to set up camp.

"This was my favourite place," I explained. "Right near the water but high up, where it never flooded. I loved to be here, borrowing a tent from my brother."

"We used to come here too," Pam replied, turning to look at me and smiling. "Me and my sister, Joan. I really liked it, but my favourite place was definitely the boat hire in Radnor Park." She stopped talking, allowing herself a chuckle. "I don't suppose it matters to tell you, but I always fancied the boy there. He worked with his older brother, who Joan liked. My first crush!"

"Pam," I was stunned, for a second disbelieving my ears. "That was me! The boy you liked was me!"

Suddenly, it appeared that all roads trodden had in fact been leading to this moment. Since Nan I had been cast adrift, ship-wrecked with Gwen, and now I finally understood the truth – Pam. It was always meant to be Pam. We had no destination but each other, and now we embraced for the very first time. She was the new centre of my universe. I was in the right place at the right time, at last. Love had found me for one final occasion and it was a miracle.

☾

I had always felt, on some level, that nursing would provide all the answers. Now, this proved true. And my old pal Eric Reynolds was also correct – a good woman would see me right. I met Pam as often as possible, racing to finish shifts at the hospital, changing clothes at work, laughing with colleagues at my regular new collection of shaving cuts in my haste to get away.

Meeting the lady tonight? They would joke at my expense, and how I enjoyed it. Everything in life had acquired a clarity and now made sense – I was determined to make the most of it, and suddenly saw how important it was to try and change the world in little ways, like Pat Tyrrell, with laughter and kindness, with generosity. Of these things, memories are made and friends collected. Finally, I was happy. When it happened and I eventually kissed Pam for the first time, my heart soared with a rediscovered capacity for love. I could not remove the smile from my face for days.

☽

The relationship flourished in a way I had never experienced before. It grew richer, deeper, and I was able to help Pam over her inevitable guilt concerning Don. She had acted the right way. His final days had definitely become more peaceful. My own recollections of cancer brought with them considerable pain and upset, but this was a price well worth paying. I felt glad to offer assistance, those bad years at last proving beneficial.

Pam and I walked back to the Warren often, and through the villages and parkland near to Kearsney Court. The sea was always a constant between us. Pam also loved to be near the water. She told me that just once she had lived away from the coast, abroad, and this had been an unhappy experience. I did not push her for any details. We had all the time in the world; she would tell me everything when she was ready.

We went to concerts at the Leas Cliff Hall, and enjoyed regular trips to the cinema where my father had worked as an attendant. I had become a big fan of Capra and James Stewart, and saw hope everywhere as mirrored in these films. Pam's favourite actor was Robert Taylor, who she loved with a passion, and I could never fully understand this. But anything was fine with me – I was the one who got to sit beside her, I was the one who held her hand.

We were both keen readers, able to swap books and recommendations. Pam's favourite author was also John Steinbeck, another good sign, and I knew that my mother would have approved of her. She was nothing like Gwen, and I felt sorrow that they should never be able to meet. Pam took me to visit her sister in Capel, Peg, and it was obvious to notice the importance of this relationship. Of family. We took to calling in whenever we were passing, on our way into Folkestone or down to the sea at the Warren.

Peg was smaller than Pam, maybe tougher, and certainly protective in her role as older sister. I made sure that we should become friends, and this was easy – I liked her. Peg had lived in the same house since the war, never once turning anyone away, providing an island of security for all those who should need it. I admired her fortitude, her humour, and the familial kindness. Pam insisted that this was passed down to them from their mother, and I felt sorry that she was departed. I would have liked to meet the lady who could raise such fine daughters, apparently single-handed. Their father had remained in South Africa.

☽

I had feared that I could not survive another unhappy relationship, with perhaps sickness and suffering of my partner all over again, the agony of having my heart broken one more time. It would break me, I felt sure, but everything had now changed. Meeting Pam, my tendency for depression that had been present since unemployment in the Twenties lifted as easily as the removal of a hat. I began to start living again, and what's more I enjoyed it.

I had been content in my own little world, not wishing for anything more, but this was finished. Now, here, I had someone that I wanted to share life with, someone who could make me happy, and it became my life's ambition to return the favour. I would never let Pam down – she could always rely on me. She came from a family background that was filled with love, cloaking her in security, and I endeavoured to add to this protection. Pam was such a good person, a kind person, and she deserved the best of everything. I wanted to make space for her in my home, as I had already within my heart. I wanted us to live together, and I hoped and prayed that she would come to feel the same way.

We began to meet every day. I needed this and I needed her. There was a certainty about us that even a stubborn fool such as myself could recognise. Already, I could not imagine life without her. It remained my top ambition to keep her happy.

I remember well the day that we walked along Folkestone pier, for it was glorious. We had been to the fun fair first, the electricity machine no longer present and the whole place a pale shadow of its former glory. I hadn't been able to convince Pam to join me on any of the rides, but had managed to win her a teddy bear. She decided to call it Harold immediately, and clutched it close to her chest.

It was hotter than usual, too good a day to venture inside, and Pam wore her summer dress with the poppies. It was my suggestion to stroll along the pier, and she had readily agreed. We walked past the occasional fishermen, one of them pulling up a glittering catch of mackerel, and I hurried Pam forward to avoid witnessing their desperate struggle. The sky was impossibly blue, not a single cloud interrupting the straight-line horizon. The end of the pier was deserted. The world belonged only to us.

"Come on, let's dance." Pam took hold of my hand. "Do you remember as kids there always used to be a live band here, a real show?"

"My brother Leslie used to go. You know, the one from the boat hire. He used to come here to meet girls!"

"Well he came to the right place. My sister Joan used to come and she was a stunner – I bet he fancied her!" Pam pulled me forward, closer, not realising the injury that she risked from my two left feet. She smiled and I could not resist, unable to disappoint the look that graced those wonderful eyes.

We began to move, to dance, and to my amazement I was better than expected. Pam led me like an expert, little surprise when she was used to teaching in a dance school. I felt overcome with joy and gratitude, and it seemed that life was beginning to make sense like the steps of our simple waltz. I realised that things had not felt this good since my time on Gozo with Nan. I felt determined that such happiness would not be allowed to slip away a second time, and my mind was then decided. There was only one course of action to take.

We walked slowly back to the Leas, arms wrapped tight about each other, to reach our favourite little restaurant. I was nervous and excited. I do not remember our conversation. We ate salad with roasted vegetables. I ordered an expensive bottle of wine that was imported from France.

"Why not? Let's pretend that we're on holiday," I replied, when Pam voiced surprise. She was not used to seeing me drink during the day, and it was only me who ordered a pudding. Pam said she was too full already, and bet that I would not be able to finish my own.

The date pudding was as heavy as a stone. It was huge, but my mind was made up and I had only to get through it; that was all it would take. "So if I finish," I said, "will you do what I want you to do?"

"All right then," she smiled. "Of course."

I nodded and set about the task. It took ages. I felt sick with nerves, tasting nothing, and glancing at fellow diners while the restaurant steadily emptied. People returned outside to enjoy the late afternoon sunlight. It was still hot. I chewed as fast as possible, swallowing the pudding in huge uncomfortable gulps in case my bravery should disappear. Pam laughed and questioned my intentions.

"What?" she asked. "What is it you want me to do? I told you that I was full. I couldn't possibly eat another thing."

I washed the last of the dessert down with a full glass of wine, making me feel lightheaded. Nothing could stop me now, and I reached for Pam's hand with conviction. I spoke slowly, trying to appear more confident than I felt.

"Pam, I want you to marry me."

"What?" She was definitely not expecting this.

"You heard. I want you to be my wife. I want you to be Mrs Fisher. Will you do that for me? Will you grant me the honour? It's what I've wanted for some time."

"Yes. Yes, of course."

She smiled, always beautiful, and I leaned over the table to kiss her. I loved Pam in a way I could never have loved Nan or Gwen, with a richness and depth that came only from age. From living. She said yes and I was saved. I was home, at last. I was free.

Epilogue

W HEN I look back and remember, life floats back to me like a long forgotten story. It resembles a dream, a half-remembered thought, but it is all real and this is good. My movements have become slow, unsteady. My eyes tire as they fall asleep on this world, and I watch my hands tremble constantly as if belonging to someone else. But with the past before my eyes, in front of me, I live again. I hope this is of use to you.

I used to believe that ageing is merciless. Now, I am not so sure, for with it comes understanding. Euphoria. If I had known how long I was going to live, I might have taken better care of myself – not for me, you understand, but for her. Pam.

I do not believe that there is just one person for everyone – there are different people, different lives, different stories waiting to happen. I have been in love three times, each experience unique. The first, a violent, passionate affair, blowing in and out as suddenly and unexpected as a candle flame, re-igniting at the strangest of times. The second provided warmth and security, companionship. But the third, now, is the best. It is a quiet, nourishing relationship. It runs deep. The passion remains, as does the comfort, but there is more. So much more. For me, I am glad it is Pam. To feel this, I am one of the lucky ones. My love runs deeper than any ocean.

The years roll by and I grow happier and happier. The days glow. I have reached the age when a man understands how to love a woman properly. Pam remains beautiful. Always. We moved from Kearsney Court to the village of River. Our house, once big, grew small with children. The spaces felt, the absences, all disappeared. I have a family. Friends. Time now approaches a standstill. It loses all meaning. I am ready, not scared, for old age to take me. My time here is nearly over, and yet my appetite for life remains. For Pam, I would eat that date pudding all over again. We hold hands, still, and life is a privilege. I am blessed to love and be loved. Without doubt, I am one of the lucky ones.

In this winter of peace, it is true that I spend much of my time remembering. I have my good days, when memories are precise and exact. They act as fuel to help keep me alive, as important as food, water. I recall sounds, textures, smells; the touch of a hand on bare flesh. I see the silk blue Mediterranean. I recall Gwen in her Garbo heyday, all lacquered hair and sharp cut cheekbones. I dream of my mother, her rose red complexion. And then there is Nan. Always Nan. Time slows then stops. I cannot breathe. A drowning sensation floods these ancient lungs, and my eyes flow over with tears. I have my bad days, when memories are precise and exact. My mind is now swimming with ghosts. They jostle and crowd for attention, making their strokes across time. They bring me comfort.

The circle is nearly closed. I love Pam. I still carry Dot's bear for luck – he has served me well, through the years. I am the last of my siblings who remains. Even Jacqueline is gone, claimed at the same age by the same cancer as her mother. I hope I made my father proud, in the end. I know I did some good with my life.

If I had known Pam earlier, there would be no Gwen. No Nan. But I have lived. I have suffered and cried. I have had my heart broken. I have experienced the purity of true bliss. I regret nothing – how I have lived! I would do it all over again. And now, finally, I have come home. I am with the right woman, the one I am meant to be with, where all paths were in fact leading all of the time. You are made free by love and by loving. Remember this.

Life without variation is colourless. Sterile. Friends ask what I should have done had it not been nursing, and I have considered this many times. I should have liked to work on the land – I long for a return to the pollution free environment of youth. But I have always loved nursing. It was only through unemployment in the hungry Twenties and Thirties that I stepped over the threshold of a hospital and into a career. Again, I was lucky. I found my true vocation. I remember the words of Reverend Hocking. My time at Charnwood. Hearts were more generous back then.

Walking, breathing fresh air, the sea: all remain high in priorities. My memories are good, intact. Would I have changed a thing, my children ask? If I'd known what would happen to Gwen, to Nan? I would change nothing. Nan is with me, always. She is never forgotten. Through Gwen, I learned how love can blossom and flower in the most unlikely circumstances. I hope and believe this was also true for her.

I enjoyed my time in hospitals. A sense of being needed, of serving a community, always inspired and encouraged me in care of the sick and wounded. It is a grand feeling to be able to change the world in little ways. The nightmares have stopped. Now, I dream only good dreams, the ones that lead me to home. To Pam.

I love Pam. Still. She is the love of my life. I was ready for her, waiting, and grateful. The kindness of a woman can move mountains. I hope this is of use to you.

What have I learned from it all, my children ask? What have I learned? And the answer is simple. The only correct answer is the truth, Nan's truth, and the only truth is love. Do not forget this.

To know that you are loved – I am one of the lucky ones.
I am free, at last, through love and through loving.

Pam.

Always Pam.

I slip away. I made my mark, a ripple upon the surface,
spreading outwards, touching, affecting other people, further
than I can imagine.

The circle is closed.

Time passes so quickly. Pam is old now, a little tired. She did not believe that she would enjoy true happiness again and she was wrong. She was married to Harry for thirty good years until his death. Two children are the result, one boy and one girl. Her pride, her joy.

The water is near and she can hear seabirds. She looks out of the window at a sunset of purple and gold. She smiles. She has not lived one life but many.

She remembers the kindness of Joan, her sister's frequent advice to seize the moment and live in the present. Joan was right: each day is rare and unique. She also believes the words of another sister, Peg, how we are all better people when loved. Love is the greatest gamble in life, carrying the sharpest pain, but it is also the greatest of gifts.

Pam's eyelids fall heavy with sleep. The thin night thickens and deepens, casting its net over sea darkened streets. Pam remembers everything. Each life carried its own heartbreak – would it be best forgotten, swept under the carpet of time? She is quick to dismiss this idea, shaking her head from side to side. Then, she would not hear Paul saying *I love you* ever again. He was beautiful. She would not experience the comfort and warmth of his love. He will never be forgotten.

She can picture the sea at Folkestone, each curve of coast at the Warren, the rock pools, the sway of trees about the pond, the path along the cliff tops. The railway bridge where Paul kissed her. She can see the lake on the outskirts of Pszow, the surrounding forest. Poland. She can see Harry in the restaurant, when he asked her to marry him.

She is not finished yet. There may be time for another adventure, a new life, and she is ready for this. She dreams of a peninsula, a great harbour, the ocean. The sea is a perfect blue, the sky vast and bright, her bedroom white with light. She has not lost her appetite for living. She will join her son and his family in New Zealand. Wellington. She will still be of use, a help, a grandmother. She is happy.

She drifts off to a peaceful sleep. Paul's words whisper from far away. *It has only just begun.* He loved her. He was prepared to risk everything for her. And Harry loved her. She will have that with her always. In turn, she loved them both. She was courageous and never afraid to love.

Pam is happy.
She closes her eyes.

ACKNOWLEDGEMENTS

This trilogy has been ten years in the making, and taken me on a journey around the world. A big thank you to all those people who helped and encouraged along the way, and taught me that books and stories can live forever.

In England: Pam and Stephanie Fisher, Pat and Missouri Tyrrell, Iain Sutcliffe, Nigel and Judith Robinson, Richard Neuberg, Brian McCleary, John Snailham, Mick Oxley, Sandra Francisco, John Saunders. Alison.

In Poland: Monika and Kasia Brachmanska, Sylwia Tomczyk, Henryk and all at the Restaurant Goscinna, Iwona, Wanda, Stefan and the remaining Konieczny family.

In New Zealand: Alfred Memelink, Brian and Dorothy Carmody, Andrzej Nowicki, Bruce and Janis Caddy.

These books are dedicated to my parents, in whose footsteps I tread with awe.